√

D1443160

The Fruitcake Murders

Center Point
Large Print

Also by Ace Collins and available from
Center Point Large Print:

The Yellow Packard
Darkness Before Dawn
The Cutting Edge
The Color of Justice
Hollywood Lost

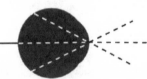

**This Large Print Book carries the
Seal of Approval of N.A.V.H.**

The Fruitcake Murders

ACE COLLINS

CENTER POINT LARGE PRINT
THORNDIKE, MAINE

This Center Point Large Print edition is published
in the year 2015 by arrangement with Abingdon Press.

The text of this Large Print edition is unabridged.
In other aspects, this book may vary
from the original edition.
Printed in the United States of America
on permanent paper.
Set in 16-point Times New Roman type.

ISBN: 978-1-62899-797-2

Library of Congress Cataloging-in-Publication Data

Collins, Ace.
  The fruitcake murders / Ace Collins. —
    Center Point Large Print edition.
      pages cm
  ISBN 978-1-62899-797-2 (hardcover : alk. paper)
  1. Large type books. I. Title.
  PS3553.O47475F78 2015b
  813'.54—dc23

                                                    2015032954

This book is dedicated to
the late Glenda Farrell
who played the reporter Torchy Blane
in the classic mystery movies of the 1930s.
No one talked faster and
entertained any better than Glenda.

Acknowledgments

Many thanks to
Ramona Richards
Teri Wilhelms
Joyce Hart
Susan Cornell
Cat Hoort

And all the Abingdon team who have
worked to make this book a success

— 1 —

Thursday, December 23, 1926
9:15 p.m.

It was just past seven, the temperature was in the teens, the north wind gusting to thirty and the spitting snow flurries hinting at a storm that would soon assure every child in Chicago a white Christmas. Though he wanted to stay home with his elderly mother and two children, love had driven fifty-six-year-old Jan Lewandowski out into the cold to make the twenty-block walk through the city's Little Italy to the small candy factory he'd started when he'd emigrated from Poland in 1905.

While his teenage son, Szymon, was too mentally disturbed to care about the weather or the upcoming holidays, Lewandowski's eight-year-old daughter had been praying for snow for weeks and today's forecast thrilled her. Thus, to make Alicija's joy even greater, Lewandowski was braving the increasingly harsh conditions to retrieve the small, red sled he'd hidden in the back of his office. Tomorrow he was going to place that outdoor toy under the tree and pretend Santa had brought it all the way from the North Pole. If only his little blonde angel could know the truth. If

7

only he could tell the always-smiling child the sled was not a gift from St. Nick, but a labor of love created by his own hands. Maybe someday he would let her know the time it took him to build it and how much love went into every facet of that job, but for the moment the credit would go solely to the jolly elf who lived above the Arctic Circle. After all, that was a part of the magic and innocence of Christmas that even a middle-aged man like Lewandowski treasured as well as the magic and innocence he felt every child needed to hang onto for as long as possible.

As the short, stocky candy maker crossed onto Taylor Street, a heavyset, finely dressed man, wearing a long overcoat and wide-brimmed hat and hugging two large paper sacks tightly against his chest, stepped out of Lombardi's Grocery and Produce and casually ambled toward a Cadillac sedan parked on the curb. A young man, tall and thin and outfitted in a beaver coat and green wool scarf to fight off the wind's bitter chill, stood by the vehicle's back door waiting. Arriving at the curb, the big man turned back toward the store, and, as he did, a street lamp revealed a deep, nasty scar on his fleshy cheek.

Standing in the shadows, under the grocery's awning, Lewandowski watched the heavyset man intently study Lombardi's showcase window before the shopper slowly spun and stepped through the large, green sedan's rear door. After the door was shut and secured, the younger man hustled around to the driver's side, got in, slid the car into first, and eased forward. As the Caddy made a sweeping U-turn, its twenty-one inch wooden wheels crunching on the fresh snow, Lewandowski stepped forward and stood under a street lamp. For a moment, his eyes met the driver's. The men briefly studied each other before the car roared out of sight and the candy maker turned and made his way on down the sidewalk.

Momentarily stopping to pull up his collar in an effort to gain a bit more protection against the unforgiving north wind, Lewandowski glanced at the tiny store the big man had just exited. The candy maker smiled at the festive holiday display Geno Lombardi had created in his front window. Illuminated by blinking, electric lights were a half dozen children's toys, a few canned hams, a small evergreen tree, four boxes of Noma Christmas lights, a basket of fruit, a can of nuts, and several rolls of wrapping paper. Circling all the goodies was a brand new Lionel electric train, its black steam engine slowly pulling five cars and a caboose around the oval-shaped metal track. While the holiday exhibit captured the spirit and wonder of December, there was something missing. Where were Lewandowski's prize fruitcakes? Lombardi had agreed to place five of the tins in the window in order to help the candy maker publicize his newest culinary creation. They had been a part of the presentation for two weeks, but now they were gone. So why had the store owner removed the cans of cake just two days before Christmas? After all, tomorrow would be the most important shopping day of the year and those cakes needed to be there.

Setting aside all thoughts of his daughter's present or the coming blizzard, Lewandowski angrily pushed open the glass-paned door and rushed into the small, corner grocery. A bell, mounted just above the entry, announced his presence.

"Geno," the visitor angrily called out. When there was no reply Lewandowski roared, "Geno, where are my fruitcakes?"

There was no still response.

Figuring Lombardi must be in his office, Lewandowski stuck his hands deep into his overcoat pockets and hurried along a bread rack toward the rear of the store. He'd just passed a display of lightbulbs when a chill ran across his wide shoulders and down his spine. Because a coal stove had driven the temperature in the store to almost eighty, the creeping cold racing along his flesh had nothing to do with the frigid outside temperature.

"Geno," he called out, his voice suddenly showing more concern than rage. "Where are you, my friend?"

10

Stopping, the confused candy maker turned to his right and studied the now empty store. The glow of six dangling one-hundred-watt bulbs bathed the room in a yellowish, almost surreal light. The fact there was no sound except for the ticking of a Seth Thomas clock made the establishment more like a church than a place of business. The grocery was never this quiet. Something was not right! Lombardi never closed before nine, so what was going on? At the very least, he should be restocking his shelves in anticipation of the Christmas Eve rush. Why was he not answering?

"Geno, where are you?" Lewandowski demanded. As an afterthought he added, "What have you done with my fruitcakes?"

Again, no one replied.

Perhaps the store owner had gone up to the apartment located on the second floor above the main store or maybe he was in the alley taking out the trash. That had to be it.

It was then that Lewandowski felt more than saw a slight, barely perceptible movement to his right. Shifting his gaze, he noted a small boy, perhaps six or seven, in a center aisle, crouching behind a five-foot-high stack of canned goods, arranged to form something resembling a Christmas tree. The child was dressed in a blue coat, black gloves, dark pants, and a fur hat. As their eyes met, the apparently frightened boy

11

darted from behind the display clipping one of the cans with his foot causing the rest to fall forward. The sudden noise in the quiet room seemed deafening. As the displaced cans rolled and bounced in every direction, the spooked youngster yanked open the door and raced out into the cold. Once more, the candy maker was alone.

As the last can rolled to a stop against the front counter, uneasiness entered the store like a late spring fog causing Lewandowski's anger to dissipate as quickly as it appeared. Now what had been so important just a few minutes before was no longer a concern. Logic had replaced emotion and he felt no reason to stay and find out why his fruitcakes were not in their spot. He could do that tomorrow morning on his way to work. There would be plenty of time then. At this moment, getting Alicija's sled and taking it home was much more important. Spinning on his heels, he began to retrace his path toward the entry, but managed only two short steps when he spotted the grisly reason his calls to the store owner had gone unanswered.

His body frozen in place by a vision too ghastly to imagine, Lewandowski's brain slogged along in slow motion trying to understand what he was seeing. As the seconds deliberately ticked by, the candy maker noted a large pool of blood around the store owner's body. The next thing that registered was the awkward manner in which

Lombardi was sprawled on the hardwood floor. Then, as he hesitantly drew nearer, Lewandowski saw the man's open, but unseeing eyes. Finally, its shiny red handle catching the overhead light, he spied a knife stuck deeply into the shopkeeper's back. Now he knew why there had been no answer. Lombardi's voice had been silenced when his heart quit beating.

"*Nie,*" the Polish immigrant whispered in his native language. As he bent closer to touch the grocer's cheek, he reverted to English, "My lord, what has happened? Geno, who has done this awful thing to you?" As Lewandowski's fingertips pushed into the victim's still warm blood . . . blood now slowly seeping out of the man's body and onto the floor, as the sticky liquid coated his fingers, the candy maker looked toward the store's open cash register. As he studied the ornate, nickel-plated machine he thought back to the stranger he'd seen just moments before.

"Did he rob you?" Lewandowski demanded.

When the grocer didn't reply, Lewandowski pushed up from his crouching position, yanked off his gloves, dropping them on the floor beside the body, and after grabbing the bloody knife handle in his left hand and pulling the seven-inch blade from the dead man's back, the candy maker strolled behind the store's main counter and looked into the cash register. With his right hand, he tapped a large stack of money still secure in

13

the drawer. As he did the blood from his fingers transferred to a five-dollar bill.

"Why did they not take the money?" he whispered while making the sign of the cross. "What good was it to kill someone for nothing? Surely death had to have a reason?" He turned back to the dead shopkeeper and demanded as if expecting a reply, "Geno, why did they do this horrible thing to you?"

Lewandowski, too caught up trying unravel a mystery he couldn't begin fathom, failed to note that he was no longer alone. It was only when he heard the bell above the front door ring that the stunned and suddenly terrified man raised the knife over his head and looked up.

Standing in the entry was not the man he'd seen just a few minutes before or the little boy, but one of Chicago's Finest. The cop's stern expression and drawn pistol dictated he was more than ready to shoot first and ask questions later. "Drop the knife down to the floor, then hands up, and don't move," came the gruff order.

Too dumbfounded to speak, Lewandowski let the bloody blade slide from his hand and to the wooden planks. The thunderstruck and silent candy maker then lifted his blood-soaked, hands over his head. As he did, the cop stepped closer, glanced down at the dead store owner and back to the cash register. Shaking his head, the policeman noted, his tone as deadly serious as his countenance, "I didn't get here in time to stop you from killing him, but at least I kept you from stealing him blind."

Lewandowski's jaw dropped and quivered as he whispered, "I did not do this."

"That's what they all say," the cop grumbled. He then studied his suspect for a moment before noting, "I've seen you. You're that candy maker with the crazy son."

"I am Jan Lewandowski," he admitted.

"Yeah, the guy who conned Geno into selling the fruitcakes. I guess you and your kid are just as nutty as what you make."

The candy maker shook his head. "I swear I did not do this. I swear on all that is holy, I could not do such a thing."

"The blood on your hands and that knife tell a different story," came the quick reply. "They'll fry you before the spring thaw, you can make book on it."

"But I did not do this," Lewandowski pleaded, tears now streaming down his face. "The child will tell you I did not do this thing."

"What child?" the cop demanded.

"The little boy who was in the store when I entered. He can tell you that Geno was dead before I got here."

The policemen shook his head, "Where's this kid?"

"He ran out into the night," Lewandowski

15

explained, his eyes looking toward the door. "You must believe me, I did not do this horrible thing."

"I'm betting a court says different," the cop snapped. "Now, turn around, and drop your hands behind your back."

Sensing he had no choice, Lewandowski did as he was told. A few seconds later, he felt the cold metal cuffs go around his wrists. Suddenly his thoughts went back to the sled and his Alicija. Why had he gone into the store? Why hadn't he just kept walking down the street? Then he thought of the big man. That man was not a complete stranger. He knew that face. He'd seen it before. If only he could remember when and where. And where was the child? The little boy could explain everything. As tears filled his dark eyes, Jan Lewandowski's chin dropped into his chest and he muttered in Polish a prayer learned decades ago in his childhood. It was a plea for a mercy that would remain forever unanswered.

— 2 —

Wednesday, December 18, 1946
9:55 p.m.

For over an hour, Lane Walker had been impatiently sitting on an overstuffed leather couch waiting for a black desk phone on the walnut end table to ring. During that time he'd read the latest issue of *Life*, worked a crossword puzzle from today's *Herald*, and counted and recounted the seven bills—three ones, two fives, a ten and a twenty—that made up the sum total of the cash in his wallet. Picking up a Montgomery Ward Christmas catalog, he spent a few minutes considering what might be the best use for those forty-three bucks before tossing the catalog to one side, taking his handkerchief from the pocket of his suit coat and knocking the dust from his black wingtips. As a mantel clock in the mansion's cavernous living room struck ten, the dark-headed, blue-eyed Walker pulled his lean six-foot frame from the soft cushions and strolled over to a large mirror. Staring into the glass, he studied his reflection.

He was no Robert Taylor, but he wasn't Edward G. Robinson either. His jaw was strong, his eyes expressive, and his mop of wavy, dark hair showed no signs of turning loose or gray. While his thirty years of living had etched a few crow's-feet outside his deep-set eyes and along the corners of his thin lips, he nevertheless still maintained a bit of a baby face. Retaining any kind of appearance of innocence after three years spent fighting battles on a half dozen Pacific islands was quite an accomplishment. During that time, many of the Marines Lane had fought beside aged a couple of decades. Worse yet, more friends than he cared to remember were buried on those islands and would never age at all. So, emerging from the war with a few minor scrapes and some mental baggage meant he was lucky. Yet, if he were so lucky, then why did he feel so guilty for making it home alive and why did his good fortune eat at his gut and cost him sleep? Why did surviving carry such a huge cost?

Checking his watch for the tenth time in the last fifteen minutes, Lane adjusted the Windsor knot on his blue-striped tie and smoothed the lapels of his gray suit before turning away to study something you wouldn't find in his cramped apartment—a six-foot cedar tree standing proudly in the room's far corner. On this night, no one had plugged in the lights, so the tinsel didn't shine the way it should and the blue and red balls looked less colorful, but, even in its darkened state the evergreen still clearly spelled out that the holidays were on their way. Smiling grimly, Lane noted that under the fir's bottom branches were a half dozen carefully wrapped presents each decorated with red bows that blended perfectly with the green-striped paper hiding their contents. It didn't take a cop's keen observation skills to deduce someone had gone to a lot of trouble to make this holiday special. Yet, some things just don't work out the way they are planned and that was a crying shame. This holiday was going to be anything but bright for the family who lived in this Windy City mansion. Death had a way of stealing the light even from Christmas.

Just to the festive tree's right was a console radio. The Zenith was almost four feet tall and at least thirty inches wide. The front veneer featured a half dozen different types of wood including maple, white oak, and mahogany, but the cabinet was mainly walnut. Strolling over to the impressive radio, Walker flipped the set on and waited for the unit's seven tubes to warm up. Forty-five seconds later the strains of Bing Crosby crooning "White Christmas" filled the eight-hundred-square-foot room and, at least for a moment, it not only looked like the holidays, but sounded like them as well. As the modern carol's lyrics spoke of hopes the coming days would be bright, the visitor leaned against the unit's cabinet and closed his eyes. In a matter of moments, he was transported to a better time and a much happier place when he still believed in Santa Claus and the holidays were filled with wonder, hope, and excitement. Whatever happened to the innocent days of his youth surrounded by family and friends? How had they so quickly evaporated into little more than faded memories? If only his parents were still alive to once more welcome him home with a hug, a cup of hot chocolate, and a cheery Merry Christmas.

Lane became so lost in thoughts of Christmases from long ago, he almost didn't hear the door-bell's chime, now just barely audible over Crosby's sincere crooning. Snapping out of a dream centering on his mother's pumpkin pie, he shook the fifteen-year-old memory from his head, quickly crossed the room, and marched out the open, ten-foot pocket doors leading to a hall. Turning left, he made his way to the towering front door. Glancing through the oval leaded glass set into the walnut entry, he saw a face he knew all too well. In an instant, for a reason that really made no sense, a very bad day had just gotten worse. Against his better judgment, he twisted the knob allowing a personal ghost of Christmas past to enter.

"It's freezing out there!" Tiffany Clayton grumbled as she pushed through the entry. "By the way, that's the strongest, coldest wind I've felt since . . ." When the visitor unwrapped the red scarf from her neck and took a moment to look up at Lane's face, her jaw dropped. Frowning, she studied her unexpected host for several seconds before taking a quick inventory of the room, and, after setting her duffle-bag-size purse on a table just to the right of the entry, demanded, in a tone harsher than the frigid breeze, "What are you doing here?"

"I could ask the same thing of you," he shot back.

Her angry blue eyes once again locked onto the unhappy doorman and, after sweeping her wavy blonde hair from her shoulder, she snapped, "As if I have to tell a dumb cop anything I'm doing. But just to keep you from putting me under a hot lamp and grilling me for five hours, I'm here to interview Mr. Ethan Elrod. I was supposed to meet him about thirty minutes ago, but the snow and all the Christmas shoppers created one long traffic jam from downtown until about a block south of my final turn. Where are the city services when you need them? The plows need to be clearing those streets! If the streets become impassable, the merchants are going to lose money."

"You always have an excuse for being late," Lane groaned. "It's as much a part of you as those blue eyes and that red lipstick you always slap on."

Glaring, the guest shot back, "You don't slap on lipstick. It is applied. Besides, I wasn't the one who missed the Independence Day fireworks

21

show. In fact, I was there early and watched it all by myself. You arrived just as everyone was leaving and you still owe me for the tickets."

"That was five years ago," he sighed. "As I remember, that same summer you weren't just late, but completely missed a play, two movies, and three dinner dates."

Tiffany set her jaw, locked her knees, and roared, "You gave me the wrong address and time on two of those." Shaking her finger in his face, she added spitefully, "It was your fault."

"I gave you the right address and times," he argued, "you just couldn't remember them. I've noticed that information pours from your mind like salt out of a Morton's box. You need a little Dutch boy to follow you around and plug up that hole in your head."

"Fine," she almost growled, "twist the facts any way you want. That's what cops do. Now I'm here for a legitimate reason, so why don't you let me go to work rather than harassing me. Oh, that's right, that's what cops do—they harass people . . . especially reporters!"

Leaning closer to her face he barked, "Yeah, I live for it. Nothing I like better than making your life miserable."

"Well," she jabbed, "at least you're very good at something. Isn't there a donut shop you could be haunting? Now where are you hiding the district attorney?"

In the light of what had happened earlier tonight, the sparring session had been mildly amusing. Yet, as the cold reality of life pushed its ugly truth back into one of life's lighter moments, it was time to end the war of words that had been going on for years and spell out the hard, cold facts to the misguided member of the fourth estate. Rather than level her with a verbal left hook from out of nowhere, Lane uncharacteristically opted to employ a bit of tact. "Tiffany, why don't shake the snow off your shoes and head into the living room."

Digging her high heels into the carpet, she demanded, "Where's Elrod?"

Lane shook his head. So much for kid gloves. It was time to blow the impertinent woman out of the water. "You're not going to be talking to the district attorney tonight or any other time."

"You can't keep the press away from him," she shot back, pushing her five-foot-two-inch frame as high as it would go by lifting her heels off the floor and perching on her tiptoes. "I have my rights guaranteed by the constitution."

Lane leaned forward to a point where they were nose-to-nose and forcefully quipped, "I'm not trying to deny you the opportunity to interview an elected official. It's just that it's pretty hard to get quotes from a dead man."

"What?" As she pushed the word between her lips, the color drained from her beautiful face and her heels once more met the carpet. The news had deflated her ego as well as taken her voice. In another place and another time, that would have been something to celebrate, but not now.

"That's the sad fact," the cop quickly explained, his tone lower and softer. "Now, if you'll pick up that steamer trunk you call a purse and join me in the living room, I'll give you what I know."

He didn't wait for a response, but turned on the heels of his black wingtips, made his way across the hall through the pocket doors and into the home's largest room. He waited in front of a dark green, velvet-covered reading chair as the woman removed her coat, laid it over the arm of the couch, dropped her bag on the cushion, and folded her arms.

"I'm guessing it is murder," she sadly observed as she pulled a pad and pen from her purse.

"Your observations always were brilliant," he cracked.

"Not much to it," she noted, "you're from homicide. They don't pull you out into the snow to investigate a death by natural causes."

He shrugged, sat down in the velvet chair, pushed his shoulders deeply into the high-backed cushion, and said, "The maid discovered the body about five hours ago. He was at his desk, phone in his hand, his head resting on his calendar, and a knife sticking out of his back."

After jotting down the information, Tiffany

looked back to Lane. "So where's the body?"

"At the morgue."

"It looks like the crime scene boys are gone," she noted, "so why are you house-sitting?"

"Because the chief wanted to make sure the scene was kept fully secure just in case the medical examiner discovered something we might have missed during our initial investigation. You know the drill, something that might give us a hint as to who killed Elrod. Therefore, rather than spending my evening visiting with interesting people, I'm listening to the radio and hosting a pesky elf while waiting for the call that allows me to head back to my office and start filling out reports." He frowned and then dryly added, "Merry Christmas!"

"Makes sense," the woman admitted as she sat on the couch, crossed her legs, and pulled the hem of her gray wool skirt down below her right knee, "at least everything but the interesting people part. Based on my knowledge of your friends, you don't know anyone even vaguely interesting."

As she allowed the heel of her black pump to dangle off her right foot, Lane noted she still possessed a dancer's legs. When his eyes moved upward, he was also reminded that as good as her pins were, they were not her best features. Not surprisingly, as his appreciative gaze arrived at her face, her full red lips, deep blue eyes, and high cheekbones dragged him into the kind of mental fog that all but caused the cop to miss her next observation.

"Not going to be a good Christmas for Elrod's wife."

"Nope," he agreed as he recovered his focus by moving his eyes from the woman to the radio, "she's downstate visiting her sister. Glad I'm not the one delivering that message."

Sounds of Dinah Shore singing "I'll Walk Alone" filled the room and for the remainder of the hit ballad neither of them spoke. When the station launched into a newsbreak, Tiffany made a rather pointed observation.

"That was Dinah's first number one record. Let me see, it has been two years since it was resting on top of the charts. You were in Hawaii on leave and were supposed to meet me at the Pineapple Club, but for some reason you didn't show up. I wonder what her name was?"

He frowned, "I drew guard duty that night."

She raised her eyebrows and slowly shook her head. "And you couldn't call? I mean was it too hard to look up the number for The Stars and Stripes? You had no problem contacting me at work earlier that day."

"I couldn't get to a phone," he explained.

"There was one in the guard house where you were supposedly patrolling." She glared at the cop. "How do I know? Because you called me from there to make the date! In fact, you bragged

26

about talking to me from a phone that was supposed be reserved for only official military use. So, Lane, I got dressed up, went to the club, and listened to that Dinah Shore song on the jukebox again and again, because I truly was walking alone."

"I'm sorry, Tiff, I was . . ."

She waved her hand, "Don't even try, none of the excuses you've ever given me held water. Let's move past what was and into what is. Since you are confused about this case, I'll move onto one that is twelve hours old. Have you made any progress tracking down a suspect in the Grogan murder?"

"Tiffany," he said, bringing his eyes back to hers, "are you making small talk or digging for information for *The Star*?"

"A bit of both, Mr. Walker," she admitted.

"For print purposes, and you may quote me, we are close to making an arrest in the hit on the known underworld figure Stuart Grogan."

She cocked her left eyebrow and smiled, "So in cop jargon that means you don't have a clue. You have found part of the body in a river and something to make an identification possible, but you have nothing else."

"I didn't say that," he hastily shot back. "So you can't print it."

She shrugged, "Okay, I'll cut you some slack. Now back to the case of the moment. Elrod was a good man. Straight as an arrow! He was trying to clean this city up. Shame this had to happen before he could reach that goal. Because if there was less crime we would need fewer cops and maybe the force would show you the door."

"So," he grumbled, trying to ignore her dig, "why are you here tonight? There has to be more of a purpose than just needling me."

She shrugged, "There's no reason to hold out on you now." Tiffany tilted her head slightly, licked her lips, and frowned. "I guess, in the light of a murder, this doesn't mean much now, but you know those Santas standing on the street corners ringing those bells?"

"Yeah."

"I began to wonder how much money they brought in for charity," she explained. "When I observed what was going into their pots and what was being deposited in the city charity account . . . you know we have that chart in the paper each day . . . well, things didn't add up. In fact, the figures the charity gave us were only about 60 percent of what I figured they should have been."

"My, aren't you good at math," he quipped.

"I'm serious," she shot back. "Someone is diverting the majority of those funds somewhere else. There are tens of thousands of dollars in donations that are not going to ever get to the orphans or widows that the blasted war created.

So, I had an appointment to give Elrod my information on this scam. He was interested."

"Why didn't you run with it?" Lane asked. "Most papers go with the story and hide their sources from the police. This sounds like a hot headline to me."

"Ah," she replied, "printing the story might have ended the scam, but it wouldn't have gotten the money back. Plus, it would have caused folks not to give donations to the legit Santas. In this case, I don't want a scoop or a byline, I just want to get the money back and have those responsible for this con game arrested."

"So, Tiffany Clayton has a heart after all."

"I also have something else you are lacking," she chuckled.

"What's that?"

"A brain."

He shook his head. Why did she have to be so beautiful? She'd be so much easier to deal with if she were just average-looking. Then his mind could stay focused. And that was the big problem. Whenever he looked at her for too long he lost his train of thought. If fact, the train almost always jumped the tracks! It was one of the reasons he'd missed a few of their dates. He was afraid she'd look at him with those baby blues for several hours and he'd then say something that would trap him for life. Though, in truth, maybe that trap wouldn't really be so bad. After all, weren't these verbal wars just a way to keep from admitting he really liked her?

"Copper, your eyes are burning holes in my new gray suit."

And they had been. Maybe it would be better if the lights were out. No, that wouldn't be any good. The darkness would just bring out her perfume. What was it? Oh yeah . . . Tabu. How he wished she'd changed to a scent that was not so intoxicating.

"Mr. Walker, do you have any thoughts on Elrod or does the cat have your tongue?"

He had to look at anything but her in order to make sense. That's the way it had been since he met her on a summer day in Wrigley Field. Clearing his throat, he once more turned his eyes to the radio.

"Lane," she all but shouted. "Speak up!"

"Sorry Tiff," he finally answered, "I was thinking about another case." Shuffling in place, he continued, "Elrod, yeah, I have some thoughts." As his eyes focused on the radio's dial he added, "I probably knew him better than you did. Like you said, he was a good man, and more importantly, I think he was about to hit the Delono family's operation with a blow that would have knocked them to their knees. Sadly, he didn't share his information with anyone. He couldn't. He knew there were spies all over the courthouse, so he kept everything in his head."

"So," she cut in, "you've got nothing to go on?"

"All we've got," he admitted, "is that somebody stuck a knife in Elrod to keep him quiet, and therefore, the one person who might have stopped Richard Delono is dead."

As he nervously looked back to her, the reporter shifted uneasily, her eyes finding a picture of Elrod and his wife hanging over the fireplace. It was easy to read the obvious sadness etched on her face.

"That photograph was probably taken on an anniversary," she noted. "She's dressed up, wearing a lily, and there are a lot of folks in the background. Must have been quite a party." Turning her head back toward his she smiled, "And speaking of anniversaries, weddings, and such, I understand you and Lorraine Day have parted company."

"Old news," he quickly replied.

"Must be," she punched back, "because she's already engaged to George Carlisle. She sure wore a dreamy look as she showed off her new rock at the Holiday Charity Ball last night. That diamond must be five times bigger than the one you gave her. By the way, did you get the ring back and have you finished your payments on it?"

"Carlisle," the cop spat, "wonder where she met that shyster? Hard to take the law profession down a notch, but when that guy passed the bar he did it."

"Take it you're not a fan," she smiled as she applied another verbal jab. "Now don't avoid the question, where's the ring you gave her? Did the Cracker Jack Company repossess it and repackage it as a prize?"

His frown quickly turned upside-down, as he began his counterattack. "I see you're not wearing your ring either. Does that mean you're not soon becoming Mrs. Malcolm Diamonds? What a jewel he is!"

She quickly covered her left hand with her right and turned her head. Now it was her turn to change the course of the conversation. "Wonder if Mrs. Elrod will stay here in Chicago? Aren't both of their children married and living on the West Coast? And I think she's originally from Madison."

Lane ignored the woman's quick conversational detour. "Just as well he dumped you, I always thought your being called Tiffany Diamonds was nothing . . ." he paused for dramatic effect . . . "that carried much weight or class."

She turned and once again their eyes met. This time hers were filled with fire. "He didn't end it, I did."

"Yeah," he laughed, "I'll buy that just like I'd buy one of those used cars Mr. Diamonds sells."

"At least he's more honest than George Carlisle."

"Tiffany, I'd expect a more imaginative reply

from one of the city's best scribes. Anyone is more honest than a lawyer!"

"Why does it always come to this?" she demanded. "Every time we get together you have to turn it into a verbal war. A war I might add that you never win."

"I would win," he laughed, "I just don't have your stamina. And even if I did, why would I hang around for hours just so you can get in that last feeble word? And, I might add, I didn't start this, you did."

"Flatfoot!" she shouted while sticking out her tongue.

"Gossip monger," he shot back.

Folding her arms across her chest she asked, "You know what your problem is? I mean other than looks and intelligence."

He shrugged.

"Personality. When you walk into a room it feels like two people have left."

"Then, Miss Clayton, why do you always follow me? I can't make a turn anywhere in this city without bumping into you."

She set her jaw and shot out a glare that carried the explosive power of an atomic bomb. "I've got better things to do than sit here and wait for you to get a phone call."

"You know where the door is," he countered. "It works both directions. Getting out of this house is just as easy as coming in."

Grabbing her huge purse, she leapt off the couch and took four hurried steps toward the French doors. Her dramatic exit was stopped in mid-step by the ringing of the phone.

"You don't need to stay," he assured her.

"I'm not staying to talk to you, but I'm not leaving until I hear what that call's all about."

— 3 —

Wednesday, December 18, 1946
10:22 p.m.

Getting up from the chair, Lane walked quickly to the end table and picked up the receiver. He felt Tiffany's sharp eyes on his every move.

"Walker here." As he spoke, he noted his guest retrace her steps and once more take a seat on the couch she'd just occupied. Why hadn't she left just two minutes earlier? Why did she seem to live to complicate his life? Why had he ever noticed her in the first place? Life would have been so much simpler without Tiffany Clayton.

"Happy holidays, Lane, this is Morelli."

"And how's our county's best medical examiner?" the homicide detective asked as he continued to study his uninvited guest.

"Impatient. It's a week before Christmas and I haven't even begun to shop for my five kids and let's not even talk about my wife. Her list runs longer than most pieces of congressional legislation. She wants a new Hudson among other things, as if I could find one. Just be glad you're a bachelor."

After taking a deep breath and offering a prayer of thankfulness for being single, Lane smiled at the woman, glad she couldn't hear both ends of the conversation. "I'm certainly happy my shopping list is short," the cop quipped, "and I'm not planning on changing that anytime soon." He grinned at his guest. "In fact, I can't think of anyone I need to buy a present for. The only people on my list have been very bad this year and don't deserve a gift." As he watched Tiffany frown and turn her head away, he smiled and added, "Now it's late, so enough about holiday plans. Let's just cut to the chase. Is there anything you can give me about the knife that killed Elrod or do I hand this thing over to my team and let them start questioning the usual suspects?"

"You must have a date," Morelli quickly observed. "Well, if you do, you can cancel it. First of all, Elrod wasn't killed by that knife in his back."

"What?"

"Yeah, whoever stabbed him did so at least a half an hour after he died."

"Why would anyone plunge a knife into a dead man's back?"

"That," Morelli quipped, "is your problem. I just figure out how someone died, not who did it or why."

"Then tell me," Lane demanded, "what did kill him?"

"He was drugged," came the reply, "and he was likely out cold when someone tapped him with a blow to the back of his head causing enough cranial bleeding to not just short-circuit his brain, but feed a vampire for a week."

"But the coroner and his team," Walker argued.

"Ah yes, well, with the knife sticking out of his back I'm not surprised old Doc Miller missed a few things during his quick exam. Until I cut into Elrod, I would have assumed he died in what appeared to be the obvious way, too."

Looking back to the reporter, Walker noted she was leafing through the *Life Magazine* he'd read earlier in the evening, so thankfully she appeared completely unaware of what he'd just heard. At least it was a bit of good news to grasp onto. Moving to where his back was to Tiffany, he quietly asked, "What should I look for?"

"If you're asking about a weapon, nothing conventional. The damage to his head was done by something with a curved edge. It was likely red as I found a few flecks of paint in Elrod's hair. Beyond that I have no idea. Never seen anything like this before. It might help if I knew where he was when he cashed it in."

Picking up the phone and walking closer to the French doors, Walker quietly elaborated. "He was at his desk when the maid found him. He had the phone in his hand."

"Then that rules out an accident," the ME explained. "I thought he might have taken some drugs to help him sleep, then, as he was getting into bed, passed out and fallen against something, but not now."

"Why not?" Walker whispered, "He could have gotten up after the fall, realized he was hurt and was trying to make a call for help when he passed out."

"No," the doctor explained, "a blow of this type would have caused him to immediately lose consciousness. So, he couldn't have fallen, gotten up, and found his way back into his desk chair. If he was in the chair, he either had to have been struck while seated or been placed in the chair after he was struck. Either way it spells murder to me, and the knife played no part in his death."

"Got it," a confused Walker quietly replied as he rubbed his brow. This case had just become the criminal equivalent of buying a toy that required "some assembly." What had once seemed so simple was proving to be very complex. "Could you call the boys and tell them to get back down here? We'll now have to go over this house from top to bottom."

"No problem, Lane. I've got two more rush

jobs, so I'm going to be here the rest of the night. Let me know what you discover, and I'll see if it matches the damage I found."

"Thanks," the homicide detective replied. "I will."

Turning, he walked across the room to the end table. After returning the phone to its place, his eyes involuntarily went to the large oak door leading to the Elrods' study. As they did, the reporter looked up from the magazine and smiled.

"So, the knife was not the murder weapon. And don't try to deny it, my ears are much better than you could ever imagine. I heard everything Mitch Morelli said. Elrod was drugged and then knocked over the head by an unknown object."

"Then you know as much as I do," Lane complained. "So why don't you run back to your newspaper and beat everyone else to the story. You might even earn a Christmas bonus for this scoop. You could use the extra cash to take a week off and explore the job markets in New York or Cleveland or anywhere but Chicago."

"Very funny," she laughed. "You always crack me up with your wit. I'm not leaving this house until I have a look at the murder room and don't even try to keep me out."

The city normally gave the press access to crime scenes and, if the story broke, five dailies would likely soon be here and each of their reporters would be shooting questions at him, so there was no reason to keep Tiffany from seeing the study. Besides, as she was working on the story about the bogus Santas and had written about the Delono operation, she might actually have a lead on who was behind this murder. Maybe this time the beautiful little pest could actually help him. That would be a first.

"Come on," he grudgingly announced, walking slowly toward the door, "but don't touch anything."

"My hands will stay in my pockets," she assured him as she rose from the couch.

Moving across the room, Lane pulled a handkerchief from his pants and twisted the brass knob. He used that same handkerchief to flip the wall switch connected to the overhead light. He then stood in the doorway, with the woman just to his right, and studied the room.

Across the back wall was a built-in floor-to-ceiling bookshelf filled with everything from law books to novels. To the right was a double door leading to a patio overlooking the estate's polo-ground-size side yard. On the opposite wall, were two large red leather chairs separated by a huge wooden globe. Elrod's desk was in front of the bookshelf. It was ten feet wide and five feet deep and constructed of tiger oak. On it was a phone, a green-shaded brass lamp, a calendar, a legal pad, two recent issues of *Time* magazine, one declaring James F. Brynes "Man of the Year," an address book, a well-worn Bible, and a half-empty cup of coffee.

"Well, the knockout drug was likely in the coffee," Tiffany noted, as the cop continued to survey the study. "Now, what do you think was used as the murder weapon?"

"Not sure," Lane admitted, his gaze moving from the desk back to the bookshelf. "But I do know this, what I need to find is not hiding in plain sight."

As the cop slowly moved further into the room, the reporter asked, "How about giving me a hint as to what's on your mind? Oh, wait, your mind is always a blank."

Ignoring the woman, he again used the hand-kerchief, this time to pick up the phone and study both the base and receiver. They both had round edges, but were clean. Besides, Bakelite might be a hard material, but if it was used as a weapon there should have been a crack. There wasn't. After setting the phone back on the desk, he examined the metal wastebasket. It looked much too perfect. If it had been used as to strike the DA the sides would have been dented. Obviously, the books with their square edges were not employed in this crime either. Perhaps the murderer took the murder weapon with him.

Taking a seat in the chair where Elrod's life had slipped away, Lane again used the handkerchief to carefully open each of the desk's nine drawers.

Once more, he struck out. None of the many objects he found could have made a rounded wound.

Tiffany, now seated in a chair just to the right of the large wooden globe, said nothing until the cop closed the final desk drawer. "I might be able to help. I've got a nose for this kind of thing."

Ignoring her, he leaned back and examined the paintings and awards hanging on the wall. Nothing was out of place and nothing was missing. Besides, once again, there were no round edges.

"Listen, Flatfoot," the reporter whined, "I know he was murdered with something round and red. I heard that part of the phone conversation. There's nothing like that in this room, so the murderer must have taken it with him."

She was likely right, but the last thing he wanted to admit to Tiffany was that he was drawing a blank. Getting up from behind the desk, he strolled back into the living room and took a quick inventory. Nothing jumped out that could have been used in the crime. In fact, there was nothing red or round in the room. Strolling back into the study he moved toward the patio. Flipping a switch beside the door, he unlocked and pushed the entry open, then stepped out into the cold night air. There were impressions in the snow. He expected them to lead out to the yard, but they didn't. Instead, they turned to the right and disappeared along the side of the enormous gray-stone mansion. Lane pulled a small flashlight from his suit pocket and shined its beam where the porch light faded.

"Still cold," Tiffany observed as she stepped out and joined him. "Do you have something or you just trying to put some distance between us? Which, don't get me wrong, I don't mind."

"I may have something," Lane explained. "Look at the footsteps in the snow. They show a man walked quickly to the area around that bush and for some reason he stopped there. Note how he shuffled back and forth. Look at these prints over there." He pointed to where his flashlight was shining. "A few of those impressions indicate he was on his toes for a while. Then you'll note by the length of his strides, he must have sprinted around the house, across the back drive, and probably to the street. With the erratic nature of the prints and the fact they hang close to the house, I'll bet this wasn't Elrod. Besides, a man of his age wouldn't have raced. I mean, look at those long strides; our mystery man was running."

"Couldn't it have been one of your cops?" she suggested. "I mean, didn't you and your men explore this area?"

"No," he admitted, "the door was latched from the inside. The only way it could be locked from the outside is with a key. So, we figured the killer must have left through the front door."

"Or just taken Elrod's keys," she added.

"His key ring was in his pocket," Lane smugly replied.

"They could have taken the one they needed," she said, rubbing her arms in an effort to stay warm. "I mean, that's what a smart person would do. Did you check to see if all the keys were there? Or did you bother finding out if anyone else had a key to those doors?"

He disregarded the woman's observation and instead moved toward the place where the man had seemingly shuffled on his feet. "You'll note," he continued, "the evening snow has partially filled the impressions. Therefore, we won't be able to gauge the kind of shoe the man was wearing, but we can probably get an idea of the size. Just looking at it compared to mine, I'd say he is somewhere between an eight and nine." As he continued to stare at the spot where a majority of the impressions were, he rubbed his chin and asked, "Why did he stop here? Even if this were the moment when the maid came into the room, she wouldn't have been able to spot him no matter where he was on the patio. So her appearance shouldn't have caused him to pause."

"And why was he on his tiptoes?" Tiffany asked.

"Why indeed?"

"And," the woman added, "Maybe this is the guy who knifed Elrod rather than actually the one who killed him."

"That's bound to be a crime, too," Lane grumbled. Looking up from where the suspect had paused, he studied the house. There were no windows to peek in, nothing to grab or reach, so why would anyone have gotten up on his tiptoes? "Tiff, it just makes no sense. There's nothing he could have seen by making himself a few inches taller."

"You're thinking just like a man," the woman grumbled while moving over to join him. "There are two reasons to be on your tiptoes. The first is to reach something high or see a bit further, but the other is when you hunker down. He might have been in a crouching position." She demonstrated by stooping over. As she balanced on the balls of her feet, her heels came off the ground.

Lane nodded, then mimicked the woman's stance and position. Not only was she right about his heels coming off the ground, but he found he now had a completely different view of the world. He could even see under the bushes. Yet, shining his flashlight in that direction revealed nothing unusual underneath the evergreens.

"Look at that, Copper."

His eyes darted to where the woman's hand was pointing. Just behind the nearest bush was a basement window. The snow on the frame had been disturbed. Moving to the spot, Lane leaned forward until his arm was fully extended and he pushed on the window's wooden frame. It moved easily. Dropping to his knees in the cold snow, he shoved the glass open. Shining his light into the basement he saw a hundred different items that had, at one time or another, been relegated to storage. Among these castoffs were furniture, three old steamer trunks, stacks of books, an ancient pedal car, a high-wheeled baby buggy and two bicycles, but there was something else resting on an old mattress just below the window that really caught his eye.

Springing to his feet, he rushed back across the patio, through the office and to the telephone. After taking the receiver from the cradle, he dialed a number he knew well. On the third ring, Morelli picked up.

"Morgue."

"Doc, this is Walker, I think I've got something."

"You found our murder weapon?"

"Maybe," he replied. "Could the damage you discovered on Elrod's skull have been made by a fruitcake?"

"What?"

"You know one of those round, foot-wide, four-inch tall tins that are filled with the stuff nobody eats."

"I hadn't expected that," Morelli answered, his voice indicating mild shock.

"There's a fruitcake can in the basement," Lane

explained. "I saw it from a window. Now I haven't gone down there and picked it up yet, but I've got a hunch somebody recently ditched it through an unlocked outside window. It's not nearly as dusty as everything else that is stored down there. In fact, it shines like it just came off a store shelf."

The line went silent for a few seconds before the ME came back on. "Yeah. When the cake is in the tins those things are pretty heavy and, if Elrod had passed out due to the drugs in his system and wasn't offering any resistance, that container could be swung with a lot of force, too. Did the can you saw have green and red stripes on the side and a Christmas tree painted on the front?"

"Not sure about the tree," Walker replied, "but I remember it had stripes like you described. Those were real obvious."

"Then I believe I know that fruitcake," Morelli offered. "If it's the one I think it is, it's part of a joke between Ethan Elrod and Ben Jacobs."

"The federal judge?"

"Yep. They've been trading that old cake back and forth each Christmas for more than a dozen years. Everyone who knows them has seen that old can. I've seen it a half dozen times myself. And that sucker is made of really thick tin, so it could well have created the damage I observed."

"So," Lane chimed in, "murder by fruitcake."

"And not just any fruitcake," Morelli wryly noted, "but one that was first purchased by Ben

Jacobs long before he was a federal judge. At least, I assumed he bought it. So we're talking about an antique fruitcake."

"I'll get the cake tin," Walker assured the examiner, "and when the boys get here to reexamine the scene, I'll bring it to you to look over."

"Thanks, I'll be waiting. Good work, Lane."

The investigator had all but forgotten he wasn't alone until he placed the receiver back in the cradle.

"So, Lane," Tiffany announced, "you've established two things."

"What's that?" he asked as their eyes met, and he was again forced to realize how intoxicatingly beautiful she really was.

"The first is, you've finally discovered a purpose for a fruitcake. The second is this was not a murder to cover a robbery because no one would steal a fruitcake. Now all you have to do is find the fruitcake that used the fruitcake to murder the crusading district attorney. That really makes this case nuts!"

Lane was contemplating a verbal comeback to her lame pun when the phone rang. Thus, as he was drawing blanks in trying to come up with a witty and biting reply, he was literally saved by the bell.

— 4 —

Wednesday, December 18, 1946
10:58 p.m.

Grabbing the receiver on the second ring, Lane pulled it to his ear and barked, "Hello."

"Okay, Elrod, this is the payoff. Have your representative bring the woman with the cash to 1014 Elmwood at 1:15 tonight. Don't be a minute late or a second early. Come to the front door. I'll have what you are looking for there. If you mess this up, then kiss your representative good-bye. Got that?"

The cop considered what he'd heard but didn't answer. Looking to Tiffany, he shrugged.

"Did you get that?" the male voice on the line demanded for the second time.

"1014 Elmwood," the cop assured him.

"And the time?"

"1:15."

"You're putting your life on the line, Elrod," the man warned, "but I'm risking even more than you."

"And you've got everything I need?" Lane demanded.

"Everything," came the quick explanation, "Just make sure you've got the girl and the money.

48

That blonde's testimony could lock someone up for a long time."

"About the blonde," Lane replied.

"What's wrong with your voice, you don't sound like yourself."

The cop took a deep breath and then in a desperate action, coughed several times. After clearing his throat, he got back on the line, "I picked up a cold. Just this time of the year coupled with my health issues."

"Forgot about your weak heart," the caller replied, "and on the woman, don't mess me around. You found her. Even though I've never met her, what she tells me will give me what I need to make sure she's the real deal. If she's not then, I don't care if you are the DA, I promise that you will be fish food by Christmas. You savvy?"

Lane looked over at Tiffany. She had clearly heard everything that had been said, so he was hardly surprised when the reporter mouthed, "I'm your blonde."

"Okay," the cop announced into the receiver, "I fully understand."

"One more thing? I know the last guy you had working for you was injured in a wreck. I want to make sure this new man is someone we can work with. Can he be trusted not to rat my boss out to the cops?"

"Yeah," Lane barked, "you can trust him. Just so

you know, he's handsome, has dark wavy hair, is well-built, and about six feet tall. He kind of looks like Robert Taylor . . . the movie star."

"Good to know, but I hope tonight's the only night I ever see him." A second later, the line went dead.

"Well, Skipper," Tiffany noted, "this sounds interesting."

"Let's not go back to using old nicknames," he snapped, "especially one that brings back a lot of bad memories."

"Whatever. By working together we might be able to save Elrod's investigation after all."

She was right, because the news of the man's death had not been released to the press and had therefore not hit the papers or radio broadcasts, the caller figured the DA was still alive. That was fortuitous. They might actually be able to pull this charade off and get a line on what the district attorney was investigating. But what were they walking into? And why would Elrod agree to leave the mystery woman with this man? That thought led to a series of troubling questions. Was he wrong about Elrod? Was this man that everyone put on a pedestal in league with the very people he was supposed to be bringing to justice? Was he a part of this whole sinister mess? What better way to hide his guilt than by pretending to be the reformer and then taking payoffs?

"Why look at this," the woman called out. Lane glanced up and found her holding a leather attaché.

"Where'd you get that?"

"Now, Skipper," she teased, "while your brain was locked up, mine was working. I made a quick tour of the area and found this had been slid behind a curtain in Elrod's living room." She popped the latch and pulled it open. "How did your people miss it? I have a few guesses." She chuckled, and then her eyes grew as large as saucers. "Wow, Skipper, this thing is filled with money. I mean lots and lots of money. Looks to be all twenties." She reached into the bag and pulled out a handful of cash.

"That's probably the payoff," he announced.

"And I'm the blonde," she again noted. "So we have everything we need for tonight. I sense we're about to blow the mob wide open."

"Or we're going to get blown wide open ourselves," he countered. After crossing the room and looking in the attaché, Walker reached out and gently took the woman's chin, lifting her face until their eyes met. "This is not a game. We're playing with fire here. If something goes wrong Santa might have two less places to visit next week."

"I know," she assured him. "This is no walk in the park. Delono and his boys keep the funeral homes and flower shops in business. But I liked

Elrod and I don't want to see his work die with him."

"Neither do I," Lane acknowledged, while not voicing his sudden doubts about the district attorney. Crossing the room, he picked up the phone and dialed the morgue.

"Morelli's place, where a corpse shows no remorse."

"Mitch, that's horrible."

"Humor of my trade," the ME replied.

"Keep it in house," Lane suggested. "Mitch, have you told anyone that Elrod was murdered?"

"No," Morelli said, "but I've been up to my ears in accident victims. I called the chief and commissioner, but they were out. No one from the media knows either. So just you so far."

"What about the guys I asked you to send down here to rework the crime scene?"

"Oh, gosh," the ME quickly explained, his tone reflecting his embarrassment, "I got to working on an autopsy and just forgot. I'll do it now."

"No," the cop shot back, "don't tell anyone what you know. I don't want the word getting out that Elrod has been murdered. It has to be kept quiet until in the morning. Call Doc Miller and the boys that worked it with me and tell them to keep a lid on it, and I don't want anyone coming over here."

"Mind if I ask why?"

"You can ask," Lane answered, "but I can't tell

you. I'll come back to secure the scene here, including the fruitcake, but I have to do something else first."

"Is it tied to the case?" Morelli asked.

"Yeah. And if I turn up missing," the investigator paused, "look in the Bible on the desk in Elrod's office. I'll write a note detailing what I know there. You can find that information where the second chapter of Luke begins. Got it?"

"Sure. This time of the year that's easy to remember, but I don't like the way this sounds. Be careful, Lane! I don't want to have to determine what killed you."

"I'll do my best to not give you that assignment," he assured the ME as he hung up the phone.

After considering what he knew, he went over to the desk, opened the Bible, and spent a couple of minutes jotting down what he'd learned. Tossing the pen down and closing the Bible, he turned back to face Tiffany. Her normal smug expression was now framed by a softer, more concerned look. Her change in disposition caused him to offer the woman an out. "You don't have to do this."

She shook her head, "And if you go there without a blonde then you won't live to explain what this is all about. I've got to know what Elrod uncovered. If he was taking down organized crime and I can report on it, I have to be there. It's my job."

"So your concern is for the story and not me?" he asked.

She forced a smile, "Maybe it's for both. I know you're tired of Delono and his ilk running this town. So am I. I'm also tired of seeing kids hooked on dope and women working the street to support their habits. I'm tired of the murders and the dirty cops. But as much as I want to break the story about the big man being sent to the big house, I don't want to see a dumb homicide detective go down in the process. You've caused me a lot of grief, you don't know a thing about tact and manners, but . . ." She stopped, her blue eyes looking as if they were suddenly a bit moist.

"But what, Tiff?"

"But nothing," she shot back, "I just don't want to have to figure out a way to make you sound good in an obituary. I've never have been any good at writing fiction."

"Don't worry," he quipped, almost relieved she hadn't gone soft on him, "I'll outlive you just so I don't have to deal with your libelous prose."

"Still," she chimed in, "there's something about this mess that doesn't pass the smell test."

"What are you talking about?" he quickly asked.

Her eyes locked onto Lane's. "Delono would have had Elrod wiped out the professional way. He'd have either used some kind of drug that made it appear the DA died of a heart attack—I mean everyone knows he had a weak ticker—or he'd have had a hired gun shoot him. Hit men don't use fruitcakes as weapons and then come back a half an hour later and stab their victims."

"So," the cop asked, "what's your theory?"

"I don't have one," she admitted, "the money still being here means that it was likely not a robbery either. I just don't see this as being connected to Delono."

"Tiffany, other than your fake Santas, who else had a motive?"

"Maybe," she suggested, "our visit to the address on Elmwood will give us some insight into that." She smiled, reached over and patted the attaché, "You got a plan, Skipper?"

"Of course," he growled, "and don't call me Skipper!"

"Hey," Tiff laughed, "if you think I'm ever going to forget what you did to us in that row-boat you're sadly mistaken."

Lane shook his head, grabbed his hat, and walked toward the door. It was not the time to relive a past adventure that ended badly, instead it was time to play Santa and deliver a gift that he hoped didn't explode in their faces.

— 5 —

Wednesday, December 18, 1946
11:02 p.m.

"It's all set," McCoy Rawlings announced as he placed the phone back into its cradle. While waiting for a response, the six-foot, three-inch ruggedly good-looking man walked over to an end table and twisted a knob on a Zenith desktop radio. The dial's light immediately popped on and thirty seconds later the walnut-encased box's speaker came to life. While tapping his fingers on the wooden tabletop, Rawlings listened to the second verse of Perry Como singing "Winter Wonderland." Only after the decade-old holiday hit concluded did he turn back and study his visitor.

In the shadows beside the small living room's one door, dressed in a gray wool overcoat turned up at the neck and sporting a matching fedora pulled low over his face, a short, thin brooding man stood stone still and mute. His motionless hands were shoved deep into his coat pockets and a cigarette hung from his lips, its smoke drifting lazily toward the ceiling giving the only indication that Richard Delono was alive.

Delono was a crime lord or a "boss" as the newspapers described him. He was by nature and profession ruthless and cold. For this Chicago native, the only lives that had any real value were those belonging to him and his family. His voice registered in the tenor range and his slow, deliberate delivery was crisp and grating. He dressed, ate and lived well, but rarely smiled. He fancied himself looking like Humphrey Bogart but in truth was closer to Bela Lugosi and, like the character that actor was famed for playing, Delono was a creature of the darkness.

Though there was no hint of emotion etched on his face, Rawlings figured "The King of the Underworld" must have been pleased with the news that'd just been shared. After all, for weeks Delono's main goal had been tracking down the blonde. Still, even if he was satisfied that his goal had been realized, the man with the dark eyes and pencil-thin mustache didn't reveal it. He remained stiff and silent until Como's song finished and Nat King Cole's new hit, "The Christmas Song," began.

"Mr. Rawlings," the guest began, his voice so quiet as to almost not be audible over the music, "what do you think of that recording?"

"The one by Nat?"

"Yes."

"I like it," Rawlings admitted.

"Why?" the visitor demanded.

Rawlings shrugged, "I guess, Mr. Delono, because it mentions so many of the things that make Christmas special to me. I like thinking about the way kids look forward to Santa, a nip in the air, snow on the ground, and the sighting of reindeer. So even though I've never eaten a chestnut, for me that song captures a lot of magic in its few short verses."

Delono nodded, reached up to his mouth, took the cigarette from his lips, dropped the still burning butt into an ashtray, and moved toward the door. It looked as though the he was about to make an exit until he paused while reaching for the brass knob and slowly glanced back to his host. The words he spoke hung in the air like a summer fog. "McCoy, there's only one way this Christmas will be merry at my house, and that's if you do your job tonight."

"Can I ask," Rawlings quietly inquired as he considered what was obviously meant as a warning, "why this dame means so much to you?"

"Do you need to know?" Delono asked. "Will it matter as to how you do your job? I mean, a man working on a Detroit assembly line doesn't know who is going to buy the car he's making or why he chose that one over a dozen other models."

"No," Rawlings admitted, "you've paid me well and the money that Elrod is adding to the kitty is more than enough bonus, so, in truth, I don't really need to know. I'll assure you my knowing or not won't matter when it comes to my work. I'll snuff out and get rid of the mark even if I don't know the reason I am doing it, but—"

Delono, his dark eyes glowing, cut Rawlings off before he could finish his question. "You don't need or want to know the whys. Too much knowledge only gets people in trouble. Just do your job and send me the proof that you've done it."

"Will a photo do?" Rawlings asked.

The underworld king nodded. "A photo and that blue jade ring she always wears. It's the only one like it, and she never takes it off. You mail those two things to the post office box I gave you and then you get back to the West Coast. After you finish here I never want to see you again."

As he considered what was obviously a threat more than a suggestion, Rawlings nodded, walked over to the radio, and switched it off. Reaching into his coat's side pocket, he fingered a thick stack of bills before turning back to his guest. "Ten thousand is a chunk of change, she must mean a great deal to you."

"Let's just call her a present," Delono countered.

"A present?"

"McCoy, were you in the military?"

"Yeah, Marines," Rawlings admitted, his tone displaying a hint of pride. "I fought in the Pacific."

Delono smiled, "And what was the value of a man's life in the war?"

"I cared a lot about my own," Rawlings truthfully answered.

"What about the enemy?" the guest asked. "Or what about a fellow soldier who took a bullet intended for you? What were their lives worth when compared to yours?"

"When compared to mine?"

"Yes."

"About a plug nickel," Rawlings explained. "I was no hero, just a man trying to stay alive. My skin was much more important to me than anything or anyone else."

"Well," Delono explained, "this woman has great value to me only because she has great value to someone I need in my camp."

The host nodded, "And who is that?"

"You don't need to know," Delono explained. "All you need to keep in mind is that the blonde needs to be silenced. When her lips no longer move, when she can no longer tell what she knows, then she has no value to anyone. Her silence is the greatest present I can give this year."

Delono's words were cryptic, hiding much more than they revealed. As Rawlings turned them over in his head, he quipped, "You said *give* not *get*. I'm not following you. I thought I was doing this for you. After all, it's your money and you hired me."

The visitor smiled, "Don't you know it is always better to give than receive? That's the great lesson of this season." Delono pulled his left hand from his pocket and ran his gloved fingers over his clean-shaven chin. "McCoy, I have a wonderful wife and five children. My oldest kid is in college and my youngest is just a third grader. This year I've spent thousands of dollars on their presents and can't wait until Christmas Eve when we sit around our tree, sing a few carols, and open those gifts. That will be a day when I will make memories that I'll never forget. So therefore it promises to be the most wonderful day of the year." He paused and locked his eyes on the hired gun. "But if you fail me tonight, then my December 24 will not mean nearly as much. I might not enjoy the looks on the faces of my kids when they open their presents or my wife's smile when I hand her the keys to her new Packard. So, I have a lot riding on what goes down in the next couple of hours. And, so do you. The Japs might not have killed you at Iwo Jima, but I can make sure that you're not as lucky here in Chicago. You're not the only one who is in your line of work. You're not the only one who thinks life is cheap. I can make one call and hire someone to finish you off. So I think you understand what happens if you don't do the job tonight."

Rawlings nodded, "I understand."

"One more question," Delono announced as he turned the knob, opened the door, and looked out into the snow. "Does killing bother you?"

"I was trained for it in the war," Rawlings calmly explained. "I was a sniper. I don't know

61

how many I killed in combat, but with each kill it was easier. Soon it just became a job. I didn't even look at the man in my sights as a person; he was just a target."

"But that was war," Delono noted, "and tonight the target will not be some man in an enemy uniform, but a woman. Doesn't that make it different?"

Rawlings shrugged, "In the war I got the same pay everyone else at my rank and grade got, so I wasn't paid for each kill but for each day of combat duty. But tonight I'm getting more than I made in three years of active duty. So, let's just say I like the rewards much better in civilian life than those I had in the military."

"So," Delono soberly cracked, "there's no emotion bubbling in your heart, this is only a paycheck."

"Emotions have to be packed in your brain and carried around. I don't like luggage. I travel light."

"You're a cold man," the visitor observed as he turned to face the winter storm.

"Blame the war," Rawlings quipped. "Now you need to get away from here before Elrod's delivery boy and the target arrive."

"I have to do a bit of shopping," the visitor announced. "So I need to take my leave anyway."

"Isn't it a little late for stores to be open?" Rawlings observed.

"They stay open for me," Delono quipped, "especially when I need an alibi."

"Buying something for the family?" the host asked.

"Got those gifts," the mob leader explained. "The only man left on my list is William Hammer. He goes back a long time. He worked for Big Jim Cosolimo and Johnny Torrio before becoming an enforcer for Capone. He lives over in Cicero now, not far from the Hawthorne Race Track on Pershing. He's old, alone, and dying with cancer. I've never bought him a Christmas present before. This will be my last chance." He looked down at his feet and frowned, "Good help is hard to find and a man loyal to the organization is even harder to get. Ham has been both of those things." Delono sadly shook his head before stepping out into the night.

Rawlings walked to the still-open front door and watched his guest get into the back of a large Cadillac sedan. A few seconds after the rear door closed, the two-ton vehicle rumbled off into the night, disappearing into a thickening blanket of falling snow.

Closing the home's entry, Rawlings strolled back over to a green chair, pulled a M1911 single-action, .45 pistol from his pocket, and, for the third time in the past two hours, checked to make sure it was operational. Satisfied the weapon was ready for action, he eased it back under his sport coat and into his belt, sat down, and waited.

— 6 —

Thursday, December 19, 1946
1:07 a.m.

Tiffany Clayton, wrapped in a tweed coat and holding the attaché filled with cash in her arms, watched Lane Walker ease the Chicago Police Department's unmarked 1941 Ford sedan up to the curb. As the cop shut off the flathead V-8 engine, the woman took a moment to study the small frame house. Judging from the architecture, it had likely been built in the 1920s. With its small stoop of a front porch, painted clapboard siding, and shutterless windows, the white one-story dwelling was simple and quaint. From what she knew of similar-style homes, she guessed it to have about twelve hundred square feet of living space and possibly two bedrooms. Glancing through the snow and down the street she noted a dozen other similar houses all likely built and sold in the years just before the stock market crashed and the country plunged into a depression. The area was well-maintained and the yards well-kept. Thus, she surmised this was a safe, secure block likely populated by people with big dreams and small budgets. On most days she would have gladly traded her tiny apartment to live in this neighborhood, but, as she considered the unknowns that waited for her behind the front door of the home on 1014 Elmwood, she fought a desire to run to another block in another part of the Windy City.

"Quite a come-down from Elrod's mansion," Lane grimly noted.

Tiffany nodded, "Pretty much anything would be." She glanced from the scene outside the car to the driver. "Did you notice that every home on this street has some kind of holiday decorations except this one?"

"Yeah," he soberly replied. "I'm guessing Santa will skip this house."

She smiled morosely, "After we give whoever is on the other side of that door the cash we have in this case, I don't think Santa's visit will be missed."

"You might be right," he agreed as he glanced down toward her feet where the attaché rested. "What's haunting me is what did he do to earn this money?"

"About this plan . . ." Tiffany cut in.

The words had barely escaped the reporter's lips when the cop noted, "There's still time to walk away from this. I could tell him the blonde got cold feet and ran away at a stop sign."

"And," she quickly added, "that would likely mean you'd hand over the money and pay with your life." Tiffany again glanced toward the house, "Besides, I want to know what's going on."

"Okay," he quipped, "it's your funeral."

"I certainly hope not," she whispered. "But, with that in mind, shouldn't I have a gun?"

He chuckled, "There's no way I'd let you have a gun. If I gave you the revolver that was in the glove box you'd likely shoot yourself slipping it into your purse. Just play things the way I planned and you won't need one. I got things covered. My plan is perfect. Now, slide that attaché over here."

"Fine," she quipped as she tossed the brief-case his way, yanked up on the door handle and stepped out into the frigid night air. Glancing back to Lane, she issued a strong warning. "You just do your job and I will do mine. But if anything goes wrong and the worst happens, I'll haunt you until the day you die."

"Couldn't be any worse," he shot back, "than the way you haunt me now."

In the twenty steps between the street and the front door, the sharp wind cut into Tiffany's cheeks like a knife. She was sure it had never been this cold. As her companion knocked on the door, a stinging, Arctic blast forced tears from her eyes and down her face. They froze on her cheeks before they could fall to the ground. She was just wiping them off with her glove when the door opened and the entry was filled with a man who appeared to be a linebacker for the Chicago Bears. She was sure the last time she'd seen shoulders like that was on a gorilla at the zoo. Was it too late to back out and run? As she looked at the man's right hand, her silent question was answered. In spite of the heavily falling snow, the light from a street lamp clearly reflected chrome from a revolver's muzzle, and it was pointed at Lane.

Their host, his face still hidden by the shadows, looked from the woman to the cop before stepping aside and allowing the visitors to enter the very dark living room. As Tiffany dusted the snow from her coat, the towering figure backed farther into the deep shadows. Other than his impressive size, it was now even more impossible to distinguish any of his features. He could have been white, black, or even green and have five eyes and three noses for all she could tell.

As she tried to remember the plan Lane dreamed up for this little holiday party, the cop closed the door, stomped his feet, and dropped the attaché on the floor. Then, for what had to be the longest sixty seconds on record, no one moved and not a word was said. Finally, their host broke the silence with an unsurprising question.

"You got the cash?"

As Tiffany's eyes tried to pierce the darkness and get a better read on the mystery man with gun, Lane answered the question. "The money's in the bag. Now, where are the files Mr. Elrod needs?"

"They're on a table about ten feet to your right. By the way, I have a gun trained on you and my eyes are accustomed to the dark. If you try anything you'll be dead before your weapon clears your belt."

Though the man's voice was deep, his accent was nondescript. He could have been from anywhere.

"How can I see if the files are legit?" Lane asked. "I'll need some light to study them."

"You'll have to take my word." Their host's matter-of-fact reply firmly reinforced there would be no compromise. Thus, the stall Lane had put in his plans, those precious minutes when he would study the files while everyone waited and watched, had now been edited out of the script. It was now time to ad-lib and Tiffany had no faith in her temporary partner's ability to do that. So, in retrospect, she now fully realized she should have penned the plan.

"What about the woman?" the cop asked as he moved across the floor to a small table barely visible in the dim light.

"Grab the files, get in your car, and leave her here. That was the deal." The host paused before adding, "And don't try to be a hero. If you pull a gun, you'll die and so will the woman. The only way you're walking out is with her staying with me."

Lane picked up the documents and glanced

back toward the host, "What are you going to do with her?"

"If I don't see that car drive off in the next two minutes, I'll kill the dame. So, if you want her to keep breathing, get moving."

When the cop froze, Tiffany knew what was holding him place. He was thinking about making a play for his gun and that was definitely not a part of the plan. The last thing she needed was Lane taking a bullet for her. If he managed to live through the experience, he'd never let her forget it. So, she had to get him back on track.

"Get going," she spat. "I'm tired of having your paws on me."

"You heard her," their host growled.

Lane moved quickly to the door and took a final look at Tiffany before opening the entry and rushing off the porch and to the car. She took a deep breath as she heard the Ford's engine come to life. At least for the moment, they were back on script. Still, as the vehicle eased forward her heart leapt into her throat.

"Okay, baby," the man announced, "my car's waiting in the back alley. Move out the door and lead the way into the backyard. When we get to the vehicle, you slide behind the wheel. You'll be driving. And don't try anything. I've got a forty-five ready to blow a hole in you the size of Lake Michigan."

This wasn't the way things were supposed to

go down. Everything was theoretically to take place in this house. Their leaving now wouldn't give Lane the time to drive two blocks, park his car, make his way back to the scene to observe what was going on, and then, like the cavalry, rush in to save her. Thus, the second facet of the less-than-brilliant man's plan had been destroyed. As she considered her options, she thought about her host's warning. Would he really shoot her?

"Listen," she quipped, hoping her voice didn't reflect how much her knees were shaking, "I really need to warm up a bit before I go back out again."

"Get moving," the man barked.

"Would it be all right if I used the bathroom," she hurriedly added. "I've been drinking coffee all night to stay warm and . . ."

He didn't give her a chance to finish before spitting out what appeared to be his final ultimatum. "Get moving or die on this floor. It's up to you."

"Great plan, Lane," Tiffany muttered as she turned, opened the front door, and slowly marched out onto the porch. She momentarily stopped at the steps, grasping for a way to buy another minute, when she felt a gun in her back.

"Baby, nobody can see you," the gunman announced. "Everyone on this street goes to bed by ten. So keep moving."

Sensing she had no choice, Tiffany walked out

into the now driving snow and around the side of the small home. This time her fear kept her from feeling the Arctic cold. It was 104 steps, she knew because she counted each of them, before she arrived at a 1939 Oldsmobile coupe. After opening the passenger door, she slid across the cloth-covered seat, dragging her huge purse behind her, and over to the steering wheel. Before she could take a breath, he was beside her, the gun aimed at her ribs.

"The key's in the ignition," he barked, "start the car up and let's get moving."

Her gloved hand found the key. After switching it to the right, she pulled out the manual choke, pressed the gas pedal two times, and pushed the starter button. The car's six-cylinder turned right over and caught. After pulling out the light switch, she pushed the choke halfway in, depressed the clutch, shifted the car into first, lifted her left foot, and eased forward.

"Turn right at the corner," the man ordered. "You're going to go across town until you get to Lake Shore Drive, then you'll head north."

"Where we going?" she asked as she switched on the wipers to knock the snow off the windshield.

"Somewhere your boyfriend can't find us."

"He's not my boyfriend," she shot back.

"Fine," came the gruff reply, "he's a cop. His name is Lane Walker, there's no use denying it.

Still, he didn't get a good look at me, he's not on our trail, and as I have both you and the money, I'm not worried about much of anything now. Yet, I am sorry that I won't see his face when he discovers that the house is empty." The gunman chuckled, "I'd love to watch him as he runs a couple of blocks back to his car in a futile effort to catch up to us. Walker has always been a day late and a dollar short."

"You know him well," Tiffany quipped as she shook her head. No matter how she cut it, she was getting just what she deserved. Once again, Lane Walker was standing her up.

— 7 —

Thursday, December 19, 1946
1:07 a.m.

Within five minutes of having Lane's plan go terribly wrong, Tiffany's heart rate returned to normal. With both hands on the wheel and her eyes watching carefully for ice, she silently navigated the Windy City's all-but-deserted streets for twenty minutes until she finally made the left onto Lake Shore Drive. It was only then the driving snow let up, giving the woman a chance to relax and reflect.

Her captor obviously knew Lane. How? Had the

guy with the shiny gun been on the police force? Had he been arrested sometime in the last year? Maybe he and the cop had met in the service. Perhaps they had even been part of the same unit. Yet, before she felt she could dig into that area, she had to focus on the one thing she did know. The gunman apparently believed she was the blonde he'd been assigned to pick up. But for what purpose? Did he need information she was supposed to give him or was he going to rub her out? At this point knowing if she was living on borrowed time seemed far more important than discovering where this guy had met Lane. So, Tiffany opted to first voice a very haunting query, and, if she managed to get an answer that offered a chance at life, she'd figured she could go on from there.

"So, is this my final ride?"

She glanced over to the man as she waited for an explanation. From the glow of the car's dash lights she could now perceive he was not only broad-shouldered, but square-jawed, clean-shaven, and ruggedly attractive. His dark, bushy eyebrows framed large eyes and his sharp nose and jutting chin gave him a bit of a Dick Tracy look.

"You're a good-looking doll," he noted as their eyes met.

"Pickup lines aren't really necessary," she replied as she turned her attention back to the road. "You already have me in your car and that gun pretty much dictates I'll have to do whatever you want me to do." Suddenly feeling a bit bolder she added, "But whatever you do, please don't call me a doll. I've got a college degree and I can put together sentences in both print and verbal fashion. Dolls can't do that."

If she'd touched a nerve, it didn't show. He cocked his head and barked, "Take off your gloves."

"It's cold and I'm driving the car," she snapped, "it would be dangerous for me to let go of the steering wheel. Besides, my hands aren't my best features."

"Okay," he replied, "I'll make this easy, just use those full red lips to answer a question. Are you wearing your jade ring?"

"Listen," she cracked, "on what I make each week the only piece of jewelry I can afford is a cheap watch. Why don't you use that cash we brought tonight and buy your own jade ring? I don't have one."

He was quiet for a moment before he began spitting out words that chilled her even more than the hard December weather. "I've been paid big bucks to get rid of you, and that jade ring you claim you don't have is the key to my not getting rubbed out, too."

She considered his words and, as she did, a plan quickly came together in her mind. The guy needed a jade ring to seal the deal. He obviously figured she'd be wearing it. If she played things right, the mere fact she wasn't might just buy her some time.

"The ring's at my apartment," she lied.

"But I was told you always wear it."

"Well," she stalled, "I do, except when it's this cold. My gloves don't fit right when I have it on. So tonight, I left it home. Why's it so important to you?"

She waited for his response, but it didn't come quickly. It was a full three miles later when he finally posed a question. "How far is your place from where we are now?"

"With the streets the way they are," she explained, "maybe half an hour."

"Let's go," he suggested. "You're no good to me without that ring."

Tiffany turned right, drove around a block, and pointed the car back toward downtown. She'd successfully and unexpectedly bought a little time, but would that really matter when they got to the apartment? When she had to admit there was no ring, then what would the guy do? That was something she didn't want to consider and thanks to his breaking in with a question, she didn't have to dwell on it either.

"What do you have on Richard Delono?" he demanded.

This was interesting. Just the mention of the

gangster's name proved that Elrod had been on the right track with his investigation. But what did a blonde woman have to do with it? Why was she so important to finishing this equation? It was time to find out and perhaps the best way to get that information was to play dumb.

"What makes you think I know anything about . . ." she paused for effect, then added, "what did you say the guy's name was?"

He leaned against the passenger door and studied her for several seconds before asking, "How much further?"

"About ten minutes, unless we hit a patch of ice."

He smiled grimly. "Elrod turned you over to me or at least he used Walker to do that. That's how badly he wanted those files. On top of that, Delono paid me to make sure you didn't talk. So what is it that you know?"

She was getting someplace now. The blonde was valuable, at least to the crime boss, maybe what the mystery woman knew might even bring him down. But if that were the case, why would Elrod turn her over to the very man he was trying to expose and stop? Or was he? Maybe Elrod had been playing both sides of the street and the blonde and cash were meant to assure Delono that they were on the same team. As she rolled the theory over in her head, she turned to her captor, "What was in the files?"

"What difference does it make?" he asked.

"If those files are worth more than my life," she shot back, "then I want to know why."

He nodded, "That's fair. There was supposed to be pages of information in those files on the man Elrod has in his sights, but it was all a scam. Those files are filled with nothing more than blank sheets of paper."

She could barely believe what she'd been told. She'd put her life on the line for nothing. Swallowing hard she whispered, "You're serious?"

"Yeah," he admitted. "I looked through them. I don't know what Elrod was expecting, but when he opens those files he's going to be very disappointed. So, I guess your life is not worth the paper that absolutely nothing is written on."

She nodded and frowned. Now that was a sobering thought. Lane had sold the reporter out for a long story with absolutely no copy. Well, at least the cop could read and comprehend what he'd been given.

— 8 —

Thursday, December 19, 1946
2:01 a.m.

Lane Walker was frantic. The house was empty, there was no obvious clue as to who had been using it, and he had no idea what the mystery man was driving when he spirited Tiffany away. Worse yet, he didn't know where the gunman had taken the reporter. Thus, the cop was completely lost.

Walking over to the phone, he picked up the receiver and dialed four numbers before shaking his head and hanging up. What good would it do to put out an alarm when he had only a vague description of the man and no guess as to where he'd taken the reporter? Besides, the last thing he wanted to admit was that he'd been so stupid. After all, this guy had anticipated every move the cop had planned. In fact, his opponent had won the game in one move and kidnapped *The Chicago Star*'s top reporter. The chief was going to eat Lane alive when he found out.

Flipping on all the lights, the detective began to search and then re-search the house room by room. Except for the furniture, there was nothing in the place. There were no clothes in the closets, no dirty dishes, the trash cans were empty, and nothing was written on notepads. There wasn't even a toothbrush or a bar of soap in the bathroom.

Frustrated, Lane hurried next door and pounded on the door to find out what the neighbors knew. A man in his forties was not pleased about having a person, even one with a badge, rouse him from bed in the middle of the night. Neither were the folks in the other homes on the street. Worse yet, no one had ever seen the big man. About all they could tell the cop was that Olivia Allbright, an elderly widow, had lived in the small house at 1014 Elmwood until three months ago when she'd died. After her children removed her personal belongings, a real estate company finished cleaning the place and was now getting ready to sell it. As it was fully furnished, the company expected it to move quickly.

With no concrete information to work with, Lane returned to the house, picked up the phone, and began digging into what little he had gleaned from his nocturnal wanderings. A series of calls finally put the cop in touch with a realtor who knew something about the house. James Cantrell informed the policeman that the property had not been leased, that he'd never met the man Lane described, and that his company would not officially put a "For Sale" sign in the yard until after Christmas. The call ended with the angry real estate agent shooting out a number of off-color descriptions of policemen that made even Lane blush. After setting the phone back down on the receiver, the exasperated cop came to the conclusion the home had been chosen for only one reason; it was empty and furnished. Thus, the man had simply picked the lock or found an open window, waited for Lane and Tiffany to arrive, and after he gotten his hands on the money and the woman, he'd likely driven to his real residence. But where was that?

The clock was ticking and if Lane couldn't find out who the man was perhaps it was time to figure out why the big guy wanted both the cash and the blonde. Perhaps the papers in the files would give him a lead. Hurrying out into the snow, Lane raced the two blocks to his car, hopped in, started the engine, popped on the dome light, and opened the top file. It was filled with nothing but blank paper. Frantically he grabbed the next two and was horrified to discover nothing but three hundred more sheets of white typing paper. Elrod had evidently been conned and that made Lane look like an even bigger fool. Tossing the file onto the seat, the detective tried to come up with a new plan, but as he caught a glimpse of himself in the car's rearview mirror, he was taken back to a bit of advice from his youth. If only he'd just thought of it earlier he might not be in this fix.

His father had once told him knee-jerk reactions

usually leave a person trying to justify their actions while standing on one leg. Now if things kept going as they were, he soon wouldn't even have that leg to stand on. Why had he blindly rushed into this situation, and even better, why had he brought Tiffany with him?

Shoving the car into gear, an angry Lane aimed the Ford back toward the district attorney's house. Perhaps the only way to find out what had happened to Tiffany was to search Elrod's personal files and see if he could figure out who the real blonde was. If he couldn't get a handle on that, then the odds against finding Tiffany were likely very long. As he slid along the slick streets, as one mile became two and two, three, his overriding fear was that his stupidity and haste had signed a death warrant for the woman he might care about much more than he was willing to admit. The more he considered that possibility, the more he wanted to scream.

— 9 —

Thursday, December 19, 1946
2:22 a.m.

Tiffany's bluff worked, at least temporarily. She'd actually managed to lure her captor into her third-floor, three-room apartment. Now the man was intently watching her, with gun in hand, as she pretended to look through her dressing table for a ring she didn't have. When she moved over to her dresser, it dawned on her that her plan would have worked much better if she'd had a much bigger place with a lot more furniture.

"Surely you know where you put it," he barked at the five-minute mark of her little charade. "Either that or you're the most scatterbrained person I've ever met."

"I thought it was in a drawer," she stalled. "Maybe I left it in the bathroom." As she hurried from her bedroom into the tiny connecting bath, he followed her step by step.

"Can't you at least give me some privacy?" she pleaded. "I have dainty things hanging over the showerhead to dry."

"I know what bras and stockings look like," he sarcastically replied. "I also know when a woman is looking for an exit."

Tiffany pointed to the eight-by-four-foot room's only window located five feet over the tub and noted, "A small house cat could barely climb through that window; so I'm not going anywhere. Just let me look for the ring in peace. Your hovering around me like a mother hen is making me so nervous I can't think straight."

Leaning against the sink, he shook his head and chuckled, "I've been called a lot of things in my life, but never a mother hen. As far as my thinking goes, it seems your mind works pretty well. In fact, it's coming up with more crazy notions with each passing second." He took a deep breath before adding, "I don't like being played a fool, so either produce the ring or admit you don't have it."

Tiffany pushed her blonde hair away from her face and frowned. The gig was up, she couldn't bluff anymore. It was time to cave and give out with some bad news. But that didn't mean she had to tell the truth. There was still one way to keep the con going.

"Listen," she paused, "what's your name any-way? I mean we are sharing a bathroom, I think I should at least know your name."

"McCoy," he stoically replied.

"What's your first name?" Tiffany demanded. "I hate calling folks by their last name."

"That is my first name."

"McCoy?" she laughed. "You're the first real McCoy I've ever met."

"That line's hardly original."

"Okay, McCoy," Tiffany coyly replied, "let me level with you. The jade ring is not here."

"Where is it?" he impatiently demanded as he waved his gun toward her face.

"Well," she explained, her eyes following the moving barrel, "it's Christmas, and things have not been going real well in my world." She smiled nervously and then continued her story. "I have not been able to find a steady job, I needed to buy some presents for friends and family, and I have a really big family, fourteen brothers and sisters, so I pawned it last week."

"So, there's no ring?"

"Well," Tiffany quickly explained, "not tonight. But we can take some of that money you've got in that attaché case and retrieve it tomorrow. I can buy it back for two hundred dollars."

His smirk clearly proved he was not really buying her latest story. Keeping his gun pointed at her face, he pulled a dime from his pocket, tossed it in the air, caught it, and glanced at his palm. He continued the little exercise nine more times.

"The flip of a coin sometimes produces all the direction any of us need," he explained. "You know, when I was in the Marines that's how we decided who was going to volunteer for a dangerous mission."

Her blue eyes followed his hand as he dropped

the dime back into his pants pocket. What did this have to do with anything? After all, the only thing she'd volunteered for was to be a part of Lane's plan. She silently laughed as she realized that decision had made her a sucker. Yep, going along with anything that flatfoot suggested was always a bad idea.

As Tiffany continued to rehash her stupidity by reliving a series of horrible experiences with Lane, the gunman raised his eyebrows and noted, "You don't get it? Do you?"

Forgetting about the cop and dates that went bad, the reporter shook her head and admitted, "I'm not following what a dime has to with this."

"Heads, you're lying," he explained, "tails, you're not."

"What did the dime tell you?"

"Doesn't matter what the dime said," McCoy calmly explained, "my gut tells me all I need to know."

As she waited for him to explain, Tiffany studied the man who evidently held her life in his hands. His hair was dark, his eyes green, and his chin strong. Not only were his shoulders as wide as an axe handle, but his chest was broad and his waist thin. In a different time and place, she would have been attracted to the handsome stranger, but it was hard to warm up to man with a gun in his hand.

"What's your name?" McCoy demanded, his

question reminding her she really was in a tough spot that was getting tougher by the moment.

She licked her lips, searching for a suitable response that didn't blow her cover while also trying to latch onto a name that seemed real. She almost opted to use Brenda Strong, but that sounded too much like a comic page heroine. The next handle she landed on, Madge Wooley, seemed too old. Janie was a nice name, but what last name worked well with it? She'd just about decided on McCall when McCoy waved his left hand and frowned.

"You're not the blonde that was supposed to come to the house. By now that's pretty obvious, so who are you and what happened to her? You might want to give out with the truth and not try to dream up another fairy tale. I outgrew those a long time ago."

"I have to be the blonde," she continued to build on her lie. "Otherwise, how would I have known when and where to meet you? I mean, that Lane person sold me out. You see, he assured me I was going to meet a rich guy who had a great job for me. You might have problems believing this, but I sing a bit. So, I naturally bought into what Lane was selling. After all, I told you I had to pawn the ring. I need the money."

"Yeah," he smiled, "I can imagine you onstage, after all, I've been listening to your song and dance routine for an hour now." He shook his head, "Just quit playing games and admit you're not the real blonde."

"That's not true," she shot back. "I've never dyed my hair. I've been a real blonde since the day I was born."

"Listen lady," a now noticeably frustrated McCoy complained, "I've had about as much of this as I can stomach. Quit with the jokes and give me the real story. After all, I've got the gun and I'm not afraid to use it."

Though she didn't want to abort her performance and though she feared shelling out the truth would mean the end of her life, what other choice did she have? The real story had to be written and she might as well be the author who decided the words to employ. Shrugging, she silently marched past her captor, his eyes and gun following her every step, through the bedroom and into the ten-by-ten-foot living room. Sitting on the edge of the couch, she pointed to a chair. "McCoy, if you'll keep your hand off that trigger, I'll shoot straight with you. So take a load off, open up your ears, and I'll give you the real unvarnished scoop."

The man eased down into a second-hand Victorian reading chair and crossed his right foot over his left knee. Though he didn't aim his weapon directly at her, he kept his finger on the trigger as he balanced the revolver on the arm of the red chair.

"Okay, McCoy, I'm not only not the blonde, I don't even know the blonde. I just happened to be at Elrod's when you called. And you might as well know this, Elrod's dead. He was dead when I arrived."

"So that's why you were with Lane Walker. You're a lady cop."

"Not really," she explained, "I don't work with the guy. In fact, I usually try to avoid him. But I had an appointment with Elrod, and Lane was there when I knocked on the door. He was in charge of the murder investigation."

"Did Lane answer the phone when I called?"

"Yeah."

"Then," McCoy said, his expression and tone softening a bit, "the quiz-club final question becomes, who are you?"

She smiled. There was no longer any reason to continue the charade. If she was going to die she might as well do it under her real identity. "I'm a reporter for *The Chicago Star*. My name is Tiffany Clayton."

"That's just great," McCoy grumbled, "I was paid to kill a blonde wearing a jade ring. If I don't mail a photo of the dead girl along with that ring back to the man who hired the hit, then he's going to kill me. So it looks like you and Walker signed my death warrant."

"Well, excuse me," Tiffany quipped, "I'm sorry I'm not the woman you need to murder."

"That's the breaks," he grumbled. "If I just had the jade ring I'll bet I could pass you off as the dame."

"Well," she snidely replied. "I just seem to be a big disappointment to you. How tragic it must be to meet a woman who simply can't deliver what you need before you blow her brains out."

McCoy pushed out of the chair and walked over to the window. He peeked through the curtain and noted, "Well, it has quit snowing."

As he continued to study the empty street three floors below, Tiffany quietly rose and took two steps toward the front door.

"I can see your reflection in the glass," he noted, "so why don't you sit down and let me figure a way out of this mess."

As she dejectedly moved back to her seat, collapsed on the couch, and crossed her legs, McCoy turned, walked into the apartment's kitchen, retrieved a glass, and turned on the tap. After taking a drink of water, he marched back into the room and studied the woman for a few minutes before finally revealing his thoughts. "If I just knew what the ring looked like maybe I could come up with a duplicate and still pass you off as her. That'd keep me alive for a while."

"But that would seal the deal for me," she noted. Forcing a grim smile she added, "Well, I'm sorry I couldn't help you, but I realize your time is limited and you have another blonde to find, so why don't you just let yourself out and I'll get ready for bed."

"It's not that simple," he explained. "And, if I might be so bold, you're being a little selfish here. If I don't follow through on this hit, then I die."

"I get that," she quickly explained. "And I wish it wasn't that way, but there's not much I can do about that. So, as your killing me really won't do you any good, I think it might be wise for you to hop in your car and go and find the real blonde. Check with Santa, he is supposed to know where everyone is all the time. Maybe he can help you."

He nodded, "You might just be onto something." Moving back to the chair he took a seat and glanced back at his unwilling host. His expression revealed a cool detachment and, as both of their lives were on the line, that either made him the coolest cat since author Dashiell Hammett invented Sam Spade or a person resigned to his own fate. His next question, delivered in a monotone, echoed the man's matter-of-fact manner. "So you were at Elrod's earlier tonight."

"We've already established that," she impatiently admitted. "You're as bad about going over the same thing again and again as Lane Walker is." She suddenly smiled and snapped her fingers. "Wait a minute. A brilliant thought just hit me."

"I doubt the brilliant part," McCoy countered.

"No," she begged, "give me a chance. Here's

my idea and I think you'll see the logic in it. Lane and I probably beat the blonde there. If we had waited around, we would have surely run into her. I mean, think about this. I had a nine-thirty appointment with Elrod. He wouldn't have asked the blonde to come until he was sure I was gone." She looked back at McCoy and quizzed, "Did he have any idea what time you were going to want to get the money and the woman?"

The man nodded, "He always did business with the guy I replaced between one and five in the morning. He knew I was going to call last night."

"Then," Tiffany suggested, "maybe the woman is not there yet or is waiting for Elrod to join her."

"That's a long shot," he noted.

"I think this one is worth playing," she added. "I mean, you need the woman and the ring and I can't give you that. At least not the ring part."

"Okay," he admitted, "what have I got lose? Your hunch is better than anything I can come up with. Put your coat on, you're driving me to Elrod's."

"I really need to wrap some presents," she explained. "And you really don't need me there. I promise I won't tell anybody about what happened tonight."

"Yeah, I trust you about as far as I can throw you."

"As big as you are," Tiffany quickly pointed out, "that might be a considerable distance."

"Come on, Miss Clayton, let's move."

"I'm guessing there's no way to talk you out of this?"

"Nope. If we can't find the real blonde, I might still be able to figure a way to use your body."

"Wonderful," she sighed. Taking a deep breath, Tiffany got up, retrieved her coat from where she'd earlier hung it on hall tree by the front door, and slipped it on. After wrapping her scarf around her neck, she marched out the door and silently vowed that if she somehow lived through this adventure she was going to tear Lane Walker to pieces.

— 10 —

Thursday, December 19, 1946
2:35 a.m.

It was an increasingly worried Lane Walker who jumped out of his car and rushed up to the front door of the Elrod mansion. His plan had blown up in his face, and he was now forced to admit the plan actually had more holes than Swiss cheese. After a year on the force, he should have known better. Police work was not like war. In the midst of battle, a soldier had to often act on a hunch, but when you were a cop you planned each detail, moved carefully, and always called in backup.

Earlier in the evening, he'd been in the react mode rather than the think mode. Thus, he'd charged in ready for action, sure that his enemy could not have guessed his plans, and was made to look like a fool. That in itself would have been bad enough, but to compound it all he'd put a civilian in harm's way and who knows where she was at this moment. If something happened to Tiffany, if she died because of his stupidity, then she'd no doubt make good on her promise to haunt him forever, and that was the least he deserved.

Not bothering to stop in the foyer to remove his coat, the rattled cop raced directly through the living room and to the District Attorney's study. He was yanking off his overcoat and tossing it on a chair, getting ready to look through every file in his search for clues as to where Tiffany might be, when he suddenly realized he was not alone. Sitting on the couch, with her left leg resting on her right knee and wearing a royal blue suit was a diminutive blonde. If she was concerned about Lane's presence, she didn't show it. Her dark eyes were calmly sizing him up with what seemed like little more than a detached boredom.

"Who are you?" the surprised cop demanded. "And how did you get in?"

"The door was unlocked," she explained. "And, I was supposed to be here at midnight. Who are you? Are you my driver?"

So this was the blonde who was supposed to make the trip to the house on Elmwood. She was not what he expected. Her face was hard, expression almost hollow, and she was sporting way too much makeup topped by a few coats of red lipstick that glowed brighter than most neon signs. And to top it off, as she sat there studying him, she was also wearing out a piece of gum. It wouldn't take much longer for the smacking to drive him crazy.

"I'm Lane Walker," he announced as he moved two steps closer to Elrod's guest. "And I'm a cop."

The woman's calm demeanor evaporated as quickly as water drops on a hot griddle. In a split second, she waved both hands in front of her face, revealing nail polish matching her lipstick, and frantically declared, "I'm legit tonight. A man paid me to go meet someone. I'm not working. So you cops can't arrest me. Isn't that right? You can't pinch me unless you have proof that I'm turning a trick."

If that didn't beat all, the blonde who was supposed to take the ride was a streetwalker. Yet, in a strange way it made sense. A woman in her profession had a much better chance of witnessing something that could cause problems for Richard Delono than would a secretary or housewife. But the question remained, why would Elrod be willing to give her to the hood? Would an honest DA actually believe that even the life of a woman

94

who walked the streets had no value? There just had to be another explanation.

"Let me assure you," Lane explained, trying to calm down the now-anxious guest, "I'm not here for a pinch." He paused and edged another step forward, stuck his thumbs in his belt, and took a deeper look at the woman who obviously didn't trust him at all. She was likely closing in on fifty, but in spite of the heavily caked makeup, she looked a bit older. Her neck, cheeks, chin, fingers, and an ashtray partially filled with cigarette butts covered with bright red lipstick proved she was a smoker and likely a heavy one. She was thin, almost drawn, her skin as pale as a ghost, and her hair was only blonde until you got about a half inch from the scalp. She was apparently weeks past due for a touch-up. As the cop looked into her eyes he thought he saw signs of drug addiction, the whites were a bit yellowed and bloodshot. This woman was no "Johnny Come Lately" to this game that some called a profession; she was a vet.

"What's your name?" Lane asked as he pulled his hands together to crack his knuckles.

"You mean what do people call me?" she replied, seemingly now a bit more relaxed.

"Yeah."

"Sunshine."

That seemed an ironic choice in names for a woman who probably rarely saw the light of day.

In fact, the only vitamin D she likely ever got was from a bottle.

"Sunshine," the cop quizzed, "why are you here?"

"Like I said," she explained, "I'm supposed to go on a ride and meet someone. But the man promised that's all, I don't have to give out any favors. So this is kind of like a night off."

"Did Mr. Elrod set this up?"

"Well," she shot back, "that's who he said he was on the phone. I have no reason to doubt it. After all, I knew him from a few of my court appearances. So when he offered me a grand for a couple of hours of riding around meeting folks, I jumped. You don't ever turn down money like that."

Lane nodded as he attempted to put the puzzle together. Sunshine evidently had no idea this was supposed to be a one-way trip. It was strange that a woman with this much experience didn't realize she was being set up.

"Sunshine," Lane continued his line of questioning as he tried to uncover why she was the woman that was supposed to go to the house on Elmwood. "Do you know a man named Richard Delono?"

She smacked her gum a couple of times, smiled and, in a happy, nasal tone, more singing than speaking, replied, "Sure, everyone knows Richard. But if you're asking if I really know him . . . no way! I've just seen him around a couple of times, but I've never been with him. And I don't mean that the way it sounds."

"I understand," Lane assured her. "I knew what you meant. So, I guess that means that Richard wouldn't have any reason to want to meet you or spend time with you?"

"I'm not in his league," she admitted. She then sadly added, "I wasn't even in his league twenty years ago. You see, in show business terms, I'm not a headline act; I'm just the gal who cleans up the star's dressing room. Most of the men in my life don't even own a suit."

That was not the answer Lane expected nor the one he needed to hear. If she didn't know Delono and had nothing on him, then why was Sunshine the pawn? She had to either know something or someone. A pounding on the front door caused Lane to jerk his attention away from his unexpected guest.

"You've got company," she noted.

"Yeah," he groaned, "you stay here. I'll get that." Whoever was visiting at this hour likely wasn't coming over for social reasons. The last thing he needed at this moment was another wild card to keep him from digging for clues. After pulling his gun from his pocket, he rushed to the front door. Taking a deep a breath, an anxious Lane yanked the entry open and found himself staring into blue eyes he knew very well. Sliding his gun back into his pocket, he whispered, "Tiff."

While he couldn't begin to fathom how Tiffany had found her way back to him, he didn't care either. All he wanted to do was reach out and hug the beautiful blonde, but the cold expression on her face and her caustic tone stopped him before he could even begin to extend his arms.

"Great plan," she spat. "And you shouldn't have put your weapon away. If you'd looked behind me you'd have seen my escort has got his gun sticking in my back."

Lane immediately glanced past the woman to the broad-shouldered man behind her. The cop's look of confusion and concern quickly changed to a broad smile. "Bret Garner, how are you doing you old son-of-a-gun?"

Stepping out from behind Tiffany, the visitor slipped his weapon into his pocket and grabbed Lane's outstretched mitt. As the two men grinned and shook hands, the woman stepped away and frowned. "You know this guy?"

Lane laughed, "Bret and I served in the Marines together." The cop grinned at his unexpected guest, "Was that you at the house earlier tonight? It was so dark I couldn't tell. You should have turned on the lights and we could have saved all this trouble."

"That was me," the guest added, "and I had my reasons for not blowing my cover."

"Hold it," Tiffany cut in, as she pointed to Garner, "you said your name was McCoy."

He glanced toward the woman, "That's the name I'm using in Chicago."

"How many names do you need?" she queried. "I mean do you need one for every place you visit? Like what's your handle in Cleveland or New York?"

Ignoring the woman's question, Lane jumped back into the conversation, "Bret, don't worry about Tiff, she's touchy at times. She has an attitude. Any little thing sets her off."

"Excuse me," Tiffany cut in, "any little thing? Being kidnapped and told I was going to be killed is not a little thing. This gorilla you are so happy to see is a hit man. Don't you get that?"

As the reporter looked incredulously at the cop, Lane smirked and asked his old friend, "Are you still with Naval Intelligence?"

"No," Garner explained, "I'm a private cop now."

"A gumshoe," Lane quipped. "So you're like a walking, talking version of Sam Spade or Phillip Marlowe."

"Not really," came the quick reply, "no one is writing my scripts. I'm working for a client, who must remain unnamed—you know that whole confidentiality thing—that asked me figure out what was going on with Elrod and Delono. So, I passed myself off as a pretty well-known hit man," he looked toward Tiffany and grinned, "McCoy Rawlings. What Delono and no one else knows is that Rawlings is on the lam and living in South America."

"But," Lane cut in, "weren't you afraid Delano would recognize you?"

"No," Garner explained, "there are no pictures of Rawlings and he's never worked anywhere but the West Coast. I guess it's all for naught now as your girlfriend tells me that Elrod is dead."

"I'm not his girlfriend!" the woman bitterly explained. "Surely you realize I have better taste than that. And, now that I think about it, I liked you better as McCoy." She then stepped between the men and pointed her finger in Garner's face, "You were going to kill me."

"No," he explained, "McCoy Rawlings was going to kill you. I'm now Bret Garner and I'm one of the good guys. But, if you don't be quiet, I might reconsider my options and slip back into my other persona. I've still got the gun."

"Why you . . ."

"We'll get to that later," Lane suggested, "by the way, the blonde who was supposed to meet you is in the study. She's not as attractive as Tiff, but she's a lot better behaved and she's in a more respectable line of work, too."

"What's that crack supposed to mean?" Tiffany demanded.

Ignoring the woman, Garner looked toward the open door, "What's the real blonde's story?"

"I think Elrod hired her to be a pigeon," the cop

explained, "she has nothing on Delono. She's never even met the man."

The private investigator nodded. "Interesting. When this hit was set up, Delono wanted proof that she was dead, but he never told me why. Now, in reading between the lines, I don't think I was supposed to kill her for him. I got the sense it was for someone else. He even alluded to her death being a Christmas gift."

"I wonder," Tiffany mused, "how Santa responded to that holiday letter?"

"A gift for whom?" Lane asked, while once again ignoring the woman.

"I have no idea," Garner replied. "Let me get the briefcase and a camera out of the car. I need those things to do my job so Delono doesn't come after me."

"Wait," Tiffany barked, "now you're going to kill her?"

The investigator smiled, "Well, that lets you off the hook, so just a take a deep breath and be happy!"

"You just can't go around murdering people," the woman spat. "Even if those people aren't me."

As Tiffany frowned, Garner smiled, spun on his heels, and hurried back to the car. He was no more than out the door when the reporter turned back to the cop. "Lane, you have to do something about that guy."

"Ah," Lane replied with a smile, "Bret is one

fine man. You know he saved my life twice in the Pacific. Imagine that, he was willing to put his neck out for me. I wouldn't be here tonight without him. I'm just glad if someone was going to kidnap you it was Bret. You couldn't have done better."

"Thanks," the woman snarled, "glad the hit man is a friend of yours. It really gives me a whole different perspective on the evening." She stuck her finger into Lane's stomach as she added, "And your plan was just peachy."

"Where's the blonde?" Garner asked, as he marched back into the foyer.

"Right through those doors," Lane explained. "Her name is Sunshine."

With Lane and Tiffany following in his tracks, the investigator waltzed into the study and studied the woman Elrod had hired. After sizing Sunshine up from every angle he posed a question, "Do you have a jade ring?"

"Never had one of those," she quickly returned. She then smiled and added, "What's your name? I like your look."

"I'm McCoy," Garner explained, going back to his cover. He then glanced over to Lane, "If she doesn't have the ring, it has to be here. Elrod knew I needed it and he'd have given it to her before she was driven over to meet me. So we need to tear this place apart and find it."

"I'll take the desk," Lane suggested, "Why don't

you search all the drawers in the tables. If we don't uncover anything there we can look through the bookshelves."

"Yeah," Garner agreed, "he might have a fake book where he stashed stuff. Or there might be a hidden safe."

"If this room has a safe," the cop explained, "I didn't see it earlier when I made my initial search. Bret, why is the ring so important?"

As Garner slid open an end table drawer, he explained, "It and the photo I'll take later will prove I did my job. Without them Delono won't be satisfied and he is a man who I need to keep in my corner or my new career won't last long."

"You probably aren't wrong on that," Tiffany quipped. "It makes sense you and Lane served together. You're both so much alike."

"Ignore her," Lane suggested, "and let's get to work."

For the next thirty minutes, the men all but tore Elrod's study apart. When they'd finished looking through the doors and examined all of the more than one thousand books, opening each and then tossing them to the side, the cop admitted the obvious, "It's not here."

"But it has to be," Garner argued. "Elrod wouldn't have sent her to the house without it." He snapped his fingers, "Was it on his body?"

"One of my team went through his pockets," Lane explained, "I doubt if Jenkins would have missed anything, but I'll call the morgue and find out. The ME would have cataloged everything he found in Elrod's clothing."

As Garner leaned against the desk and folded his arms over his chest, the cop picked up the phone and began to dial. He was on the third number when Tiffany rose from the couch, shook her head, grinned, and announced, "You two men think you're so smart. Use your heads. If Elrod was going to leave something that had to go with the blonde to the house . . ."

"My name is Sunshine," the other woman interrupted.

Tiffany smiled and nodded. ". . . to go with Sunshine to the house, wouldn't he put it in the same place with everything else that was going there?"

"The attaché case!" Lane all but shouted as he started to move toward foyer.

Before he could make a full step, Tiffany opened her hand and revealed the blue jade ring. As it sparkled in the room's light, she added, "It was in a small jewelry box beside all of that green stuff."

"When did you find it?" Garner demanded.

"About the time you opened the first drawer," the reporter explained. "You were too busy tearing this place up to notice me or what I was doing."

"But . . ." Lane cut in.

"But," the reporter parroted, "I didn't tell you because both of you men have treated me horribly tonight. Lane, your plan made it is easy for this lug," she pointed at Garner, "to kidnap me. And, if I'd had this ring then, he was going to kill me."

"I wasn't really going to kill you," the agent explained. "But as I was undercover, I had a role to play."

"Yeah," Tiffany grumbled, "and that's supposed to make everything all right."

"Would flowers help?" Garner asked.

"By the way," Sunshine cut in, "do I still get paid?"

"I guarantee," Tiffany declared, "that you are going to get paid."

"In fact," Garner suggested, "we ought to do that right now." Retrieving the attaché, the agent reached in, grabbed a handful of cash and looked back to the blonde. "How much were you promised?"

"A thousand."

Garner quickly counted through the twenties as he walked over to Sunshine. "Here is fifteen hundred, but for you to earn it I need for you to do something."

She eagerly grabbed the cash, "Like what?"

"Play dead." Looking back to Lane, Garner explained, "I've got a bottle of blood in my camera bag, let's go to the kitchen, pose Sunshine on the floor as if she'd been shot, have her face away from the camera, pour the blood on the back on her head and shoot a few photos. Then I'll take them to a lab, get a print made, and send it and the ring to the post office box I was given. That will prove I did my job and keep my cover as McCoy Rawlings intact."

"We can make the print at the police lab," Lane suggested. "A private lab might get suspicious and foul things up."

"Fifteen hundred just to play dead?" Sunshine whispered.

"Yes," Garner said, "and I'm also going to need to visit with you to find out why Richard Delono paid me to kill you."

"But," the woman argued, "I don't know Delono."

"But," investigator interjected, "you have to know someone or something important or this whole thing wouldn't have been set up. And don't worry, you'll get paid for any information you can give me that will bring Delono down."

"Okay," Sunshine announced as she happily got up from the couch. "Wow, fifteen hundred, this night might just be the best of my life. Let's go play dead."

Grabbing his camera bag Garner took the woman's arm and led her through the study door. As they strolled into the foyer, he almost glee-fully announced, "Let's see if we can find the kitchen. In a house this size it might take a while."

Tiffany watched the pair disappear down a hall before turning her attention back to Lane. She glared at the cop as she coldly announced, "I'm never listening to one of your plans again. It's one thing standing me up on a date, but allowing a hit man to grab me is another thing altogether."

"He's a friend of mine," Lane argued, "not a real hit man."

"You didn't know that back at the house," she noted. After taking a deep breath, the reporter added, "And you wouldn't let me have a gun. If ever I needed a gun, it was tonight."

"No," Lane argued, "then you might have shot Bret. That wouldn't have been good. After all, he's not really who you thought he was."

She shook her head, "I'm not so sure. Anyway, there are two other things that bother me even more than having you hang me out to dry."

"What's that?"

"The first is why would Elrod knowingly send a woman, even a prostitute, to her death? He had to understand what was in store for Sunshine. Did her life have that little value to him?"

Lane nodded, "So you think the DA was no better than Delono?"

"Maybe," she admitted.

"Tiffany, what's the other thing that's digging into your skin?"

She crossed her arms and frowned, "Nothing I'm ready to share right now, but believe me I'll let you know about it after I do some homework."

"For the moment," Lane suggested, "why don't

you go give Bret a hand staging the photo? I'd help, but I've got a fruitcake tin I need to retrieve from the basement."

"I'm tired of your plans," she grumbled. "I'll skip the play acting, I've had enough of that tonight. I've got a story, and if I call now I can still make the first edition." She turned and glared at the cop, "And nothing you can do or say is going to stop me this time."

He held his hands up, "I wouldn't even try, but please leave out the way in which he was killed. Just say the police are investigating what appears to be a murder. I don't want some copycat killer imitating this one."

"Fine," the reporter agreed, "I will say Elrod was murdered in his home and inform my readers that the police will be releasing more details after doing an extensive study of the crime scene."

"Perfect," Lane replied.

As the woman moved over to the phone, the desk lamp caught the glow in her Carolina blue eyes. The cop studied them for a moment before shaking loose from their spell and hurrying to the basement to get the fruitcake.

— 11 —

Thursday, December 19, 1946
6:09 a.m.

As Lane looked on, the ME, a short, pale man weighing no more than one-hundred-and-forty pounds, dressed in a white shirt and dark slacks, his tie loosened at the collar, stood beside Ethan Elrod's body. After parting the DA's thick gray hair to more closely study the scalp, he frowned. Drawing his face a bit closer to the wound, Morelli sighed before slowly walking back to a table on the large gray room's far side. The examiner's eyes focused on the dented fruitcake tin, and he sadly nodded. After running his thin fingers gently along the can's dented edge, he looked back to his visitor.

"This is the murder weapon," Morelli explained. "There can be no doubt. It fits perfectly in the area crushed on the backside of Elrod's skull."

"Amazing," an exhausted Lane hoarsely announced. "Hard to believe you can kill a man with something like that. I'm not even sure how I write this one up in the case files without becoming a laughingstock."

"Not so hard to believe," the ME argued as he picked up the holiday cake. "This thing is huge. It weighs over five pounds, and with that ancient cake reinforcing the thick tin, it is as hard as a rock. If you came from the right angle and delivered a blow with full force, you could kill a gorilla with this baby. Write it up that way and nobody will laugh. And, if they do, send them down here and let me give them a demonstration."

"By the way," Lane asked, "is this the fruitcake you guessed it was? I mean is this the gag gift that floated between Elrod and Jacobs each year?"

The ME shrugged, "I can't say for sure. What I can tell you is that the brand is the same and the can matches that one perfectly. Did you find any fingerprints on it?"

"No," the cop sadly admitted, "it had been wiped clean."

"I'm not surprised," the usually smiling man replied. "You know, people are not as considerate as they used to be. Fifteen years ago, when I first moved into this position, only a few folks bothered wiping away their prints, now almost all do it. I blame Hollywood for that. Those crime movies give a person a primer on how to avoid being caught."

"You think so?" Lane replied.

"Not really," Morelli answered with a grin. "Movies are not nearly as a good a source for that kind of information as are books. Sir Arthur Conan Doyle found a hundred different ways to do people in, and if it had not been for Sherlock Holmes, each of those folks would have gotten away with murder, because Scotland Yard didn't have a clue."

"You do know those weren't real cases?" the cop asked.

"Sure," the ME said. "But have you ever thought of this? Why is someplace in London, England, called Scotland Yard?"

Lane shrugged, "Do you have an answer for that?"

"No," Morelli admitted, "I was hoping you did. Still, the fact is that as criminal science improves, those who want to get away with murder have to get smarter, too. The person who knocked off our DA was no dumb cookie."

"Was that meant as a clever pun?" the cop asked. "If it was, you failed."

"No, the reference to cookie was not supposed to be linked to cake. Anyway, whoever this guy was, he planned well and he executed that plan to perfection. He knew exactly where to strike, he knew how hard the blow had to be, and he knew how to set things up to be able to exactly orchestrate what he wanted to accomplish."

Lane stuck his hands into his pockets as he noted, "No crime is perfect. It seems to me criminals, even those who study criminal science, still always make at least one mistake."

"Okay," Morelli cut in, "where is the mistake

here? You've already told me you have no motive, no prints, and no witnesses."

"We do have a dented fruitcake can," the cop suggested. "So, that's a start. I've had a bunch of cases where I didn't have a murder weapon. Now, where can I buy a fruitcake like the one used to knock off Elrod?"

"Well," Morelli laughed, "right now you can pretty much buy fruitcake everywhere, but who actually pays attention to the brands when they pick one up? So you'll likely have to check with a few of the stores and to see who carries Jan's Old World Fruitcake."

"Why?" the cop demanded.

"Lane, are you asking me to search for what stores carry this brand? I kind of figured we knew where it came from. It has to be the one that Jacobs gave to Elrod and then it was reversed the next year. I just figured it was the cake they always passed back and forth as a gag gift."

"Mitch, you are likely right on the origin of the so-called weapon. So, I probably don't need to know where I can purchase Jan's Old World Fruitcake. You misunderstood me, I'm just wondering why it was used as a weapon. Does anything you learned in college give you an insight into that?"

The ME picked up the tin, studied it one more time, then set it back onto the table and casually strolled over to Elrod. He studied his guest for a few moments before glancing at five other bodies lying on slabs in his private lair. Using his right hand as a pointer, Morelli took on the role of a college professor. "Counting your victim, there are six people who started yesterday alive and now aren't. They are here rather than at a funeral home because they just didn't die of natural causes; in one way or another they all died under suspicious circumstances."

The examiner slowly strolled over the body closest to Elrod's, grabbed a sheet, and pulled it back to reveal the face of a man who looked to be in his fifties. "This guy was shot from close range. The .32 slug went right through his heart. From what his wife told the investigators, they were robbed and the old boy was a bit too slow pulling out his wallet. In other words, he thought about if he should give into the demands of the crook. You know far too many people believe their money is worth more than their lives. I would bet if this guy had it to do over again he would have reacted much faster. Life is filled with second chances; death is not."

Covering the man's face with the sheet, the ME moved to the next victim. After repeating the unveiling process, Morelli sadly noted, "Little kids are always the hardest. When their bodies come in I always cry before I start cutting on them." As Lane watched, the usually upbeat ME touched the small boy's forehead. "They haven't found out who he is yet, so his parents don't know he's gone. When they do locate this little guy's folks, thanks to my work the cops can at least explain how the boy died. My findings were his chest was crushed so badly his ribs punctured both his lungs and his heart. He was a victim of a hit-and-run. He was crossing Sixth Street and never made it to the other side. I'm guessing he was about six when he took his last breath. I'd also have to believe that somewhere there are wrapped presents waiting for this guy that will never be opened. Did you ever think about that? Imagine buying Christmas presents, wrapping them up, putting them under a tree, and then finding out the loved one who was going to receive that gift is dead."

A now very sober Morelli didn't bother uncovering the next two bodies, but that didn't prevent him from explaining the cause of each victim's demise. "The guy under that sheet was twenty-five and his ticket was punched by a knife. From what I've been told, two rival gangs were having a powwow that turned into a rumble. Someone yanked out a switchblade and a second later this guy found out what's on the other side of this world." He paused and pointed to the other gurney, "And the woman over there was beaten to death. I've seen punching bags hanging in boxing gyms that weren't hit as much or as hard. They arrested her boyfriend. Seems the argument was over money and all he can say was that he didn't mean to hurt her."

The ME turned back to his guest, "None my guests died in the same manner, but each of those I've just introduced to you have one thing in common; their deaths were sudden, quick, and unplanned. Each was killed with something that was not so much a weapon of choice as an instrument of convenience. As you know, most homicides happen just that way. Something is said, someone reacts, they grab whatever is close, and before they can think about the consequences of their actions it is over. Even the man in the hit-and-run didn't ever plan on using his vehicle to murder someone. Now that I have given you the cause of death of four of my guests, let me digress and say I think your case is the exception to the rule."

Lane walked over to his friend's side, and after studying the form of the beaten women hidden by the white sheet, asked, "What drives you to that conclusion?"

"It doesn't take Sherlock Holmes to explain this one," Morelli began. "Something was placed in Elrod's drink to knock him out. That one element means this thing was planned. Our unknown suspect then waited until the DA was helpless and delivered the blow to the head. As the wound was to the left side of the skull, you can make a pretty good assumption the killer was left-handed."

"So," Lane asked, "are you saying the murderer planned on using the fruitcake can as a weapon?"

"I can't say that for sure," Morelli qualified his earlier statement, "but unlike the four victims whose stories I just shared, someone planned to kill Elrod and they carried out that plan. Maybe they had a gun jam, and thus, they picked up the can to finish him off, but whatever way it fell together, I believe they walked into the room intent on snuffing out the DA's life."

"What about the knife?" Lane demanded. "What did it have to do with anything?"

"Here is where I channel Charlie Chan and Philo Vance," Morelli explained. "Logic tells me the knife plays into this situation in one of two ways. The first would be as a symbol."

"Explain," the cop cut in, "what would plunging a knife into an already dead man's back symbolize?"

Morelli held up his finger and smiled. "Well, I might just be sounding like a radio detective, but when you hear the phrase 'stabbing someone in the back' what does that mean to you?"

The cop nodded, "It's an act of betrayal."

"Thus," the ME continued, "I'm thinking whoever killed Elrod used the knife to symbolize why the man had to die."

"Elrod betrayed someone."

"Could be."

Lane nodded. "What's your second theory?"

"The other one," Morelli grimly announced, "is that two people wanted to kill the DA. The first accomplished the deed with the can. The second entered the room, thought Elrod was asleep at his desk, and plunged the knife into his back. At this particular point, as the press had not gotten the story of how Elrod died, that person likely still thinks they accomplished their mission. Thus, you might be looking for a real murderer and a wannabe murderer."

"So," Lane remarked, "in this case, there is no symbolism."

"No," the ME agreed, "but rather than being an act driven by either hate or passion, this, too, had to be planned. The red-handled knife that was used was taken from a kitchen, and, as your team found out, it didn't come from Elrod's home. So it had to be brought to the location. Oh, and as the knife's blow was delivered in such a way the blade went directly through the heart, the murdered knew exactly where to strike. That murderer was also likely left-handed."

"Could the knifing have been a hit?" the cop suggested. "As the blow was so perfect, do you think it might have been the mode of operation used by a hired killer?"

"It doesn't matter," the ME answered. "After all, you can't hang a man for trying to kill someone who is already dead."

The sleep-deprived Lane rubbed his eyes. This

case was getting more bizarre by the moment. He suddenly found himself heading up an investigation looking for two different left-handed people with two different motives. Worse yet, the list of enemies made by the DA was long even before he started his very public campaign against Richard Delono.

"There's something else you ought to know," Morelli cracked.

"What's that and will it help me identify either of the suspects?"

"Probably not," the ME admitted. "Elrod had a weak heart and the knockout potion he was served was secobarbital sodium, better known as Seconal. It is prescribed for several conditions including insomnia and epilepsy. You don't give it to men with known heart conditions. The amount in that coffee I tested suggested that even if the fruitcake killer hadn't struck when he did, the drug would have likely finished our victim off anyway. Thus, you might just have three different people who used three different methods with the same goal in mind."

"I suppose," the cop grumbled, "you're going to tell me that the person who laced the coffee with the drug was left-handed, too."

"I don't know about that," the ME announced with a wry grin.

"Let's get back to what you said earlier," Lane interjected. "You told me that the killer used the drugged coffee to render Elrod helpless before he was struck."

"Well," he suggested, "let me amend what you heard. I said the coffee was drugged, causing Elrod to pass out and then he was hit with the fruitcake. Did the same person do both of those things? My friend, that is what you will have to prove. I've told you all I can."

Lane shook his head, "You sure know how to wrap and deliver some holiday cheer. Don't expect a thank-you note for this one." The cop paused and glanced toward a covered body at the far end of the room. "You didn't tell me that one's story."

"It has yet to be written," Morelli explained. "They just brought that guest in a few minutes before you arrived." The ME covered the thirty feet to the rolling gurney and pulled back the top of the sheet. He looked at the body for a moment, standing as if to block the cop's view, and then turned toward Lane.

"The cause of death was obvious. This victim was about forty when she was strangled. The murderer used his hands rather than a scarf or rope, so this was an act of real passion. He wanted this woman to see who was killing her."

"Does the victim have a name?" Lane asked from across the room.

The ME turned and picked up a clipboard. As he scanned the information, he smiled grimly.

"What's up?" the cop asked.

"Nothing funny," Morelli soberly explained, "just ironic. In all the years I've been in this windowless basement room, the one thing I've missed more than anything else is the sunshine. I never expected it to come into this room via a victim's name."

A suddenly shocked and now very much awake Lane quickly marched over to view the body. It was her! And this time she wasn't faking a death like she'd staged in the Elrods' kitchen.

"You know this woman?" the ME asked.

"I saw her just a few hours ago," the cop explained. "She was at Elrod's."

"So," Morelli observed, "she's a part of all this, too."

"I guess she is," Lane dryly noted.

Picking up the clipboard the cop studied the information written by the investigating officer. As no money was found on Sunshine, the working theory was she'd been murdered in a robbery. Pulling the sheet further down, the cop examined the woman's right hand. On her pinky was a blue jade ring. Another theory shot down. If it had been a straight robbery they would have taken that, too. Maybe Sunshine knew a lot more than she realized or admitted. Maybe she *had* been the blonde Garner was supposed to take out.

— 12 —

Thursday, December 19, 1946
11:33 a.m.

"A little different than eating K-rations while dodging Japanese bullets," Bret Garner noted as he surveyed the out-of-the-way diner Lane Walker had chosen for lunch. The private eye had turned his attention to an image of a snowman, complete with stovepipe hat and red scarf, painted on the window beside their booth, by the time the cop finally answered.

"In some ways it was easier back then," the cop mused. Glancing toward the menu posted behind the counter and over the twenty-foot-long mirror, he added, "We didn't have to choose our food from such a long list. We just ate what was in the cans."

"My burger was better than anything in a K-ration," Garner noted, "and I never had fresh potatoes during my entire three years in the Pacific."

"Yeah," Lane admitted with a slight nod, "but, even though I don't miss it, life was easier then, too. I didn't have to think, just react. Everything was black and white. There were no mysteries to solve or reports to fill out. Each day I knew our only objective was to gain ground. We were told to just keep pushing west until they didn't push back anymore."

Garner shook his head, "I don't miss those days. If fact, I don't even like to talk about them." In an attempt to change the course of the conversation, the investigator chimed in with a question. "Now, why did you call me and set up this little meeting? Do you have some new information on the Elrod case? Did you find a connection to Delono? Because I have a feeling the mob is going to be hunting for me very soon. If we can put Delono behind bars that gives me a much better chance of actually seeing another Christmas."

"I don't know what I have," Lane admitted as an attractive, slightly overweight redheaded waitress waltzed towards their booth.

"You gents need anything else?" she asked.

"No," Garner answered for both of them, "we're fine. By the way, who did the art on your windows?"

"I did," she grinned. "I used tempera paint. I think my best one is the big Santa on the window by the cash register."

The investigator glanced at the waving St. Nick and nodded. "You really captured his smile." He looked back to the woman and grinned. "You know I think Santa's other job might be as a cop."

"Why do you think that?" she asked.

"He looks like he's eaten a lot of donuts," Garner quipped.

Her brown eyes lit up as she laughed. "You are the funny one. Sure you don't need anything else?"

"Just leave the check and we'll be fine."

After the woman dropped the paper onto the table, turned, and sauntered off, the investigator looked back at his friend and picked up the conversation where it was dropped a few minutes before. "What is it that you don't know?"

"You name it," Lane quickly replied. "I have no leads and no hunches." The cop paused and when the two men's eyes met, the homicide team leader posed a question of his own. By his tone, it appeared to be one that he didn't want to have to ask. "What happened to Sunshine after you finished staging that photo in the kitchen?"

"I gave her a ride," he quickly replied. "It would have been impossible for her get a cab that time of night in that neighborhood and she'd have frozen before she got to a bus stop. Besides, I wanted to probe her mind and find out what she might know about Delono. It seemed she knew absolutely nothing."

Lane remained stern, almost as if he was in his full investigative mode as he tossed out another query. "Where did you take her?"

"I dropped her off at the Palmer Hotel."

"The Palmer?" the look on the cop's face was

priceless. A flashing neon sign couldn't have spelled out disbelief any more clearly.

"Yeah, the Palmer," Garner shot back. "She said with all the money she was carrying she wanted the chance to spend a night in luxury." He paused, took a sip from a six-ounce bottle of Coca-Cola, and shrugged, "Who was I to say no? It was her life."

"So you just dropped her off?" the cop demanded, his voice becoming more accusing with each new question.

"Yeah, I wanted to get back to my room at the Regis and grab some shut-eye. Now why the third degree?"

Lane licked his lips and lowered his voice. "Someone strangled Sunshine about dawn. They found her body in an alley a block from where you claimed you dropped her off."

"Are you accusing me?" the investigator demanded.

"You left Elrod's with her," Lane noted, "as far as I know you were one of the last people to see her alive. You'd even been hired to kill her. Do I have to go on?"

"You batting .333," Garner quipped, "but you whiffed on the last two curve balls. Yes, I did leave with her, but I also watched her walk in the front door of the Palmer. That means someone else had to see her after I dropped her off. And, let me make this very clear, I was not hired to kill Sunshine. I was hired to kill the real blonde, whoever that is. You know as well as I do that I was never going to kill her."

"Why didn't you take the ring back?" Lane shot back. "She was still wearing it when they brought her into the morgue this morning."

"Okay, Lane, I'll admit I forgot it. I staged the photo, gave you the film to have developed, and then took her to where she wanted to go. It was only when I got back to my place I realized she still had the ring. So, on the way over here this morning I dropped by the Palmer to meet with Sunshine and get it back. She wasn't there. In fact, there was no record of her ever checking in. And believe me, I know how all of this sounds."

"That doesn't look good for you," the cop calmly suggested. "I could arrest you right now. I've already got enough to have you spend some time being grilled under a very warm light."

"This is ridiculous," Garner complained. "You know me a lot better than that." As he considered the poor woman's fate, he studied the few dozen patrons who'd crowded into the mustard yellow booths and were filling the chrome stools in front of the counter. They all seemed to be glowing with the spirit of the season. One man was even going from table to table handing out candy canes. The mood in Bill's Diner was so festive the investigator figured he could stand up and shout out the news that a streetwalker had died and a minute later everyone would have forgotten. It seemed no one was thinking about anything but joy to the world. Sadly, there was very little joy in his.

"Who's Bill?" Garner asked as he once more looked deeply into the cop's eyes.

"You'll have to be a lot more specific, I know a lot of Bills."

"So do I," the investigator shot back, "a half dozen of the Bills I knew got killed in the war. But what I'm asking is, who is the Bill who runs this place? I mean, it's called Bill's Diner."

Lane shrugged, "I don't know. Guess I never thought about it."

"Maybe you need to think a lot more," Garner snapped. "We were together for three years in the Pacific. We fought, ate, and slept side by side. Now you look back to those days and tell me I could kill a woman."

"War changes people," the cop suggested.

"It sure changed you," came the quick reply. "Now Lane, tell me, how did Sunshine die?"

"She was strangled," came the blunt explanation. "The method used was the same we learned in our combat training except this person likely looked into her eyes as he killed her."

"That narrows it down to about a million vets," the investigator suggested. He paused and added, "Let me explain something to you that you might not understand. I felt sorry for Sunshine. On the trip to the Palmer, she leveled with me. Her parents died when she was kid, she was then placed with an uncle who abused her. So, at fifteen, she ran away. With no skills and no family, she used the one thing she had going for her, her looks, to keep from starving to death. It didn't take me long to figure out that in her forty-four years she didn't have a week of real happiness. Her face showed every year and then some. She told me that the money she walked into last night was the very best moment of her life. And," he raised his eyebrows to emphasize his point, "if I had killed her I would have certainly remembered to take the ring. After all, I need that to make sure I hold onto my skin. The photo's not enough."

The cop started to speak, but Garner cut him off. "Listen, I forgot the ring because I felt sorry for the gal. I was so caught up in her sad story, I even dipped into that attaché and gave her some more cash. When I drove away, I felt more like her sad brother than I did a private eye. I don't care what she did for a living, she was still a human being. I fought a war to save her just like I fought a war to save the Rockefellers."

"Okay," Lane replied, "for the time being I'll buy that you might have a big heart. But let me get this straight, I don't care if you did save my life on Iwo Jima, if I come up with anything more that ties you to that woman's death, I'll use it." Frowning, he reached into his inside suit pocket. When his hand came out it was holding a white envelope. "Here's the photo you need and the jade ring."

Taking the gifts from the cop Garner grimly replied, "Thanks. This will buy me at least a few days." After slipping both items into his suit coat pocket, he looked back to Lane. "My two weeks inside the organization assured me that the only person who really had the goods on Delono was a Stuart Grogan."

"He's dead," Lane announced, "it's all over the papers today. Surely, you read it."

"I saw the headlines," the investigator replied, "so I'm guessing you have the body."

"No," the cop admitted, "We have pieces of it. So far we have a torso and a leg found in the Chicago River. The clothing contained his bill-fold. Until the ice thaws, we likely aren't going to find the rest."

"You sure it's him?"

"Two witnesses saw Grogan plugged. They watched him fall into the water. They saw some-one shoot him."

"Who were the witnesses to the hit?"

"Now who's grilling who?" Lane demanded. "Okay, I don't mind you knowing, but don't give the information to any reporters and that includes Tiffany. One of the witnesses was a woman, about forty, who lived in the area and was walking her dog. The other was a night watchman. Their stories were solid, they don't have criminal records, and they easily picked out a photo of Grogan. There's no reason to doubt them."

"What did they say about the shooter? How did they describe him?"

"They never saw his face, it was too dark," the cop explained. "But there was a light at the end of the pier where Grogan fell into the water, so they got a good look at him."

"So," Garner noted, "the investigation is dead in the water."

"If that is a pun," the cop observed, "it's a bad one. Sounds like something Morelli would make up."

"Sorry, didn't think before I spoke."

"Ah," Lane smiled, "now you are sounding a lot like Tiffany."

"And who's Morelli?"

"Our ME," Lane explained. "His sense of humor is a bit dark."

Garner shrugged. "He lives in a dark world, so that's to be expected. Since you brought up Tiffany's name, what's the tale on you two?"

"Why do you want to know?"

"I just get the feeling there is a there is much more to the story."

The cop glanced out the front window. He studied the street scene for a few seconds before deciding to level with his old friend. "Bret, she's the gal I talked about that night we had leave in Honolulu."

"I kind of figured she was."

"Yeah," Lane replied as their eyes once more met. "Whenever I'm away from Tiffany I want to be with her. But whenever I'm with her, I'm looking for an exit."

"So you're not a couple?"

"If, in war terms, you are asking if she is rationed, the answer is no. She and I butt heads too much to ever hold hands for long." He glanced across the diner to an empty phone booth. "Speaking of Tiffany, I need to catch her up on the case. I owe her an exclusive after putting her through what I did last night. Besides, I find it's a lot easier to talk to her on the phone than it is in person."

"Yeah," Garner grinned, "those eyes hook you and reel you in before you can say hello. A man would have to be blind to not get a bit dizzy when he's around her."

The cop rose, stood by the table, and intently studied his old comrade before speaking in a hushed tone. "You have to level with me. Did you have anything to do with Sunshine's death? I've got to know that beyond a shadow of a doubt."

The investigator took a deep breath, rolling his neck and stretching his broad shoulders before answering. "Yes, I had something to do with her death." He paused for effect before adding, "Without knowing it, I likely set her up. I'm pretty sure Delono had someone watching my every move and I should have realized that. Thus, my dropping her off at the Palmer likely set her up for the kill."

"If that's the case," Lane warned, "then you have a target on your back right now."

Garner nodded, "Could be, but I'll send the photo and ring anyway. I'll also include a note thanking Delono for financing my date last night. Thus, he might just buy that I picked Sunshine up and the woman in the photo is the real blonde. That also might stop the search for the woman who Delono wanted to kill as a present for our mystery man." The investigator took a deep breath before sadly adding, "I'll pay the check and then go down to the post office and mail this little package. Give Tiffany my warmest greetings."

As Lane strolled back to the phone booth, the investigator grabbed the check, slipped out of the booth, and walked up to the register. As he paid his bill, he looked into the mirror behind the counter and noted a small man, in a blue suit, white shirt and black tie, sitting on a stool intently watching him.

"Keep the change," Garner told the manager. Turning on his heels, the private eye moved quickly back through the diner and over to the counter. Poking his finger into the small man's chest he softly said, "This will make it easier on you. I'm driving to the post office, and after that I'm headed back to my room at the Regis to grab a nap. My room number is 417. I'll get up in time to grab a bite at the café across from Marshall Fields. Randolph Scott is starring in *Abilene Town* at a theater two blocks east of my hotel, so after I eat, I might just go and catch that movie. If I go and you want to join me, I'll attend the eight o'clock showing and I'll even share my popcorn with you, as long as you wash your hands before you sit down." As the stunned little man tried to make himself even smaller, the muscular private eye added, "The man I had lunch with is a homicide cop. He was grilling me about my date last night. It seems the woman was strangled early this morning and I'm under suspicion. What does that mean? It means I can't leave town like I promised." Garner reached into his pants and retrieved a dime. "Use this, call your boss, and give him the full rundown on what you just heard. Make sure he knows he can pick up a package later tonight at Post Office Box 1032. You got that? 1032! Also, tell him, because of the police investigation into the death of a hooker, I'll have to put off my trip to Los Angeles for a few days. Now, haven't I made your job so much easier?"

Garner spun around and marched to the door. After stepping out into the cold wind, he looked back into the diner. His new acquaintance was standing outside the phone booth waiting for Lane Walker to finish his call. For the time being, it appeared he'd lost his tail.

— 13 —

Thursday, December 19, 1946
1:17 p.m.

Even though the temperature was in the twenties,
after mailing the ring and photo, Brent Garner
spent forty minutes walking the streets of downtown Chicago. From time to time, he would duck
out of the cold wind and into brightly decorated,
crowded stores to both warm up and observe the
madness that was the holiday shopping scene in
post-war America. The reason for his stroll was
twofold. He needed to make sure he was no longer
being followed, and he wanted some time to come
to grips with the fact he might have been the
reason Sunshine was murdered. Even for a man
who'd seen so much death in war, the latter was
hard to stomach. When the investigator was
finally convinced he no longer was being
shadowed, he made his way to 17 East Monroe
and marched into the city's most famous hotel to
try to dig up some information on the guest that
seemed to walk into the hotel but never registered.

The first Palmer House had been built in 1871
but as a victim of the Great Chicago Fire, it had
burned less than two weeks after opening. The
second Palmer House was completed in 1875 and

was advertised as The World's Only Fire-Proof Hotel. By the 1920s it was time to expand again and the newest version of luxury jumped up twenty-five stories and sported almost two thousand rooms. In 1945, Conrad Hilton purchased the Chicago landmark for twenty million and added his own name on the sign and stationery, but ignoring the business marriage, the locals still just called the grand lodge the Palmer House.

The business's main lobby made most of Europe's royal palaces look like well-worn tenements. It was three stories high and had almost as many lights as Times Square. The carpets were imported, the ornate walls covered in detailed paintings, and the artwork on the ceiling might have been more complex than that found in the Sistine Chapel. The room's liberal use of brass likely required the hotel to purchase Brasso by the truckload.

As Garner entered, several hundred well-heeled people of all ages milled about the lobby and a small choir sang carols on the stairs. It was a scene begging to be etched onto a Christmas card, and, the visitor mused, there were likely cards with that image on sale in the Palmer's gift shop. Unlike earlier in the day, when he'd been in a hurry, this time the investigator tried to imagine what Sunshine must have been thinking when she strolled into the place earlier in the day. After all the nights she'd spent in flophouses and cheap dives, checking into the lap of luxury would have been a dream come true. Therefore, he couldn't believe she would not have carried through on her plan.

As a now determined Garner crossed to the main desk, a small, well-dressed man, sporting slick-backed dark hair and a thin pencil mustache, greeted him with a forced smile and two short words. "You're back."

"I am."

"As I told you this morning," the clerk explained, "we have no Sunshine registered here."

"I'm not surprised," Garner quipped, "who needs sunshine when you have all this artificial light. But, as I told you earlier, I dropped Sunshine off at your front door and watched her walk in last night. She had enough money in her purse to set up residence in your place until well into 1947. Now, before you shake your head at me, let's go over this again. She was a small, frail bottle blonde wearing too much makeup and a bright blue suit. She was also chewing gum."

"That's not our kind of customer," came the quick response. "We only cater to the best. Our clients do not smack on gum."

"What's your name?" Garner demanded.

"Smith."

"Okay, Smith, I want to look at your register from early this morning and talk to your people who were working in the lobby then."

"I can't show you the register," came the curt reply, "that is against company policy. And if you want to visit with our overnight crew come back at midnight. Now, if you will excuse me, I have business that is actually important calling me."

As the man turned his shoulders to start back to an inner office, the investigator reached over the counter, grabbed Smith's right arm at the bicep, and spun him back to where they were face to face. Leaning close, Garner smiled and made a suggestion. "You *will* be helping me. Do you know the reason why?"

"Let me go or I'll call the house detective," Smith whispered.

While continuing to tightly grip the hotel employee's arm, Garner reached into his inside coat pocket and grabbed his investigator's badge. He pulled it out and flashed it just long enough for Smith to see it, but not so long that the clerk realized it only identified him as a private cop and not a member of the Chicago Police.

"Now, do you still want to make that call?"

Smith slowly shook his head.

"Good, let me see the register."

"So," the clerk asked, as he pulled his coat down and smoothed the wrinkles, "this is an official police matter."

"Let's just say," Garner coolly explained, "this involves a murder and I don't think you and your establishment want to be seen as impeding the department's search for the party or parties responsible."

Smith nodded and motioned for the investigator to follow him down to the far end of the counter. Grabbing a large book from under the desk, he opened it and spun it to where the visitor could easily read the page. "You'll find the early morning entries on the right. The times they registered are in front of the names. The list won't be long as not many folks check in after midnight."

A quick search of the seven who registered around the time he dropped off Sunshine proved a disappointment. There were five men and two women and none of them matched his needs. Yet, as he studied the register a second time, something jumped out.

"What room is this woman in?" Garner demanded as he pointed to a rather unusual name.

"Oh, my," Smith cracked, "do you suppose that is her real name?"

"I doubt it," the investigator assured him, "but we can figure that out later. For the moment just let me know the room number for Mary Noel."

The clerk checked the hotel log list of registered guests, nodded, and chuckled. "You're not going to believe this, but Mary Noel is in room 1225."

"If," Garner solemnly answered, "this woman is the person I am looking for, she probably requested it. She came in here last night convinced Christmas had come early for her."

"Do you want to go up and see her?" Smith asked. "Or would you rather call her room?"

"We'll need to go up."

"We'll?"

"Yes," Garner explained, "you will need to come with me and bring your pass key. I doubt she'll be there to let us in."

Three minutes later the two men were at the door to room 1225. Not surprisingly, no one answered the investigator's knocks.

"Open it up."

The clerk slipped the key into the lock and turned it to the right. Grabbing the knob and twisting, Garner pushed the entry open. As he expected the room was empty and the bed hadn't been slept in.

"She doesn't appear to be here," Smith noted.

"Would you ring the switchboard," Garner suggested, "and see if there were any calls made from this room in the hour or so after Miss Noel checked in?"

As the clerk made the call, the investigator went to work searching the room. There was nothing in the dresser's three drawers. Except for a Gideon Bible, the nightstand was empty. The guest hadn't hidden anything under the mattress either. In the bath, Garner did find a brush containing strands of dyed hair matching Sunshine's.

"Mr.—" Smith began, then paused and noted, "you didn't tell me your name."

"Garner," the investigator barked as he walked out of the bath. "Now what did you find out?"

"Mr. Garner, there was one call to this room at just after four this morning. It originated from the phone in our lobby."

"How do you know that?" the investigator demanded.

"While we can't give you locations for outside calls, the switchboard shows where all the calls originate in this building and makes notes on those."

Garner grimly nodded. That likely meant that he'd been tailed everywhere he went last night. If that were the case, by simply giving her a ride and dropping her off at the Palmer House he'd set up Sunshine to be murdered. That wasn't the news he was hoping to uncover.

"Will there be anything else?" Smith asked.

"Don't rent the room," Garner suggested. "And don't let anyone come in or go out."

"I'll make sure that we block this one off," the clerk assured him. "Should I close the door on the way out?"

"Please."

Garner rubbed his chin as he sank onto the bed to think. The man tailing him must have not only seen Sunshine but also the blue jade ring he forgot to retrieve from her hand. That ring marked her as the blonde the crime boss had hired him to kill, and since the investigator had dropped her off very much alive, Delono must have felt he was being double-crossed. After all, the crime boss had earlier questioned if Garner could kill a woman. Therefore, to ensure the hit was carried out, Delono must have had a second man ready to do the job just in case Garner went soft. It appeared the crime boss had every angle covered.

Glancing down to the nightstand the investigator once more noted the Bible. From this angle he observed that it was not completely flat. Something had been placed between some of the pages. Retrieving the book, Garner flipped it open to the eighth chapter of John. Marking the spot was the money he'd given Sunshine. Setting the bills to the side, he scanned what was printed on the page. Someone had underlined the eleventh verse. Was it the woman? Had she read the story found on that page?

Putting the money back into the Bible, he closed it and returned the book to the drawer. He then picked up the phone and asked for an outside operator. When the phone company's employee came on the line he said, "Please connect me with the homicide department. I need to speak to Lieutenant Lane Walker."

The cop answered on the third ring. "Walker here."

"Lane, it's Brent. Come over to the Palmer House and meet me in Room 1225. I think I can fill you in on what happened to Sunshine. By the way, it looks like her murder had nothing to do with robbery."

"What makes you think that?"

"Just get over here. I'm in the room and I'm not going anywhere. Once you see what I found, I doubt if you'll need any explanation."

— 14 —

Thursday, December 19, 1946
7:15 p.m.

Tiffany wasn't completely surprised when Bret Garner called her at work, after all, even when he held a gun on her she still observed a glint of approval in his eyes. Yet, she was more than a little caught back when, after he apologized for kidnapping her, he asked her out for dinner. That didn't happen every day. She was about to turn him down until he mentioned he'd like to take her to J. H. Ireland's Oyster House. In fact, in hopes she'd say yes, he'd already made reservations for the high-class joint's Lobster Grotto Room. In the Windy City, the elite met at Ireland's and a reporter didn't get into that place unless there was a murder. So, even though her date was with the same man who threatened to rub her out the night before, suddenly she was more than willing to dig out and iron her nicest evening dress, bundle up to fight off the Arctic cold, and ride with the investigator over to 632 North Clark Street.

Six finely dressed employees greeted them at the door, and just inside the lobby, Tiffany spotted a half dozen millionaires, two professional athletes, a Broadway star, and a member of President Harry Truman's cabinet. As they were escorted into the Lobster Grotto Room, she picked out at least two dozen members of Chicago's high society and two semi-famous Hollywood actors. When the couple was seated at their wall-side table covered with a blue tablecloth and lit by an ornate lamp, she realized that her date had seemingly missed the long parade of Who's Who. For the moment, he seemed to only have eyes for her.

Garner studied her as if she were a work of art, then took a deep breath and announced, "Your dress is amazing." He paused for a moment allowing his eyes to linger on her floor-length, dark green holiday frock before adding, "it hugs your curves like a Rocky Mountain road."

"Is that good?" she asked.

"No," Garner replied, "it is well beyond good. My goodness, you're a vision. Your eyes are as blue as the Pacific Ocean in late summer and, might I add, it should also be a crime to have skin that creamy."

"Let's go back to the eyes and the sky," she suggested, "the cream comment reminds me of my teenage years living on a farm in Wisconsin. Let me assure you that getting up on cold mornings before school to milk the cows is not the way to spend your childhood. So please stay away from any compliments that have cream, butter, milk, or cheese references."

"Got it," he laughed.

Throughout the meal, as Garner entertained her with stories of growing up outside Little Rock, Arkansas, and his days of playing football at Ouachita College, Tiffany found herself becoming more fascinated by the man's wit, surprisingly gentle nature, and intelligence. By the time they'd finished their dessert of New York cheesecake and coffee, she'd almost given into his charms. Yet, each time he leaned close enough for her to smell his bay rum aftershave, she remembered the previous night and the way he'd allowed her to believe he was going to kill her. Thus, just like a room with a faulty thermostat, she was running hot and then cold and then back to hot in a matter of minutes. Sensing a need to gain control of the conversation, she shifted the subject away from his old stories and her appearance to the much more pressing subjects of murders and mayhem. Surely, guts and gore would make him forget love and romance.

"You know, Bret, Lane still considers you a suspect in Sunshine's death."

She immediately realized her ploy had worked,

as Garner frowned, leaned away from the table, and looked across the room. A few seconds later, he rested his elbows on the table while touching the fingers from both hands together in front of his face. As if frozen in place, he remained that way for several minutes, until he finally shifted his eyes back to her. His verbalized thought was short, but hardly sweet.

"Lane thinks like a dumb cop rather than a smart one."

"When he called me this afternoon with an update," she explained, "he said you could have planted the money in the Bible and the brush in the bathroom."

The investigator dropped his hands back onto the table and shook his head. "He doesn't really buy that for a moment. He's just trying to plant suspicion in your mind. He doesn't want us getting too close."

She laughed, "Lane doesn't really care about me, he just likes to string me along. He's stood me up more times than he's actually taken me out."

"If you buy that," the investigator quipped, "you really are a dumb blonde." He let his words hover in the air for a few seconds before asking, "What's he told you about the war?"

"Well," she snapped, "that came from out of left field." She paused and looked deeply into the man's face. For the first time tonight, it was etched with what looked like concern. After tracing the rim of her coffee cup with her index finger, she admitted, "Other than the fact we won, he's not mentioned it."

"I'm not surprised," Garner quietly answered. "Let me fill you in on a couple of things. I sold myself to Delono as a hit man by pretending I had Mr. Walker's war experience. Lane was such a crack shot the Marines made him a sniper. He picked off countless men who never knew they were in his sights. One minute they were alive, the next, after Lane squeezed a trigger, they were dead. They had no warning their lives were about to be snuffed out. Most times it happened during lulls in battle." The investigator loosened his tie and frowned before explaining, "There are some snipers who love their jobs; he didn't. It gave him nightmares. So, while he avoids talking about those days, he can't escape thinking about them. For that reason, he's likely never going to let himself get too close to anyone. So he's not playing a game with you, he's playing a game with himself. You just happen to be in that game from time to time."

"I didn't know," she whispered. She carefully considered what she'd just learned before adding, "I just thought he was a jerk, because that was his nature."

"Well," the investigator laughed, "maybe he is that, too. But you need to know this. There are a lot of men, and I'm one of them, who can take what we saw and experienced in war and leave that baggage behind. There are others who carry it with them. Lane carries it with him. Inside that suitcase are the faces of every man he had in his sights and killed."

A suddenly chilled Tiffany looked away from her date, rubbed her arms through her dress, and studied the bright red lobster painted into the opulent dining room's ceiling. There had been a change in Lane. She'd noticed that in Hawaii during the war and even more so when he'd returned to Chicago last year. In the past, he'd been inconsiderate and irresponsible, but he'd never been cold and distant.

"Back to the present," Garner suggested. "Lane tells me while we are trying to smash organized crime, you have your sights set on a Santa ring."

She smiled now, thankful the investigator had changed the subject. "There are too many Santas in Chicago right now."

He chuckled, "More every year it seems."

"I'm serious," she resolutely explained, "there's too much money coming into those charity buckets and not enough making it to the city funds designated to buy gifts for war orphans and widows. So, to find out what's going down, right now I have newsstand operators and paperboys secretly watching those Santas and taking notes. I'm going to find out which of the jolly elves are being naughty and which are being nice."

He grinned, "The bad Santas really better watch out."

"It's no joke."

"I get it," Garner assured her. "Maybe I'll do some digging, too. If I find anything, I'll let you know." He leaned close enough for her to once again get a whiff of his aftershave. "How about catching a movie with me tomorrow night?"

She almost agreed, but the thought of the bogus Santa racket caused her to shake her head. "I've got to work late tomorrow. In fact, I need to be getting home right now and catching any calls that come in from my spies. Maybe we can do it another time."

"Maybe," the investigator cracked, "if Lane doesn't toss me in the slammer or Delano doesn't pick me off."

— 15 —

Friday, December 20, 1946
9:25 a.m.

Tiffany Clayton, dressed in a gray suit, light blue blouse, charcoal pumps, and carrying her huge black purse, was escorted by a law clerk into the plush office of Judge Ben Jacobs. The tall, distinguished man was seated behind his paper-covered desk reading what looked to be a law journal, but when he became aware of her presence he immediately set the magazine to the side, stood, and smiled. His thick, mostly dark hair was streaked with gray, his eyes were small and brown, his brow pronounced, and his jaw firm. Though he was well into his fifth decade, the man most felt would soon be the state's next governor maintained a slim, athletic body. He wore a dark, pinstriped suit, white shirt, and conservative black and red tie. His black shoes sported a military shine and his only jewelry appeared to be a thin, gold wedding band.

"Miss Clayton," he began, his tone as charming as his smile, "it is so good to finally meet you. I read your work everyday in *The Star*. In fact, I look forward to it. You are a very talented writer. In fact, I think you're almost as good as many of the men on your paper."

Almost? So much for her casting a vote for Jacobs in the next election. Most of the men she worked with had barely gotten out of high school while she had graduated with honors from Northwestern. In her mind there was no *almost* to it; she was a better scribe than any of them even if they often got the best assignments.

As Tiffany chewed on the backhanded compliment, the judge pointed to two chairs situated on each side of a small, round wooden table by the window. It was obvious he was unaware he'd verbally stepped on the reporter's toes as he suggested with a broad smile, "Pretty lady, would you please sit down and then we can get to business."

The reporter nodded as she shot out a luke-warm, "Thank you." After easing into the soft, brown leather chair, she reached into her purse, pulled out a pen and paper, and waited for her host to take his place. When he was seated, she began to dig. "Your honor, I know you are very busy, so I will try to not take much of your time. I came to get your thoughts on the murder of Ethan Elrod."

"Oh, my goodness," the judge began as he pushed a bit of hair up and off his forehead, "Ethan was not just a great man, but an even better friend. I was the best man as his wedding and he filled that same role at mine. I was the godfather to his children. There was hardly a day over the past fifteen years when we didn't either visit in person or over the phone. I already miss him more than I can begin to express. What a tragedy! Sadly, I understand the police have no idea as to who did this. Such a shame! I have spoken to both Mary and the children and have been so inspired by their strength during these difficult days."

As she jotted down his statement, Tiffany marveled at the way the man so quickly summed up more than a decade of friendship. Most men would have searched for words, stumbled in their delivery, and failed to fully define the relation-ship, but not Jacobs. In one paragraph he'd hit a home run. And, as she quickly found out, he was not finished.

"Ethan's most dynamic quality was his integrity. He would not bend his principles for anyone or any reason. In his years as a lawyer, I never knew him to compromise on the truth. Not once!" He waved the index finger on his right hand to emphasize the point. "That was a lesson he learned when he interned at the DA's office and will no doubt be his legacy." And so it began.

For the next forty-five minutes, starting with tales from college, when Jacobs was a student and Elrod a teacher, and ending with a lunch meeting just last Monday, the judge related story after story painting a detailed picture of his admiration, respect, and even his love for Elrod. Though the words tumbled from his lips as easily as rain spilled off a steeply pitched roof, it was in the man's dark eyes where the real depth of his loss could be seen. Though he never completely broke down, several times Jacob teared up. Finally, when he paused, pulled a handkerchief from his suit pocket, and dabbed at his eyes, Tiffany tried to steer the conversation in a new direction.

"Judge Jacobs, as I write this profile piece on the late district attorney, I want to know a bit more about why you think he might have been killed. Did any of your recent conversations with Mr. Elrod hint at any reason someone would want to take his life?"

Jacobs crossed his right leg over his left, then placed his hands over the raised knee and frowned. "He was investigating organized crime. It was his mission of the moment. Therefore, there was not just one man that was gunning for him, but scores of men. On top of that, Ethan had put a lot of people in jail over the years. So, when they got out after serving their time, a few might have still held a vendetta against him." He paused, glancing out the window to the traffic some four stories below before posing a question of his own. "None of the newspapers have listed in what manner Ethan met his demise. Do you have any idea?"

"The police are withholding that information," Tiffany explained without revealing she knew exactly how Elrod had died. "Now, can we move past the death and possibly end our conversation with a more uplifting story . . . something that might make my readers smile a little?"

"What do you have in mind?" His tone indicated he was both surprised and perplexed with her suggestion of a new direction for the interview.

"There was an annual present the two of you gave each Christmas."

Folding his hands together, the judge smiled, "You mean the fruitcake?"

"Yes, it seemed almost everyone who knew the two of you also knew about the tradition of passing it back and forth each year. How did that begin?"

"Gosh," Jacobs chuckled, his eyes drifting toward the ceiling as if seeing another time and place, "I got that old fruitcake way back when I was a kid here in Chicago."

"By *kid*," Tiffany asked, "what do you mean?"

"I guess I was likely in my late teens, it was Christmas break, and I working some odd jobs. I'd been given the fruitcake and I just hated it. I kept it because it carried some special memories for me that I didn't want to forget. Later on, when Ethan and I became friends, I found out that he hated fruitcake, too, so I wrapped it up and gave it to him. Lo and behold, rather than toss it in the garbage, the next year he gave it back to me. Over the years it just continued. Of all the traditions of the season, it might just be the one I have cherished most." He smiled and looked directly into her eyes, "It was actually one reminder of how far we had come. When I first gave him that cake, neither of us had a spare dime in our pocket. Over the years, we escaped the poverty of our youth, became well-known and respected, and even traveled all over the world. We ate in the best restaurants and even visited the White House. Yet, each year at Christmas that cake brought the past back into sharp focus. That way we never forget . . ."

As his voice drifted off, she stopped, held the top of her pencil against her cheek, and asked, "Who was supposed to give the cake this year?"

His face grew ever sadder. "I guess I'm stuck with it forever." Getting up from his chair, he slowly crossed the room to a filing cabinet, slid open a drawer, reached in, and retrieved a large, round, red and green tin. Retracing his steps, he set the still unopened container on the table and frowned. "Not sure what I should do with it now."

Jan's Old World Fruitcake was painted on the top of the tin proving it was the very same kind as the one Lane had shown her at Elrod's house. Yesterday, on the phone, the cop had even guaranteed the gag gift had been the murder weapon. Now it appeared that theory had been riddled with holes. Lane would not be pleased when she shared this scoop with him.

"Where can you buy these?" Tiffany asked.

"Nowhere," Jacobs quickly explained as he once more eased down into his chair. "The company that made this cake went out of business a long time ago. This is likely the last one left in the whole world. I mean, think about it, who would keep a fruitcake for twenty years?"

"Who indeed?" the reporter asked, her mouth framed by a wry smile.

— 16 —

Friday, December 20, 1946
3:25 p.m.

Mary Grant Elrod was fifty-seven, but looked a decade younger. She was five-four, and thanks to playing tennis and swimming on a regular basis, was within five pounds of what she weighed when, thirty-six years before, she led cheers for the Fighting Illini. Her face was not as much strikingly beautiful as it was motherly pleasant. Her best feature was likely her brown eyes sprinkled with flecks of gold. When she smiled they lit up like Independence Day fireworks. As she led Lane Walker from the Elrod mansion's front door to the spacious living room, she walked ramrod straight, her perfect posture even more emphasized by her black sweater and tailored gray slacks.

"I'm sorry to bother you," the cop apologized. "I wouldn't be here if I didn't have a job to do."

"I realize that, Lieutenant," she announced, each of her words seemingly carefully carrying a dose of tact, grace, and elegance. "Why don't you take a seat on the couch; I will sit in the chair by the Christmas tree."

As his host slowly eased down, much like a

bird lighting in a tree, Lane took a quick look around the room. Except for the tree's lights having been plugged in, it looked much the same as it did the other night, but it felt much different. The shock of murder had now been replaced with an overriding sense of grief. There was an invisible hole in this room and this hole could not be filled. As long as some member of the Elrod family lived here, the house would be haunted by the events of December 18.

"He was a giant," she announced without prompting.

Lane, caught off guard, turned his attention back to his host, and nodded. Though her eyes were clear and fixed on him, he sensed that her heart might be broken beyond repair. He figured that Mary and Ethan must have been very close. Yet, with her next words, that illusion was shattered like a fine crystal glass dropping on a marble floor.

"You need to understand something," she continued, her voice surprisingly strong. "My husband lived to work. He focused on his job ten or twelve hours a day and sometimes seven days a week. I raised our children. Yes, he was there for birthdays and holidays, but he didn't have the time to read them stories or play with them." She shrugged, "He really didn't have time for me either. He promised a few times that he would cut back, slow down, and focus more on family, but I knew that wasn't his nature. It was funny, he always kept his campaign promises, but he never managed to keep his promises to me or the children."

"I . . ." Lane muttered, unsure as to how to respond.

"I'm only telling you this," she explained, "so that you will understand why I am reacting as I am. You see, I haven't cried. In fact, because we rarely spent time with each other, I don't even feel he's really gone. So, while the city of Chicago has been tossed into a deep, dark time of mourning, I'm just numb. But maybe that's the way it should be, the city feeling more of a loss than I do. After all, he was more married to the city than he was to me. That's really where his head, heart, and focus were."

Lane had been blindsided and was now completely unsure how to respond. Seeing no possible answer that would cover his shock, he opted to avoiding commenting on what the woman had shared and chose to plunge directly into the reason he'd come to the house. After clearing his throat he asked, "Mrs. Elrod, did your husband have any enemies?"

The woman glanced toward the window, smiled, but remained strangely mute. Even when she finally spoke, she continued to stare at the home's huge, snow-covered front yard. "Ethan was one of the most beloved men in this city. He was both esteemed and respected. We have already

156

received hundreds of Christmas cards and in the next four days hundreds more will come in." She turned her gaze back to her guest, "But a man who has that many friends also will have many enemies. His job was to put people in prison. I have no idea how many men and some women have served time or are serving time in places like Joliet because of Ethan's work."

"I understand," Lane assured her, "but had he recently gotten any serious threats?"

The widow softly laughed, "He got them every day, but they never worried him. He assured me that those who took the time to let him know how much they hated him for who he was, what he did, or what he had done were not a problem. Let me explain what I mean. If you see a snake first, you likely aren't going to get bit. Ethan felt that if anyone ever tried to kill him there would be no warning. So written threats didn't bother him. He never lost a moment's sleep over the hate mail."

"So, Mrs. Elrod, you have no idea who might be behind this?"

She pushed her hand through her light brown bob and shook her head. "Lieutenant, if I had to make a guess, it would be someone connected to his crusade against Richard Delono and his organization. I mean that's what makes the most sense at this moment, but in truth, I don't have any idea who did this horrible thing."

"I am very sorry," Lane added. "Everyone at

the department is bent on solving this case."

"If," Mary Elrod said, "you manage to find the killer, will that bring Ethan back?"

He shook his head.

"So," she noted, "then it really doesn't matter to me, because the time he promised to give me and our family is never going to be realized."

Lane nodded, pushed off the couch, and moved toward the door. He paused there for a moment, debating if now was the time and this was the place for the question that was hanging between his mind and lips. He was about to opt to wait until after the holidays, when the woman broke the silence.

"There is something else you want to ask me. Isn't there?"

He turned back to face his host and nodded. "We're looking for a blonde woman with a blue jade ring. For reasons we don't understand, your husband was supposed to deliver that woman to someone representing Richard Delono in exchange for files that were to help him in his investigation into organized crime. We don't know who she is."

The woman rose from her chair and slowly made her way to where he stood. As she fiddled with her wedding ring, she sadly shook her head. "I wish I could help you, but I have never seen a blonde woman wearing a blue jade ring. If I had, I'm sure I would have remembered it." She looked up to his eyes as she continued. "If you think about it, it's a very strange combination. Jade is usually worn by women from the Far East not by someone with blonde hair. I've always been told that blondes prefer diamonds. In truth, I think that goes for all American women."

"I hadn't thought of it that way," he admitted.

"Lieutenant, you're a man, of course you wouldn't. You probably believe that all shades of blue can be worn at the same time."

Rather than show his ignorance and ask why shades of blue shouldn't be mixed, Lane posed another question. "There is something else I need to ask. May I?"

"Certainly."

"Did your husband have a fruitcake tin in his office or did you have one in the house?"

She smiled, "Not this year. Neither of us eats fruitcake. Now every other year, Ethan got one from Ben Jacobs, but this is one of the off years in which we didn't have to find a place to store the thing until we could give it back to Ben."

"Thank you for your time," Lane said, "and I just want you to know that I have men working overtime and they will keep working until we have gone through all your husband's case files. Be assured, we are running down every lead and questioning anyone who might have had a motive. We'll catch this guy."

Mary Elrod shook her head as she made a

159

suggestion. "Don't work so hard that you and your men fail to stop and remember Christmas." She paused and looked back toward her tree. "Please, wait just a moment."

As a curious Lane looked on, the woman marched as if on a mission. She quickly crossed the room and retrieved a small, wrapped package. She held it in her right hand for a moment, almost as if weighing it, then smiled and then retraced her steps. "This is for you," she announced as she pushed the gift into his right hand.

"I don't understand," the suddenly perplexed cop said.

"I bought this for Ethan," she explained, "and he won't be using it now. But, based on what I have observed today, I think you might just need it."

"I couldn't . . ."

"Of course you could," Mary Elrod scolded, "and you will. But don't open it until at least Christmas Eve. A part of the magic of the holidays is wondering what is hidden behind the paper."

Lane looked down at the small gift, "Thank you."

"Merry Christmas," she replied.

As he walked to the door, he couldn't help think of the irony of her words. How could Mary Elrod have any happiness during this holiday season? Her husband, one of the city's most beloved men, had been murdered, and she had barely known him. Was there anything sadder than that?

— 17 —

Friday, December 20, 1946
8:30 p.m.

Tiffany Clayton put the finishing touches on a story profiling the life of Ethan Elrod, turned it over to the copy editor, grabbed her coat, and stepped out into the cold night air. Rather than hail a cab, as she normally did when getting off work, the reporter turned to her right and made a six-block walk down State Street to a newsstand run by a World War I vet named Thomas Tacker. Little Tommy, as he was called, was now closing in on sixty, but he had crowded a lot of living into those six decades. Though just five-one and likely not more than one hundred and twenty pounds, the diminutive man had once been a star. For more than three decades, Tommy had traveled all over the world as a circus performer. While walking the high wire for Barnum, he'd met kings, queens, and presidents. It all ended in 1935, when a fifty-foot fall smashed his right leg. It took him a year and five surgeries just to get back on his feet and to this day, the tiny man dragged his foot whenever he took a step. His career finished, he'd taken what little savings he had left after his extensive medical bills, bought a newsstand and now worked twelve hours a day, seven days a week to make enough to afford a rundown basement flat located below a pool hall. Yet, as sad as his life seemed, Little Tommy never complained. Whenever Tiffany saw him, she was greeted with an ear-to-ear grin and hearty, "How you doing?" This night was no exception. Even with the windchill close to zero, the man was still happy to be alive.

"How you doing?" he announced with a smile and wave, "Happy holidays, Miss Clayton."

"It is?" Tiffany asked.

"If you're breathing and eating," Tommy explained, "you've got reason to celebrate. Listen to the sounds of the season. You can hear Christmas music playing over store loudspeakers, parents are walking the streets shopping and dragging giggling children by their sides, church carolers have been coming by all night long, and there are Santas everywhere."

"And," Tiffany quickly replied, as she leaned under the awning to try to escape a bit of the damp wind, "those Santas are why I am here."

"Can I get a copy of *Life*?" a heavy-set man asked, as he sidled up to the small outdoor store's counter.

"Got one right here, Mr. Rice," the newsstand owner announced. "Do you need anything else, cigarettes, gum, or a candy bar?"

"No," came the quick reply, "just the magazine."

"Okay, that will be fifteen cents."

The customer flipped a quarter to Tommy and said, "Keep the change."

"Thank you, sir, and have a Merry Christmas."

"You, too."

After the big man lumbered off, Tommy turned back to Tiffany. "That's Jonathan Rice. He owns the drugstore down on the corner. They sell magazines and newspapers there, too, but he always buys his copies from me. It doesn't make a lick of sense, but he's just a grand guy who wants to see an old carny keep eating."

Tiffany smiled, "People like you, because you are a quality person. Anyone who doesn't smile when they come to this newsstand doesn't have a heart."

"I'm just happy," he replied, "that's the way God made me." Tommy leaned a bit closer and said, "I know it's too cold for you to hang out on this corner for long, so let me show you what I got." He pulled three pieces of paper from his pocket and pushed them toward the reporter. As she picked them up, he explained. "Those are the permits the city hands out to the charity Santas who work the streets. The guys in the red suits could be arrested if they didn't have those. Let's just say I borrowed them tonight. Slipped them right out of their pockets when they stopped here to visit."

"They all look the same to me," she noted.

"They are," he assured her. "In fact, you'll notice that two of them even have the same name on the permits. And guess what?"

She looked up, "Fill me in!"

"Neither one of those guys is named Max Boyd."

"You got a theory?" Tiffany asked.

"Don't need one," he explained. "I've seen this kind of scam before. Someone has stolen a batch of signed permits and they have also secured the names of all the real Santas working the streets. Then they use their blanks to make up extra permits with duplicate names. That way if a cop checks on one of them and then makes a phone call to city hall, the name always rings true."

She smiled, "So, thanks to you, I've got something to run with."

"I hope so," he answered. "I don't like to see little kids being cheated at Christmas."

"Tommy, do you have any idea where the fake Santas are taking their cash?"

"No word on the street about that," the little man explained. "That makes me think this is a real professional operation. The big cheese behind this caper must be someone that has the power to make sure no one talks. And there is only one man who fills that bill in Chicago."

"Delono?"

"Miss Clayton, you said it, I didn't."

"But why?" she argued. "For the mob this is a small-time operation. I mean, there is not a huge bankroll made from coins folks are tossing in pots."

Tommy pulled his green scarf tighter around his neck and nodded. "On the surface is seems that way, but in the circus things also appeared one way and in reality were another. Consider the acts that sawed women in half or made tigers disappear. So you need to be looking for a slight-of-hand trick. I don't know what that is, but I've got to believe more than just a handful of change is disappearing right before our eyes."

"Interesting," the reporter said, her mind trying to grasp the scenario that Tommy had just laid out.

"Miss Clayton," the newsstand owner suggested, his expression now much more serious, "This could be very dangerous. You might want to reconsider your investigation. After all, some-times it's best to accept that the tiger disappeared and not question how it was done." He paused as if letting her carefully consider his words before adding, "Now please give me those permits back and I'll make sure I get them to our Santas tomorrow. I'll just tell them they must have fallen out of their pockets and I was fortunate enough to find them. I know the corners where each of them works. It will be easy for me to give them back with no suspicion falling on me or you."

"Tommy," the reporter asked, as she shoved the documents back his way, "Did you know any of these men before they were playing St. Nick?"

"Yeah, I know two of them real well," he assured her. "Benny is a retired bookkeeper and maybe the best grandpa in the world. He's like a big teddy bear. Horace is an old bachelor, a steady churchgoer who never drinks anything harder than grape soda. I can't believe either one of them would be hooked in with a scam. But, I worked in the circus for all those years and never figured out the disappearing tiger trick either. I guess what I'm hinting at is that things are not always as they seem. Even good people can fall on hard times and then are forced into doing things they normally wouldn't do."

Tiffany shook her head, "You never know."

"Miss Clayton," there was a frown now framing the man's expressive face, "why don't you just drop this? As my friend who buys the racing forms would say, the odds aren't in your favor."

"I'll think about it," the reporter lied. "Now I've got twelve blocks to cover before I get to my apartment building and it's not getting any warmer. Thanks for taking a risk for me."

"It was easy," he laughed. "And I'd pretty much do anything for a woman as classy as you."

Tiffany leaned forward, kissed Tommy on the cheek, and began the long walk home. She had something to go on now. It might not have been much, but at least she'd made some progress and, no matter the little man's warning, she was in this game until the finish.

— 18 —

Friday, December 20, 1946
9:15 p.m.

Four blocks into her walk, Tiffany realized that as soon as she left her meeting with Little Tommy she should have grabbed a cab. It was far too cold for a woman in a skirt and heels to be trudging through the snow. Yet, as she was now a couple of blocks past where the open businesses and the city's nightlife ended, she was stuck. At this time of night there would be no taxis venturing down the lonely streets she was walking. Thus, she was going to have to duck her head, gut it up, push on, and hope she got home before frostbite set in.

Two blocks further down the all but deserted street, the reporter stopped in front of a closed grocery, stepped out of the ferocious wind, and looked into the mirror on a pennyweight and fortune machine. She didn't like what was reflected in the dim light. Snow was caked in her hair, under her eyes, and around her cheeks. Her lips appeared to be blue, but, in an attempt to be positive, she did her best to convince herself that was likely just the dark lighting on the street. Her brain might have bought the rationalization, but her chattering teeth didn't. Still, blue lips or bad lighting aside, what the mirror really reflected was a woman who hadn't used her common sense. No one with any brains walked twelve blocks on a night like this. That fact she'd tried it pretty much spelled out how smart she wasn't. If she managed to live through this experience, she vowed to never let another living soul know about this long walk home. A shiver went down her spine, shaking her from head to foot, as she considered the grief Lane Walker would give her if he knew what she'd done.

Turning up her coat collar, she stepped away from the store and back to the curb to cross the street. An oncoming car, its lights reflecting off the snow and ice, forced her to wait.

"Come on," she whispered as she stamped her feet in an attempt to get her ever-thickening blood moving. As a blast of wind all but knocked her over, she glared toward the car and screamed, "Get moving. I can't wait here forever."

Tiffany was caught off guard when the sedan slowed down rather than sped by. She was even more shocked when the car pulled to a stop right in front of her. What was this all about? Was someone actually taking pity on her? She didn't have to wait long to find out.

A tall man, his face covered by a dark scarf, pushed open the passenger door and stepped out. He stared down at her for a moment before barking, "Get in the car."

Tiffany glanced from the man giving the orders to the dark, four-door Buick. There were three other men in the vehicle and none of them appeared to be knights in bright armor coming to her rescue. She'd been around Chicago long enough to know hoods when she saw them.

"I'm fine," she answered, mustering as much strength in her tone as a freezing woman could. "I live right up the way, I don't need a ride."

"You're taking one, anyway," came the gruff reply.

"I don't need to bother you," she snapped.

"Lady, you need to be taught a lesson. Now get in."

"I've got a college degree," she shot back, "I've learned enough lessons to last a lifetime. Now move on or I'll call a cop."

The man shifted his eyes up the street and then back to the woman, "Scream all you want, there's no cop to hear you. Now get into the car or I'll pick you up and throw you in."

As the man reached out to grab her arm, Tiffany dug her heels into the snow, spun in her tracks, and brought the full weight of her large purse against his face. Due to the buildup of ice on the sidewalk combined with the force of the blow, he lost his balance, fell against the car, and slid down to the street. That was all the time the reporter needed to turn and race down the sidewalk in the direction of her apartment. As she ran, she considered her options. If only there was a store or diner open, but one glance proved there were no businesses with lights on. For a change, the city had no crews out working on the street or fixing water main breaks, either. And where were the cops when you needed them? Just her luck, the only folks awake at this time of night in this part of town were the quartet of goons and the reporter.

Tiffany covered about twenty-five yards before the man she'd knocked down recovered enough to reach into his coat pocket and retrieve a gun. He squeezed off four rounds, but his aim was bad; all of them went well over her head. He must have sensed she had too large a lead to catch on foot, because as she turned back to check, the thug opened the door and jumped back into the old sedan. A second later, it was rolling down the street in her direction.

As she tried to pick up her pace, her heels slipped and slid on the snowy concrete. At this speed, just keeping her balance required all her concentration. It was just a matter of time, perhaps seconds, before the heavy sedan would soon catch up with her again. So, if she couldn't outrun them, she had to find a way to get some cover. But where? Most of the alleys in this area were dead ends. If she picked the wrong one she'd hit a wall and be cornered, yet the open street offered her no cover or options. Once again, where was a cop when you needed one? If she lived through this, she was going to have that saying made into a plaque and present it to Lane to hang on his wall.

As she raced by a closed drugstore, she stopped and tried the door; it was locked. The next three doors on the street were also shut tight. As she approached a corner, she took a deep breath and looked to her right. There was a snowplow just a hundred feet away and moving fast. Wisdom dictated she wait for the truck to cross, but with a quartet of men now just forty feet behind her wisdom was no longer a part of this equation. Digging her heels into the snow, she shot off the corner and rushed directly in front of the oncoming plow. It was moving faster than she'd figured. It was now so close she could hear the machine's scraping blade grating against the pavement and feel the heat being generated by the truck's roaring engine. As the lights caught her small frame, the driver hit the horn and the brakes. Tiffany ignored both and kept moving forward. She was almost safely across the street when she hit a slick spot, slipped off her feet, and landed on her stomach.

The truck was now ten feet away. One glance to her right was all it took to convince her it was not going to be able to stop. Rather than wait to be hit, Tiffany clawed at the street, moving forward about six inches a second. Then, as the shadow of the snowplow's huge blade crossed over her, luck swung to her side. The truck's driver managed to gain a bit of traction and jerk the wheel to the right, pushing the five-ton vehicle just far enough from the curb that the far side of the blade tossed about ten pounds of snow onto her body, but the blade never struck her. Picking herself up, now looking more like a snowman than a woman, a winded Tiffany turned and watched her luck continue. The Buick's driver did not react quickly enough to the unfolding situation. The snowplow's eight-foot-wide and three-foot-tall blade rammed into the car's passenger side, tearing into the metal as it pushed the Buick more than fifty feet up the street. For a second, Tiffany thought she was safe, but that moment passed far too quickly. The thugs' ride had no more than come to a stop when a short man dressed completely in black leapt out of the back driver's side door and charged in her direction. It was now three blocks to her apartment and safety. Could she beat him?

For two blocks, she maintained about a forty-yard lead, then she caught a piece of ice with the heel of her left shoe, slipped, and fell. Though it only took fifteen seconds to push to her feet, it seemed like a lifetime. Glancing back she noted the man, all but his eyes hidden by a scarf, now just thirty feet away, had stopped and pulled out a handgun. As if frozen in place, she watched him squeeze off three rounds. Maybe it was the weather or the slippery surface, but all three went high, striking and bouncing off the brick building behind her. Saying a quick prayer of thanks, she turned to her right and took off again. If she could just make it another block and a half she would finally be safe.

Tiffany's lungs now ached as each new breath brought searing pain. Her legs, scraped from her falls, were failing her, too. Her strides were shorter and her pace slower. As her body continued to break down, there were also cracks in her resolve. With each new step, her mind was screaming that she simply couldn't continue. And though she didn't look back, she sensed the predator was getting closer and, in fact, she could now clearly hear his footsteps in the snow. A few seconds later, she swore she could even feel his breath on her neck. Surely, at any moment, she would feel his hand on her shoulder and he would drag her to the pavement. Just as she neared the corner, an Oldsmobile motored up the far side of the street, swerved across to the curb, and slid to a stop. With the car now blocking her path, she knew it was over. The race was lost just one short block from home.

As she slowed to avoid running into the car, the vehicle's passenger door flew open and from inside a man's voice screamed, "Get in!"

Too tired to argue, an exhausted Tiffany ducked her head and literally fell into the Olds.

"Shut the door," the man demanded.

With her last ounce of strength, the reporter yanked it closed. When it was secure, the driver hit the gas and rapidly motored away from the curb. After taking a deep breath, Tiffany pushed herself upright in the seat and looked toward her left. She was shocked to see Bret Garner behind the wheel.

— 19 —

Friday, December 20, 1946
10:00 p.m.

"Where do you want to go?" Garner asked, as he flashed his eyes to the rearview mirror. So far, things were fine. No one was following them.

Tiffany took a deep breath and muttered, "I guess my place."

"No problem," he shot back. "Let me drive around a few blocks to make sure no one is on our tail, and then I'll head back in that direction. Meanwhile, why don't you see if you can catch your wind and rub some of that snow off your face and your clothes. I'll turn the fan up a notch and you can open the heater doors to help you warm up faster."

"I'm so cold my head hurts," she moaned, as she leaned forward and reached up to the dash to swing the doors wide open.

"That's what you get for playing in the snow," he sniped.

"Yeah," she shot back, "that was it. If only you knew the whole story."

"Time for that later," he suggested. "There's a blanket in the back seat. Grab it, wrap up, and try to keep your teeth from chattering. I hate the sound."

"Well," she cracked, "I'm sorry. I'm not a big fan of it either."

Garner made a right turn and again checked the mirror. So far so good! As he pulled up to a red light, he glanced over to his passenger. If she was injured, at least it was not too badly. She already was feeling well enough to wrap herself in the Indian blanket, huddle close to the heater, and pour snow out of her shoes onto the floorboard. In truth, all things considered, she looked pretty good. Maybe the worst that would come of this would be a few scrapes and bruises and perhaps a cold.

"You warming up?"

"Yeah," she assured him. "At this rate I will be up to zero by Easter."

The investigator wanted to press her for information. He wanted to find out why the guy had been chasing her and what had happened before he came along. But for the moment, it was enough that she was safe. Now, if she would quit chattering her teeth.

Garner drove around for ten minutes before

turning the Oldsmobile south and heading back to the reporter's apartment building. After parking the car on the street, he walked slowly around the car, his eyes darting to every dark doorway and alley. Satisfied they were alone, he opened the woman's door and silently escorted her up three flights of stairs. The investigator's eyes locked onto the stairway as she dug through her huge purse and found her keys, unlocked, and opened the door. He then shifted his gaze to Tiffany as she switched on the overhead light, yanked off her coat, dropping it onto the floor, kicked the shoes from her feet, and collapsed on the couch. Grabbing a throw pillow, she hugged it close to her chest and closed her eyes. He could sense she was not sleeping, but saw no reason to interrupt her. She needed some time to sort things out and evaluate what had happened. He was perfectly willing to give it to her.

After closing and locking the door, Garner strolled over to a bookshelf and turned on a small Philco radio. As he waited for it to warm up, he studied a photo of a much younger Tiffany, perhaps twelve, with what appeared to be her parents. Outfitted in bib overalls, her father looked every bit the dairy farmer while her mother, with her wholesome attractiveness still evident in her housedress, was a more rural version of her daughter. The picture seemed to verify his hunch that she was an only child. He studied the photo for a few seconds before shifting his attention to the bookshelf's contents.

Stacked beside the radio were a half a dozen issues of *Life*, *Time*, and *Newsweek*. Lining the shelves were at least two dozen books, all nonfiction and most of them biographies. He was running his finger over a copy of *The Wit and Wisdom of Will Rogers* when the radio's tubes finally warmed up and the strains of the Andrews Sisters' new cut, "Christmas Island" filled the room. Forgetting the book, Garner adjusted the radio's volume and walked back across the room to the chair he'd occupied just two nights before. After falling into it, he was content to watch the clock, listen to the music, and wait. Five songs later, his host finally opened her eyes and spoke.

"How did you happen to be on the street?"

He smiled as he looked into her blue eyes, "I was coming to see you. You might have turned down my movie invitation, but I thought I might be able to tempt you with a late supper tonight."

"So it was luck," she suggested as she pushed herself upright and leaned against the cushion while still hugging the red throw pillow.

"I don't really believe in luck," Garner said. "I just happened to be at the right place at the right time."

"Actually," she corrected him, "you were ten minutes late! The right time would have been before the big guy tried to grab me and long before I almost became a sacrificial offering for a snow plow."

He paused for a moment to consider her story. Evidently, he had missed some stuff. "Who was after you?"

"I don't know," she admitted. "Maybe it is that Santa thing I'm looking at. I found out some stuff tonight and my source suggested I back off. He thought it was too dangerous to pursue."

Garner hadn't expected that angle. Why would someone skimming a few bucks off a charity make Tiffany a target? This was hardly big-time crime; it was just penny-ante stuff. "Who knew you were working on it?"

"Lots of folks around the paper," she explained. "And I've made some calls to officials at the city who put together this fundraiser, so they knew. But who kills someone over a few thousand dollars in charity receipts?"

"There are some who would," he assured her, "but I can't buy into it being the reason for what happened tonight. I think this might be more on me."

She frowned, "Not sure I understand that."

"Did they just try to nab you?" he asked.

"Well," she quickly replied, a bit more life now flashing in her eyes. "When I wouldn't take ride with them, they got a little upset. Before you picked me up two of them shot at me, too."

He'd only seen her being chased and this new

178

element ramped up the nature of tonight's events. She'd gotten into some serious stuff, and it was a much different road than he figured she'd traveled to get into trouble. He frowned, "Okay, scratch my theory."

"What do you mean?"

It was a good question, and he wasn't real sure he had a full answer for it. Yet, rather than swallow his tongue, he spilled out a theory he was making up as he went along. "I figured that Delono might have sent his boys out to get you, because they'd seen us together. Thus, the mobster either thought you were the real blonde or knew you were a newspaper reporter and was afraid I'd given you information you might use in a story to hang him."

"That sounds logical to me," Tiffany cut in. "These guy acted like torpedoes."

"It only makes sense," he explained, "if you were dead."

"I don't like the way that sounds," the woman said, pushing her still slightly wet blonde hair away from her face.

"Here's what I mean," Garner continued. "I saw enough of Delono's hired talent to know his boys are professionals. These guys are good. When they shoot, they don't miss."

Tiffany waved her hand, "Then why did he hire . . . what was the name you were using in your role as a hit man?"

"McCoy Rawlings," Garner answered, "and Delono told me the only reason he hired an outsider to take care of the blonde was that he didn't want to take a chance on one of his guys being recognized by a witness. While it sounded good at the time, I think that using an outsider was a part of the deal he made with whoever really wanted our mystery woman dead."

"So," Tiffany asked, "why did four supposedly amateur thugs go after me?"

"Beyond the Santa deal," he asked, "Have you stirred up any other hornet's nest? Are you working on anything else that could mean jail time or worse for anyone?"

She shook her head. "The only other person I've talked to is Judge Jacobs."

Garner pushed out of the chair and walked over to the radio. After he turned it off so he could fully concentrate, he once again studied the family photo. He was still looking at it when he popped a question that had nothing to do with the evening's events. "Do you ever wish you'd stayed on the farm?"

Tiffany soberly replied, "Not until I was sprinting down that street tonight. It did pop into my mind for a moment then."

He turned and faced her, "What happened to the kids you went to school with?"

Tiffany looked back toward the front door, "Two of the guys were killed in the war, but most of the others stayed close to home and got married. My closest girlfriend has three kids now."

"Doesn't sound like such a bad life," he suggested.

She looked back at her guest and shrugged. "For Debbie, it's not. But I'm not cut out for that sort of thing."

He smiled, "That life's a lot safer than the one you're living now."

Tiffany grinned, "Let me put it this way, until I met you no one ever tried to kill me." She let her jab land before adding, "Bret, what if this has something to do with Elrod? Maybe I've got information and just don't realize it."

"I guess that's possible," he said as he moved back across the room and to the chair. After sitting down and resting his elbows on the cushioned arms, he added, "But, once again, someone associated with that case wouldn't have missed when they shot. By the way, when was the last time you talked to Lane?"

"This afternoon," she replied, "I called to try to get him to help me on the Santa investigation and he cut me off. He had to go out to the river. He said something about maybe finding another piece of Stuart Grogan."

"That's a grim thought," Garner noted. "Have you got anything to drink or eat?"

"Got a couple of Cokes in the fridge and some bacon. I could make us a sandwich."

"Tiffany, that's the best offer I've gotten all day. We can talk while I watch you cook."

As she pushed off the couch she bragged, "I'm a farm girl, so I'm pretty good at it."

"We'll see," he announced as he watched the now seemingly energized woman bounce toward the kitchen. She was both durable and resilient. Yep, she was something special.

— 20 —

Friday, December 20, 1946
11:35 p.m.

Garner leaned against the cabinet as Tiffany set a skillet on the stove and retrieved bacon from the fridge. After turning on the gas, she dropped the eight pieces of meat in the pan and smiled, "You know, I'm pretty hungry, too. I guess running for your life works up an appetite."

"If you've ever been in combat," the investigator noted, "you'll never take eating a hot meal for granted again."

"You want some eggs?" she asked. "I can scramble or fry them."

"You got another skillet?"

"Sure. The first door on your right."

"Okay, Tiff, I'll grab that second burner and do

the eggs while you work on the bacon. We just might make a pretty good team."

"Bret."

He waited until he pulled butter and eggs from the refrigerator and set the pan on the burner before answering. "What do you need?"

She looked over to the man now cracking four eggs into the cast-iron pan. "It sounded like you felt a bit sorry when I mentioned Stuart Grogan. I didn't expect that. I mean, he was a hood. You know the old biblical saying, you live by the sword you die by the sword, so he got what he deserved."

"Maybe," the man sighed, "or maybe not." As he used a fork to stir the eggs, he explained. "I knew Grogan. I got to know him toward the end of the war when I was transferred over into Naval Intelligence. He was smart and charismatic. The first few weeks we worked together, I thought he had the potential to be a dynamo. I could see him working in Washington or in post-war Europe. But in time, cracks started to show."

"What do you mean 'cracks'?" she asked, as she used tongs to flip the sizzling meat.

"Tiffany," he continued, his eyes still focused on the task at hand, "he was kind of like Lane, except even worse. What happened to him in the war gave him nightmares, even when the sun was shining. At times, he just fazed out and when he did, he'd see things and hear things that weren't a part of the real world. There were three times I saw him snap and without warning pull out his gun and fire it into a wall. After he did it, he'd be fine again. A couple of other times, when we were out at a nightclub in Honolulu, someone said something that set him off. With no warning, he grabbed them and lifted them up by their necks. Then, a few seconds later, as if was realizing what he was doing, he'd let them back down and pretend it was a joke."

"He sounds like a killer," she noted.

"Yeah," he admitted, "why don't you get a couple of plates and I'll dump the eggs on them." As she turned and retrieved the dishes, Garner continued, "Grogan was a time bomb. I saw a lot of men like that in my days in combat. There was always something eating at them that made them that way. So I did some digging and found out more about Grogan. What I discovered wasn't pretty. He had witnessed his whole unit wiped out early in the war. Somehow, he was the only one who lived, and I guess he blamed himself for surviving."

"Like a guilt complex?" she asked as she held out the plates. "Give yourself the biggest portion."

After dumping the eggs onto to the plates in near equal amounts, he took the dishes as she dropped five pieces of bacon on one plate and three on the other.

"Why don't you take those over to the table,"

she suggested, "and I'll grab the bread, mayo, and see if I have any lettuce and tomato."

"It's okay if you don't," he assured her.

When they were both seated at the tiny metal table set between the kitchen and the living room, Tiffany asked the evening's most logical question. "If he was crazy, how could Grogan keep his position? Why didn't they put him in a hospital?"

"I served under generals and admirals crazier than he was," Garner explained. "In times of war, sometimes crazy is actually something the military loves. I've seen crazy men do some incredible things in combat. I guess what I'm saying is this . . . sometimes crazy just makes you the perfect killing machine." After eating a forkful of eggs, the investigator picked up his story. "Anyway, toward the end of our days together, Grogan seemed to calm down. In fact, the day he mustered out he told me he wanted to right wrongs and do something really noble. He said he was looking at going back to college and perhaps even to a divinity school."

"That's not the path he took," Tiffany noted, as she dropped a slice of tomato on her bread.

Garner hadn't bothered with anything besides the bacon and was chewing on his sandwich when he sadly admitted, "I lost track of him after that day. I mean, that happens when you get out of the service. You swear you're going to stay in touch, but you don't. You just get on with your life! In October, I heard he was working for Delono. That just didn't square with my last conversation with the guy. I figured that he might be acting as a mole. Maybe he was feeding the cops information. If that was the case, I knew he was in over his head. So I blew into town with my cover as a real West Coast hit man to see if I could at least protect him. It seems I got here too late."

"Who hired you?" Tiffany demanded, as she ate her eggs.

"Well," he shrugged, "I'd just cracked a big case for an insurance firm, had money in the bank, so, I took this case on myself."

"That's not what you told Lane," she noted accusingly.

"No," he admitted, "you're right. But I figured that a trumped-up story would make him actually believe I was working for client who needed to keep tabs on Elrod's investigation. He'd like that better than my trying to protect a guy he felt was a real killer. But that's the strange part about this whole caper."

"What is?" she asked.

Garner took a long swig from his Coke before explaining. "While he acted tough, Grogan never really killed anyone while he was with Delono. In fact, the reason he was knocked off was due to Delono's belief Grogan was actually biding his time until he got a chance to kill him. And in a strange sort of a way, that actually makes sense. Grogan, and his warped mind, might have believed that taking out the big guy and ridding the city of that mobster was a noble act."

"And you haven't told any of this to Lane."

"No," he admitted.

Tiffany pointed her finger at him and frowned, "You just can't stand for Lane to know you are on the up and up."

"Ah," he laughed, "it works better with him being the good guy in the white hat and me being the misfit. So, I'd appreciate it if you didn't mention that I gave you a ride tonight." He paused and glanced back to the family photo. "Now, there's something that's been bugging me since I found out your real name."

"Hold that thought," she suggested. "Are you finished?"

"There's nothing left on the plate," he pointed out.

"Let me put the dishes in the sink and then, Mr. Garner, you can share what is bothering you. Go over there and take your place in what seems to have become your chair."

The investigator moved to his assigned seat and listened as Tiffany rinsed off the plates. She must have forgotten about having to run for her life, as the entire time she worked she was humming, "Have Yourself a Merry Little Christmas." After the last dish had been put up, she returned to the living room, fell into the corner of the couch, grabbed the throw pillow, and pulled it to her chest.

"Now, what is your question?"

He smiled, "How does a farm girl from Wisconsin end up with a high-society debutante's first name?"

She shyly grinned. "Now we are diving into family history. You sure you want to go there?"

"Absolutely."

"Well, Bret, to make a long story short, I was named after a place in New York where my dad worked."

His jaw dropped, "The jewelry store?"

"That's it," she admitted. "The one at Fifth Avenue and Fifty-Seventh. My father was an important part of that establishment for some time."

"You don't say," Garner shot back, as if deeply impressed.

"I don't like to brag," she laughed.

"So your father's farm is just kind of a hobby?" Garner asked.

"Well," she explained, "Daddy didn't want me growing up in New York City, so he bought the place in Wisconsin. We moved west when I was in sixth grade. I know he still misses working with diamonds. It was in his blood. I'm sure Mom misses the parties, the shows on Broadway, and the friends she made in all the city's social circles.

But they gave it up just to make sure I had a normal American upbringing." She raised her eyebrows as she almost sang, "Yes, my life could have been so much different. But I do understand why they did what they did. Their hearts were in the right place. Still, I miss the Big Apple."

"Must have been tough," the investigator chuckled, "to go from the penthouse to the farm."

"It made me who I am today," she casually added.

"Tiffany, it's a great story."

"What do you mean 'story'?" she demanded. "It's the way it really was."

He laughed. "My dear, sweet almost-debutante, I used my skills as an investigator and did a little homework today. I made a few calls to Wisconsin and then backtracked to New York. While it is true your father once worked at the famous jewelry store in the Big Apple." He paused and grinned, "He didn't exactly run the place. He was a night watchman when you were born, and a few weeks later he was fired for sleeping on the job."

"Why you . . ." She finished her sentence by throwing a pillow directly at her guest. He caught it in his left hand just before it would have struck his face. Standing, she stomped her foot and screamed, "You let me go on all that time knowing the real story! That was cruel even by your fake hit man standards."

"It's a good story," he softly replied. "And, you

tell it well. In fact, it's obvious you have had some experience sharing it over the years."

Dropping back onto the couch, she pouted and sighed. "I hope you don't give this information to Lane. He's believed that story for six years. I couldn't bear looking like a fool in front of him."

"I'll let it be our secret," he said with a smile.

"That was just mean," she quietly added.

"Tiff, in my mind, you're a lot more of a jewel than any diamond in that store in New York." He allowed his words to sink in before pushing out of the chair, moving over to the couch, leaning down, allowing his lips to briefly brush hers, and then walking to the front door. As he pulled it open, he glanced back and let his eyes linger on the woman still glued to the corner of the couch. She was something else. He wasn't sure what yet, but he hoped he'd get to find out. Stepping out into the hall, he pulled the door shut and hustled down the apartment building's three flights of stairs. After studying the seemingly empty street, he walked over and slid into his Oldsmobile. He sat in his car for thirty minutes studying the apartment's back window until Tiffany's lights went out. Garner then remained there, huddled in the front seat with the Indian blanket wrapped around him, watching the street for the rest of the night.

— 21 —

Saturday, December 21, 1946
9:15 a.m.

After surviving a race for life less than twelve hours ago, it was a cautious Tiffany Clayton who emerged from her red brick apartment building on a cold, but sunny, Saturday morning. Dressed in gray wool slacks, a red sweater, long black overcoat, and red scarf, she opened the door of a well-worn, 1942 yellow and black Desoto, and slipped into the backseat.

"Where to, lady?" the cab driver asked as she closed the rear door.

"City Hall," she quickly replied.

"Aren't they closed today?" the middle-aged, portly man inquired.

"Yes," she assured him, "but the person I need to see is there, so don't worry about it."

The reporter quickly discovered her driver, like a lot of the city's cabbies, not only loved to talk but also felt a need to share all the personal details of his life. Within just four blocks, the reporter had learned that Melvin was forty-one, had three kids, one nine-year-old boy and two teenage girls, and a short, dumpy, red-headed, freckle-faced wife who was sweet, but didn't fully understand him.

"I met Mabel at a square dance when we were both sixteen," he noted. "She was a little thing then. Her green eyes matched her dress. I wasn't as much taken by her looks as I was by her laugh. She just loved to cackle. Our daughter Millie is like that as well. Now Jessie is a quiet one. She nods more than she opens her mouth. Anyway, Mabel and I got married right out of high school. I think she would have liked to have stayed in little old Muncie, but I had a yearning for something bigger and we ended up here. I got a job driving a taxi and been doing it ever since. Now this life's not for everyone, no sir, but I like it. I get to meet lots of good folks, see the best and worst parts of the city, and listen to music hours each day."

"That's interesting," a still-exhausted Tiffany lied.

As they passed through the business district, which on this final Saturday before Christmas was packed to the gills, Mel noted, "You know, old St. Nick is likely wrapping up the last of the toy making at this very moment. He might even be resting up. Meanwhile the clerks at Marshall Field's are probably close to experiencing the retail version of battle fatigue. Look at those shoppers. There's a line just waiting to get into the stores and they look well prepared to fight over the last stuff on the shelves. You got your shopping done yet?"

She nodded while noting his eyes looking back at her via the car's mirror. Sensing he was waiting for an answer, she gave out the information. "I only had to buy two things and I've already mailed them. So, I have started and I've finished and did it all in one easy trip."

Mel glanced over his shoulder, "You mean a beautiful dame . . . excuse me . . . I mean, a lovely woman like you isn't having a big Christmas?"

"I figure I'll just use the day to rest up," she explained. "I've got no family in town and I kind of enjoy spending a bit of time alone every now and then."

"You got a tree?" he asked.

"No," she admitted.

"It's not Christmas without a tree. You just gotta have a tree. There's a tree stand about a block up the road. Why don't we stop and get you one?"

She shook her head, "No, I really don't need one, but thanks for the offer."

"Seems a shame you don't have a tree," the cabbie mournfully said. "There's nothing like a tree with tinsel, lots of ornaments, and lights. Mabel always uses all blue lights on ours. Those blue lights just make my holiday a lot brighter."

"Sounds pretty," the reporter noted.

"What do you do?" Melvin asked.

"I write for *The Chicago Star.*"

"Not sure I ever had a reporter in my hack," he

laughed. "Now I've had some pretty important characters. A couple of years ago Bing Crosby rode with me. He was really a nice guy. It was the middle of July, but we still talked about Christmas. I mean when you think of the holidays you have to think of old Bing." Mel glanced into his mirror and popped a question, "You know what?"

"What?"

"Bing told me that Irving Berlin didn't think he'd done a very good job writing 'White Christmas.' Isn't that screwiest thing? The best song scribe on the planet didn't know 'White Christmas' would be a hit." He patted the steering wheel and shook his head. "Don't that just beat all?"

As Melvin began to hum the Crosby standard, Tiffany thought about her favorite holiday hit. "I'll Be Home for Christmas" was a secular carol she saw as a prayer. When she was working for *Stars and Stripes* during the war, she'd seen grown, battle-tested men cry when they heard that song on a jukebox. Though she didn't like to admit it, she'd shed a few tears as well. That song nailed it. The holidays really were about home and family. That was when Christmas was sweetest and best. Yet, she hadn't been home to help trim the tree or bake cookies for five years. That was just after Pearl Harbor and being home meant more that year than any other.

"So," the cabbie asked, "Do you have family somewhere?"

"Wisconsin."

"So why don't you take off and go see them?" he suggested.

"I can't," she explained. "Reporters work on the holidays; that's the way it is. News happens on December 25 just like it does on March 10 or September 15, and someone has to be there to put those stories together."

"Maybe Congress should pass a law outlawing news that day," he offered.

"Maybe," she replied, "but lots of others work, too. It's not just me."

"What's your best memory of Christmas?" the cabbie asked as he turned onto Randolph Street.

"I don't know," she admitted. "There are so many. I guess it was being in church with my mom and dad on Christmas Eve. We always lit candles when the service ended and we carried those candles home with us as a reminder to light the world with hope."

"You going to light a candle this year?" he asked.

"No reason," she explained. "I'll be alone and no one would see the light."

Mel nodded, but didn't say anything else until they arrived at City Hall. As Tiffany got out of the car, the cabbie slid across to the right passenger door, rolled down the window, and made an offer. "Our place isn't much, just a little house on the west side, but we always have room at the table for one more. Why don't you join me, Mabel, and the kids for Christmas dinner? We've got a real tree and Mabel even decorated our windows using stencils and tempera paint. Everything is real nice this year. And we can all light a candle together."

The reporter leaned into the car and smiled, "That's sweet, but, really, I'll be fine. Now what do I owe you?"

The talkative man with the big smile shrugged. "Just consider the trip my gift to you. I hope you find a way to have a Merry Christmas. In fact, I'll get Mabel to pray about that. She's real good at praying."

Tiffany was about to argue about the fare, but before she could say a word, Melvin slipped back behind the wheel, dropped the car into gear, and eased away from the curb. The reporter watched until the big car made a right turn and disappeared. The cabbie was right. Christmas needed to be special and shared with folks you cared about. It wasn't meant to be spent by yourself.

— 22 —

Saturday, December 21, 1946
9:45 a.m.

Shaking thoughts of Christmas past from her head, Tiffany marched up to the Randolph Street entrance of the nine-stories tall City Hall. After pulling open one of the building's ornate entry doors, she climbed two flights of worn marble stairs to the third floor. After a sixty-second walk down a long, tiled hallway, each of her steps echoing off the walls and ceiling, she pushed on the frosted glass and hardwood door of the city's licensing and permit department. The man she'd made the appointment to meet was waiting behind the counter and holding a file.

"Miss Clayton?" he asked.

"I hope I haven't kept you waiting," she quickly replied. "This is a horrible time of the year to ask someone to come to work on Saturday."

"No, I was actually going to be here anyway," he answered. "I have some things to catch up on. Anyway, my name's Collins."

The tall man had graying hair, blue eyes, and a quick smile. He was dressed casually, in a blue shirt and black slacks, and unlike almost everyone else in the city, he didn't seem to be in a hurry to get anywhere or do anything. If only all folks could be this relaxed during the holidays.

"I believe," he began, "you wanted to know about the Santa project."

Tiffany nodded, unbuttoned her coat, and leaned up against the chest-high counter opposite her host. She watched intently as he opened the file and glanced at the first page.

"This campaign actually began three years ago," he explained as his eyes came up to meet hers. "At that time, the mayor was made aware of how many men from Chicago had died in combat and how many of their widows and orphans were having a hard time during the holidays. So we put a dozen Santas on the street that year to raise money for presents for the fallen servicemen's kids. We've been doing that same thing every year since. Last year, we raised over twenty thousand dollars. This year it looks like we will even top that."

"That amount will buy a lot of gifts," she noted with a smile.

"Not just gifts," Collins pointed out. "We also buy food and clothing for the families in the greatest need. So while churches and other organizations take care of the needs of the very poor, we focus on those who have suffered due to the war. Now that peace is really here, I hope things will improve enough in 1947 so that we won't have to do this next year. In other words, I hope peace brings prosperity and security to those we reach."

"Let's hope so," the reporter echoed. "How many Santas do you have this year?"

Before answering, Collins glanced back to the file and flipped to a second page. "We have forty-three. They are good men, too. They work long hours in the cold and are paid nothing. Most of them are retired. A couple of local churches and the Salvation Army do bring them food and coffee a few times a day, but that is all they receive. In other words, they are giving their time because they believe in this cause."

Forty-three . . . *The Star*'s paperboys had counted over one hundred working on corners. So, without the city's knowledge, the population of jolly old elves was up this holiday season. How had the extra men in red suits not been noticed?

"Mr. Collins," Tiffany asked as she pointed to the file he still held in his hand, "who issues the permits for these Santas? And how does this process work?"

"Well," he explained as he dropped the file onto the counter, "the volunteers meet in our office in mid-October. They fill out an application form and give us references. We then carefully check them out before we designate them as one of our Santas. It might sound like a waste of time, but you have to do that in order to weed out folks who might steal from the kitty. And, as we have the only Santas allowed on the city streets, we want them to represent Chicago in a manner that makes our citizens proud."

"So," she asked, "do you issue the permits or does someone else do it?"

"Actually," he explained, "the mayor likes to get involved. So our Santas go to that office to obtain the permits."

"And," Tiffany continued to probe, "there are only as many permits as there are Santas?"

"No," he admitted, "We've found our men lose the permits pretty easily. You can understand how. For over a month, they are working in the wind, rain, and snow. So, the mayor signs a bunch of them and that way when one of our Santas loses or damages a permit they can come back to the mayor's office and quickly pick up a replacement. All they have to do is give the clerk their name."

Tiffany smiled. The scam was much easier to pull off than she had figured.

"Where do you get the costumes?" she asked.

"Mellon's on Fifth Street. They have outfitted us since we began this campaign. They make good suits, too. Our Santas look real and not cheap."

"They do indeed," the reporter agreed. "Thank you for your time."

"Merry Christmas," Collins sang out. "I hope I have been of some help."

"It is almost like you've written the story," the reporter announced as she turned and waltzed toward the door. As she pushed it open, she called out, "Happy Holidays!"

After hurrying down the hall and the stairs, Tiffany stepped into a phone booth and grabbed a directory. She scanned the listings until she found Mellon's Costume Shop. Dropping a dime into the phone, she called the number. A man answered on the third ring.

"Mellon's."

"Hello, I'm Tiffany Clayton from *The Chicago Star*. I understand that you supply the costumes for the Santas that we see on our street corners."

"Yes, we do," he proudly admitted. "I think those costumes are some of our best work."

"They are beautiful," she agreed. "Do you have them on hand or do you order them?"

"We actually make them," he explained. "The men playing Santa come in, we measure each person, and he comes back two days later and picks up his suit. That way we know just how much padding to add to make each man look like the real Santa." He giggled, "In a few cases, we actually don't have to add padding."

"How many Santas did you fit this year?" Tiffany asked.

"We made one-hundred and twenty-one costumes. That's a lot more than in past years. In fact, it kind of surprised us. We had a lot of men come into our offices in late November for fittings. Normally, they all come in just before Thanksgiving."

"Do they just ask for the outfits and then are measured?" she inquired.

"Yes," he admitted, "but they also have to show their city permit."

"Who pays for them?"

"Oh, we donate the labor and an outside donor pays for the materials. So there is not really any cost to the city."

"Thank you for your time," the reporter said.

"Happy Holidays," the man announced as he hung up.

As she considered what she'd learned, Tiffany drummed her fingers on the small wooden shelf under the phone. The scam was so easy to pull off that any person with a lick of sense and an eye for observation could have cooked it up. If twenty thousand was raised last year, then using three times the Santas the total might top sixty this year. That extra forty sounded like a lot until she factored in the seventy or more men working the scam. Their payout would be less than six hundred bucks and that hardly seemed worth the risk of getting caught and doing jail time. So, there had to be something else at work here, but what was it?

Getting up, she dashed out the front door and was shocked to see a familiar Oldsmobile parked at the curb. After waving, Bret Garner smiled and asked, "You need a ride?"

"I need to go to my office," she quickly answered. "So no time to goof off."

"You got a lead?"

"Yes," Tiffany assured him, "And I'll fill you in on the trip."

— 23 —

Saturday, December 21, 1946
12:21 p.m.

"Walker," Lane announced as he picked up his ringing desk phone.

"Are you with homicide?" a woman on the other end of the line asked.

"Yep, I'm the lieutenant in charge of this division, who I am speaking with?"

"My name is Sister Ann, I'm a nun. I run the feeding center about five blocks south of the stockyard."

Lane nodded. "If it is the one I think it is, you're in the old Townson shirt factory building?"

"That's the place."

"What can I do for you, Sister?" the cop asked. "But, you need to know, my division can't really offer you much help. If you are having a problem with one of those who comes in to eat there you need to get ahold of your beat cop."

"It's nothing like that," the woman assured him. "There's a guy who helps me down here. He's probably about fifty . . . maybe older, maybe younger . . . kind of scruffy, but he has a good heart. He doesn't even ask for anything in return for his work and he will do anything for us. Everyone calls him Joe."

Lane picked up a pencil and pulled a pad over by the phone. After cradling the receiver between his shoulder and ear, he asked, "Did something happen to Joe?"

"No, he's fine. But he seemed rattled today. So I asked him if there was something bothering him. That's when I heard his story and that's why I called you."

"I guessing," Lane noted, "there must be a death or you wouldn't have called homicide."

"Joe took me down to the old Cattlemen's Hotel," she explained.

"I know the place," the cop cut in. "It used to be pretty nice, but that was a long time ago. Last time I was there it was home to unemployed men and retirees who didn't have pensions. I guess you would call it a social club for bums and hobos."

"It's still that way," the caller agreed. "Joe led me to Room 233. The door wasn't locked. Sitting in the room's only chair was a man. His head was resting on a table and there was a knife sticking in his back. As the blood under his head was drying, I'm guessing he'd been dead for a while."

"Did you touch anything?" Lane asked.

"I just checked on the man, he was cold, so I said a prayer, and I backed out of the room."

The cop scribbled the room number on the page, tore off the paper, and stuck it in his pocket. "Okay, Sister Ann, I'll get right down there with a team. Where are you right now?"

"At our kitchen."

"What about Joe?" Lane asked.

"He's with me."

"Let me ask you something," the cop continued, "and answer it using what you have observed and your own instincts. Could Joe have done it?"

Her answer was quick and precise, "No."

"Then why was he there?"

"I sent him to deliver a meal to the man who lived in that room," she explained.

"So you knew the man?" Lane asked.

"Yes," the nun admitted. "He was a retired policeman named Henry Saunders."

The fact the victim was one of the city's veteran cops suddenly made this case even more personal. "Can you and Joe meet me at the hotel in twenty minutes?"

"We can," she assured him.

"Thanks, I will see you soon."

Slamming the phone down, Lane jumped up,

opened his office door, and looked at those working at the desks in the building's center room. "Stan, Tyrone, and Lester, we've got a body at the Cattlemen's Hotel and it's murder. Let's grab our gear, a car, and get out there. I'll call Doc Miller and tell him to meet us."

— 24 —

Saturday, December 21, 1946
1:05 p.m.

Lane Walker intently studied the scene in Room 233. Except for the location, it looked very similar to one from earlier in the week. As he stood in the door, the homicide cop's main focus was on a short man in an ill-fitting suit examining the body.

"What was the cause of death?" the cop asked the coroner.

Leroy Miller was a fair-skinned balding man, fifty-five, and perhaps a hundred and fifty pounds. His two most dominating characteristics were his deep-set dark brown eyes and his small pug nose.

"Well, Lane," Miller began, "logic would tell us that the man was killed when someone plunged that red-handled kitchen knife into his back, but if I told you that I would be making the same mistake as I did the other night with Elrod."

"Let me guess," Lane cut in, "the knife was inserted well after Henry Saunders died."

"Yep," the coroner announced as he pointed to a deep gash on the rear of the victim's skull. "The back of his head was bashed in with one single blow."

Lane pointed to a tin of Jan's Old World Fruitcake resting on the nightstand. "Could that have been our murder weapon?"

"Based on the paint flecks I'm seeing in the victim's hair," Miller noted, "I'd bet on it."

Lane walked across the room and looked at a half-empty glass of a brown liquid setting beside the fruitcake. "Stan, I want Morelli to test that glass for us. If my hunch is right, there will be some kind of knockout drug in it."

"Got it, Lieutenant."

"And we need to dust this room for prints," Lane ordered, "and the can too."

Stan nodded before offering an observation. "It will be the first time this joint has been dusted in a long time. What a horrible place to die."

"It's a worse place to live," the lieutenant noted. Turning his attention back to the victim, Lane signaled for tall, thin older cop to join him. "Tyrone, you've been on the force a long time, did you know this guy?"

"Almost forty years," Tyrone Jordan noted, "and, yes, I knew this man. His name was Henry Saunders."

207

As Lane studied Saunders's unshaven face and dirty, alcohol-stained tan slacks; torn, gray flannel shirt; and scuffed shoes, Jordan filled him in on the life story of the very dead cop. It was not a happy tale.

"He joined the force before World War I. As I remember it, he served about thirty years and never did much other than walk a beat. He lost his job because he had a problem with booze and it got so bad it cost him his family, too. None of us could help him either. He just had to have the stuff. Said it was the only way he could sleep at night. Based on all the empty bottles tossed over in the corner, I'd say he'd been sleeping a great deal."

Lane shook his head, "Could he have had any connection to Ethan Elrod?"

"I don't see how," Jordan replied. "The difference in the two men is like day and night. I'd be shocked if they'd ever met. You ready to get the body back to Morelli?"

"Yeah," the Lieutenant answered, "I'll talk to the nun and the guy named Joe and then meet you back at the station."

Lane exited the small, dirty room and stepped into the dank hallway. Waiting for him was a disheveled man who looked to be somewhere between forty and fifty, a small nun, her blue eyes shining in spite of what she'd witnessed, and a very familiar reporter.

"Tiffany," he jabbed more than asked, "How did you find out about this little party?"

"I have my sources," she assured him. "I had a chance to peek in the door and this sure looks familiar."

"I'll fill you in after I visit with these two," Lane announced with a frown.

The lieutenant looked toward the man who found the body. Joe was dressed in all black, about six-foot four, his thick hair partially covering his ears and collar. If he was nervous, he didn't show it. His dark eyes were clear and focused and his thin lips relaxed. "So you discovered the body."

"I was bringing him lunch." Joe's voice was so strong and steady the cop figured this wasn't his first encounter with death.

"And you didn't touch anything?" Lane asked.

"I knocked," the man explained, "and when he didn't answer, I let myself in. I found him the same way he is now."

"Was this your first visit to Mr. Saunders's room?"

"No, I've been coming here bringing him meals for a couple of months. So, I was here two times a day almost every day. In fact, I was here last night about six."

"And he was fine then?" the cop inquired.

"He was inebriated," Joe explained.

"Did you talk to him?"

"I sat with him for a while as he ate. He knew

me well enough to realize I carry a Bible with me, so he asked me to read the story of Christmas. I read a few chapters out of the Gospel of Luke and left when he fell asleep in that same chair."

Lane glanced to the nun. She was a small woman with a gentle but strong face. "How well did you know the victim?"

"He'd been coming to our kitchen for about two years," she said, her voice clear and inviting. "About two months ago, he got to the point where he had problems walking that far. So, I had Joe bring him his meals. I'd come and visit with him about once a week."

"Did he have any enemies?" the cop asked.

She sadly smiled, "There was only one I know of."

A suddenly hopeful Lane leaned closer, "Who was that?"

The nun nodded, "Himself. He never talked much about his past, but it was easy to see that it haunted him. Maybe it was because he was an alcoholic who couldn't stop drinking, maybe it was that he lost his family, or perhaps it was something else he just couldn't get over, but whatever it was, it constantly ate at him. At least now he has found some peace."

The cop nodded, "His finding peace is not bringing any into my life. Thank you for your time."

Sister Ann reached out and took Lane's hands

and whispered, "Merry Christmas and may God bless you."

As Joe and the nun walked down the stairs, Tiffany stepped to the cop's side and posed a question. "You can't have twin killings and no connection. It can't be a copycat as no one has printed how Elrod was killed. So, an alcoholic former cop and the city's most beloved leader have to be tied together in some way."

"But how?" Lane demanded.

Lane knew even the talkative blonde would not try to answer his question. In fact, the only people who might have a clue were either dead or the killer.

— 25 —

Saturday, December 21, 1946
3:05 p.m.

With two identical murders that on the surface had seemingly no connection, it was time to put the "Case of the Fake Santas" on the back burner and dig through what was now becoming the top story of the holiday season and perhaps the most explosive series of murders to hit Chicago since the days of Al Capone. So, while Lane turned to Morelli for possible clues, Tiffany Clayton opted to check out Sister Ann's soup kitchen.

The charity operation was not much to look at. Located in the front part of an old factory building, the dark dining room consisted of little more than forty wooden tables and two hundred chairs that had been salvaged from a closed stockyards café. The walls were brick, the floors wooden and sagging, and half the building's windowpanes were covered with plywood. The nun's staff consisted of Joe and four older men who cleaned up the place and served the meals. For those few hours of labor each day, Sister Ann let the men eat as much as they wanted and sleep in a bunkroom on the second floor.

Unlike many charity kitchens there were no sermons before the meals and those who entered came and went as they pleased. The only rule, clearly spelled out on a three-by-three-foot hand-scrawled sign, was there was no alcohol allowed on the premises.

A quick inspection revealed the food served at Sister Ann's was hardly fine cuisine. Depending upon donations from grocery stores, meals consisted of baloney sandwiches on day-old bread, some watery soup, and weak black coffee. Yet, as unappealing as it seemed to the reporter, for the men and a few women who lived on the streets and had nothing, the kitchen was a lifesaver and the meals were as much appreciated as the one she'd had just two nights before at J. H. Ireland's Oyster House. And this place of charity and hope, a light in one of the darkest sections of the city, was open three hundred and sixty-five days a year simply because of the drive of one, small, determined woman.

As Tiffany sat at a corner table and watched the nun work, the reporter tried to get a line on Sister Ann. Hidden by her habit and its hood, the woman could have been anywhere from twenty-five to fifty, but, even though only a small portion of her face showed, what was clearly obvious in her sparkling eyes and ready smile was her passion for the work. It seemed she knew each of the sad souls who wandered into her establishment. They had no more entered when she called out their names and asked them a question about their lives. As Tiffany observed the nun interacting with those she described as "the least of these," the reporter made a mental note to do a feature on the woman when this fruitcake mess was put to bed. Perhaps this was a bigger story than even the Santas and with a bit of publicity maybe this mission could be ungraded and expanded.

At three-thirty p.m., after hugging a small man, his face twisted as if in pain, and his movements almost spastic in nature, Sister Ann finally made her way over to where the reporter was sitting. Tiffany allowed the woman to catch her breath before noting, "I can tell you love what you do."

The nun nodded. "Caring for those no one cares for is not a job for everyone." She turned her eyes from the reporter to the half dozen men sitting in various places in the room. "Old Sam over there is from Mississippi. He was injured in a railroad accident a dozen years ago. He came north looking for someone who'd hire a man with a bum leg, but sadly he didn't find much. He sleeps in alleys and digs through trash for things to sell to pay for clothes. He might not look it, yet under all that dirt and grime he's as honest as the day is long."

The nun subtly shifted her gaze to a small, thin man dressed in a coat four sizes too large. "That's Elmo, he's from Chicago, he grew up on the South Side, he's a good guy when he's sober, but he just can't stop drinking. Thus, he can never hold a job for long."

Tiffany glanced to the man the nun had just hugged, "I guess he has a story, too."

"They all do," came the quick reply, "but he's a pet project and has been one for a long time. Because of a childhood accident, Si's mind is warped, he doesn't always think straight and he has fits. You don't have to worry about him, he's not dangerous, but with the crazy things he says and the wild look in his eyes, he scares people. Like all the others he's just looking for a place to fit in and be accepted." She shook her head. "That's the real problem. These people just don't have anywhere they do fit in. As a society, we have standards, and folks have to meet those

214

standards to be accepted. Thankfully, God doesn't have standards that have to be met to be considered a part of His family."

The reporter nodded, "And what's your story?"

"I was orphaned," she explained, "and nuns raised me through my teen years. That was likely what saved me from a pretty bleak life. So I guess it's just natural I look out for those who weren't as fortunate or blessed as I was." Sister Ann, her blue eyes misting, tapped her fingers on the table and added, "Life is not fair. The good don't always win and when they don't, when they get ready to give up, they need someone just like I needed someone twenty years ago. That's why this place is here."

The conversation died for a few moments as both women studied those coming in and going out of the soup kitchen. It was a sobering scene. In the midst of so many spending so much on holiday gifts, there were so many others who had nothing. Finally, pulling her eyes from hopeless faces back to the nun, the reporter remembered her reason for coming and posed her first meaningful question.

"What about the man who was killed? Did you know him well?"

The nun shrugged, "As well as I do any of the others who come in here. Mr. Saunders never opened up much. About all I uncovered was that he used to be a cop who fell upon hard times. I just assumed his life was ruined by his battle with the bottle. Of course, there's usually something else that drives men to drown themselves in booze, but whatever that was he never shared it with me."

"I know this will sound a bit off the wall," Tiffany continued, "but did you ever meet Ethan Elrod?"

Sister Ann smiled. "He used to come in at least once a week."

"Really?" The reporter's tone revealed her shock.

"He was one of my biggest donors," she explained. "He could have mailed his gifts to us but for some reason always brought them in person. I'm not sure why. He didn't interact with anyone but Joe and me, and the look on his face showed he received no joy from his visits, but he kept coming back anyway."

"So," Tiffany cut in, "you didn't know him before you opened the kitchen?"

"Not that I remember," she admitted, "his and my social circles are very different, and, as Elrod was a Methodist, I wouldn't have run into him at church. I guess he just had a soft place in his heart for people like this. He did tell me once that he was poor as a kid and the Salvation Army had served him a few meals when times were really tough."

"Do you remember," Tiffany asked, "If he ever talked to Saunders?"

She shook her head, "As I said, Mr. Elrod didn't really mingle with the folks who came through those doors. He pretty much sat where we are sitting and talked to either Joe or me. In fact, he never stayed more than fifteen minutes." She smiled. "He did have one funny habit."

"What's that?"

Sister Ann shrugged, "Don't understand why, but he wouldn't leave without praying with me."

"Anything specific?" the reporter queried.

"Not really," the nun answered, "he just wanted me to ask the Lord to forgive him for his sins. When I assured him that they had been forgiven, he always left seeming to be feeling better."

"Sister Ann . . ." Tiffany began.

The nun cut her off with a whimsical look and a wave of her hand and asked, "Are you a Catholic?"

"No," the reporter admitted.

"Then why don't we just treat this as two women talking to each other? You just call me Ann."

"Okay, Ann," Tiffany agreed. "I feel there has to be a connection between Elrod's and Saunders's murder. I can't fully explain why—the police are asking the press to hold back certain details about the deaths in order to dig a bit deeper into the motives and their bank of suspects—but my guess is that the two victims had to have known each other. Are you sure they didn't meet and talk here?"

The nun didn't reply. Instead she looked toward the serving line and waved. A few seconds later, Joe laid down a soup ladle, stepped around the counter, strolled over to the table, and sat down.

"You remember Joe?" the nun asked. "He was with me at the hotel."

"Yes," Tiffany assured her. "I do remember him."

"Then ask him the question you just asked me. He knows these men as well as, if not better than, I do." The nun looked toward the man and announced, "This is Tiffany . . . what was your last name again?"

"Clayton."

"Tiffany Clayton," Sister Ann continued. "She is a reporter with *The Chicago Star* and would like to ask you a couple of questions."

Tiffany turned her face toward the middle-aged man dressed in the black clothes. Though he was a bit untidy, he still carried himself with a sense of dignity that she hadn't noted on the other men and women who had slipped into the soup kitchen.

"Joe," the reporter said after catching the man's eye, "did Ethan Elrod and the man whose body you discovered today know each other? Did they ever talk?"

"No," Joe quickly answered. "I don't even remember them ever looking at each other." He paused and rubbed his mouth, "Mr. Elrod was a fine man. He spent so much of his life trying to do good things, and I think the burdens of his job weighed on him. Meanwhile, Saunders was just a lost cause. He really didn't want any help. His desire was for absolution."

"Forgiveness for what?" the reporter demanded, all the while wondering why the man had used a fifty-cent word in describing the now-dead cop.

"He never said," Joe replied. After glancing toward the door and watching a bent, elderly woman dressed in a blue coat and using a tattered blanket as a scarf enter the front door, he pushed his chair back and stood. "I need to get back to the counter. Betsy is going to want some soup."

As Joe walked resolutely across the room to his station, Tiffany noted the sad state of his wardrobe. The knees of his black pants were patched and the patches were so old they were shiny.

"I've got a friend who's about Joe's size," the reporter offered. "I'll see if I can't get a couple of pair of slacks and give them to Joe. They wouldn't be new, but they'd be in much better shape than what your worker is wearing now."

"He's got five pair of trousers just like that," Sister Ann explained, "and I've given him a dozen better pairs of pants to replace them. He always passes along what I give him to one of the other men. When I ask him why he keeps wearing those old black rags he just tells me they remind him of who he once was. For some reason that memory is very important to him."

"Strange," Tiffany observed as she watched Joe spoon up a bowl of soup and hand it to the old woman.

"Not really," the nun answered, "each of these folks have memories they hang onto in some way or another. Their trigger to those recollections might be a photograph, a handkerchief, a house key, or a newspaper clipping, but it seems they all have something that connects them with who they were a long time ago."

"Did Saunders have anything?" Tiffany asked.

Sister Ann nodded. "A tarnished badge. I once offered to polish it for him, but he wouldn't let me."

The reporter looked from the scene at the counter to the nun's eyes and posed another question. This query was driven by personal curiosity, not a quest to unravel a murder mystery. "Do you have anything you hold onto?"

The nun smiled, "I have one thing, but I can't carry it with me. Still, like a photograph, it brings back a moment in time that remains very dear to me."

"Ann, can I ask what it is?"

"Miss Clayton, you can ask, but I'm not going to answer. Even a nun has secrets. Now, I need to start preparing for our supper crowd, so if you will excuse me."

"Thank you."

"God bless you," the woman answered.

Tiffany watched Sister Ann get up from the table, walk through the room, and back to the kitchen. Once more alone with her thoughts, the reporter spent a few moments looking at the faces of the city's forgotten men and women before getting up and strolling out into the cold Chicago wind.

— 26 —

Saturday, December 21, 1946
5:30 p.m.

Against his better judgment, Brent Garner had been out in the cold wind and below freezing temperatures for a half an hour. As the minutes ticked by, he almost wished for a return to the heat and humidity he experienced in Burma toward the end of the war. Yet, even as the winter gales cut through his clothes, chilling him to the bone, he concluded that being subject to a zero-degree windchill and surrounded by frenzied holiday shoppers was much better than being drenched in sweat while being shot at by Japanese soldiers. Positioned on a street corner across from the Metro Diner, Garner was on a mission. Last week, the Met—as called by locals—plunged into the Santa fundraiser with both feet. In an ad taken out in all the Chicago papers, the diner promised to feed any of the city's official Santas between five and seven on Saturday. There would be no charge. There was no doubt that any of the jolly red-suited men who liked to eat would take the diner up on its generous offer.

After the six Santas entered the Met, the all-but-frozen private investigator casually crossed the street and pushed open the glass door. As Garner studied the scene playing out in the long, narrow building, he couldn't help but smile. From the jukebox music to the smiles on people's faces, Christmas was everywhere and so was St. Nick. Two of the Santas seeking meals were sitting in a booth on the back wall. The rest were camped side by side at the long counter. As Garner watched, a child, dining with a pair of adults at a table just inside the door, grabbed his mother's arm and all but yelled, "Mommy, which one is the real Santa?"

Ironically, that was the very same question that Garner wanted answered. As the woman explained to the confused child that these red-clad men were just St. Nick's helpers, the investigator opted for a more direct approach to separate the real Santas from the phonies. Sticking his hands in his pocket, he ambled to the back wall and paused beside the table where two of the rotund men were examining a menu. After snapping his fingers to gain their attention, Garner flashed his badge for just a second and asked, "Can I see your permits?"

Neither man hesitated pulling out the pieces of paper. Garner glanced at the names and handed them back. He repeated the exercise at the bar. Once again, he met no resistance. For the next hour and a half he used the same routine to study each new arrival's paperwork. By seven, he'd met and talked to twenty-two Santas.

As the time limit for the free meals expired, the investigator walked over and stood beside a booth where three of the red-clad fundraisers were munching on hamburgers and fries. He remained mute until the one sitting on Garner's left said, "You need something else? We've already shown you our permits."

"And," the investigator noted with a wry smile, "that's part of the problem. It seems two of you have the same name as a pair of other Santas I met earlier in the day. So," he pointed to the two large elves sitting to his right, "are either of you really George Kelly?"

As he glanced from man to man, the table remained silent.

"Okay," Garner demanded, "Your silence speaks volumes. Now I want the real story. I know at least two of you are playing a con game and you're going to tell me what it is. If you don't, Mrs. Claus is going to have make a long trip to bail you out of jail."

"I don't know anything about this," the man whose name was not Kelly piped up. "I can prove who I am, I have my driver's license in my pocket."

The investigator pushed into the booth beside the legitimate Santa and coldly studied the other pair of red-suited men. After letting them sweat for a few moments, he asked, "What's the story, gentlemen?"

The shorter of the two bearded men shrugged, "We volunteered to do a job, a guy gave us the permits and told us to go get a costume."

"Didn't the fact your names weren't on the permits seem strange?" Garner asked.

"He told us not to worry about it," came the reply, "something about not having time to print more. As this was for charity, I didn't question it."

The investigator dug deeper. "Where were you recruited?"

"I was notified at church." The talkative man glanced to the still silent Santa and added, "My pastor gave me the permit and instructions."

The still mute Santa nodded.

"Do all you fake Santas go to the same church?" the investigator demanded.

"No," the talker quickly replied. "There was no one else from my church, and the other men I've talked to came from a lot of other churches. They aren't even the same denominations."

That was a twist Garner hadn't expected. How did the city's churches get involved in this scam? Pointing his fingers at the two imposters, the investigator demanded, "What do you do with the money you take in?"

"We turn it over to the folks in charge," he explained.

Garner looked toward the apparently legit Santa, "And you?"

"I do the same thing."

"None of you holds any of it back?"

Three heads shook in unison.

"Jim," Garner prodded, "so if you are the real Santa in this trio, have you noticed anything screwy going on?"

"No," he quickly answered, "in fact, I've been doing this for three years and we have already raised more this year than we did last year."

The investigator nodded, "And who do you give the money to?"

"A uniformed cop drives up every night around nine," the Santa not named Kelly explained. "He takes my pot and gives me an empty one for the next day. You can look in the car tonight if you want, there are all kinds of pots already in there when he picks up mine."

"Me, too," chimed in one of the Kellys.

Once again, the quiet man nodded.

"So everything is done the same way for all of you?" the investigator quizzed.

"Same for all the Santas I've talked to," the silent member of the group finally chimed in. "When we signed up, we got a detailed copy of the city rules on how this works. The guys I know are all honest and follow those rules to the letter. I don't know about anyone else, but I wouldn't even take out a penny for a piece of gum."

"Me either," Jim added.

"Are you going to shut us down?" one of the men known as Kelly asked.

"No," Garner admitted, "you just go back to work and pretend this conversation never took place. You will only get into trouble if you tell anyone what was said here. By the way, where is the corner where you work?" The investigator smiled as he added, "Mr. Kelly."

"My name is Goldstein . . . Harold Goldstein."

"Okay, Harold, give out with the information."

"I'm at Michigan and Pershing."

Garner nodded, "If you're finished eating, why don't you go back to work."

Though there was still a bit of food left on their plates, the trio didn't argue. As soon as the investigator stood and stepped to the side, the Santas made their way out of the booth and through the front door. After they were gone, Garner slid back into the booth. What he'd discovered had done little to unravel the reason for the scam. Yes, the whole thing was fishy and it smelled, but it hardly seemed like a reason for four men to scare or maybe even murder Tiffany. There had to be more to her being attacked than a simple fund-raising scam.

— 27 —

Sunday, December 22, 1946
9:15 a.m.

Though most women wouldn't have called two men and suggested they meet for a breakfast date, Tiffany Clayton was not most women. She cared nothing about what Emily Post outlined as correct etiquette for today's proper young ladies. When it was time for action she believed protocol should be dismissed. As she had talked to both Lane Walker and Bret Garner the night before, listening to the new information both had shared, she decided a powwow over eggs and hotcakes was in order to build upon their combined knowledge. After all, three heads were surely better than one, even if one of those heads belonged to smart-mouthed cop. During this meeting the only topic she was keeping off the table was the fact someone had tried to shoot her. At this point, she didn't want the cop in this equation to get wind of that bizarre episode. If he did, he might toss her in jail for her own protection. So, when she set up the meeting via the phone, she instructed Garner to keep his mouth shut.

The two men met Tiffany at a Walgreens Drug Store counter about eight blocks from her apartment. The trio spoke mostly of the bitter cold and their lack of holiday plans until their waitress removed the empty dishes and refilled their coffee cups. Sensing it was time, as her father always said, "to fish or cut bait," the woman steered the conversation in the direction of the unsolved murders.

"Though I couldn't pin down any direct contact between Elrod and Saunders," the reporter explained, "I know they both were at the soup kitchen from time to time. Perhaps there is something there that connects them."

"I don't know about that," Lane cut in, "and by the way, I like your outfit today."

Tiffany looked down at the red and green checked wool dress and chuckled. "Have you had your eyes checked? You've never noticed what I've worn in the past."

"That's not true," he objected.

"Okay, what was I wearing when we ate at the Oyster Bar?"

"That was actually me," Garner announced. "I was the one who took you to the fancy place. Lane is more the cheap diner kind of guy."

"Oh," Tiffany quietly admitted, "that's right."

"You went out to eat with this character?" Lane asked loudly enough that a half a dozen patrons turned to see what the fuss was all about.

"Hold it down," she hissed. "And yes, Bret took me out. Not that it should concern you."

"My goodness, Tiff," Lane grumbled, "he could be a murderer. I haven't cleared him in the Elrod case yet. So you're stupid if you spend anytime alone with him."

"I'm stupid, am I?" she shot back.

"I didn't say you were stupid," Lane quickly amended. "I just implied that you were not acting very bright right now."

"I have a history of that," she shot back, "it was evident all the times I went out with you."

"Oh," he mocked, "so it comes back to that. Well, my dates with you were not my finest moments either."

"Excuse me, Skipper," she jabbed, "how many of those did you actually show up for?"

"I really don't mean to interrupt," Garner whispered, "but I'm trying to keep a low profile here. I mean, there is a price on my head. So you two need to hold it down. Right now everyone in this store is looking in our direction."

"Yeah," Tiffany suggested, "let's move on to the real reason we're here."

The cop took a deep breath, learned forward, lowered his voice, and turned his focus back to the case. "Fine with me! Here's my news. I did confirm a few things I suspected. Both men were drugged and likely out cold when they were clubbed . . . that is, if you can use a can to club someone. So their deaths were not caused by the drug, but by the blows. Also, in both cases the knife was stuck into their backs in the very same way and the very same manner."

"So," Garner chimed in, "the ex-cop had been dead for some time before he was stabbed?"

"Yep," the cop replied, "and both knives were exactly the same. They were made at the Kitchen Best Factory in Bedford, New Jersey. And they are not rare. You can pretty much buy them at any dime store in this city or any other of a thousand cities from coast to coast."

"So," the woman noted, still stinging from being insulted, "we have two murders, one killer, and no clear connection between the victims other than they might have been at the soup kitchen at the same time." Her tone indicated she was quite proud of beating the men to that fact.

"Since you shared that bit of information with me yesterday," Lane acknowledged with a slight frown, "I put my men to work on checking out everyone at the kitchen. We looked at all those that come and go and not one of them, other than Sister Ann, had a real connection with either man. I don't know why, maybe it is because it has never happened in the history of Illinois, but I doubt if the nun is our killer. Now I haven't ruled out the guy named Joe. In fact, I ran him in last night and grilled him."

"Did you find out anything?" Garner asked.

"Right now," the cop admitted, "we don't even know his last name. He refuses to give it. So we tossed him into a cell to let him think about that for a while and that's where he remains this morning."

"Surely you searched the soup kitchen?" Tiffany asked.

"Of course," Lane answered, "even a stupid cop knows to do that. You know how smart I am?"

The reporter whispered, "I'm sure you will tell us."

"Here's brains at work," he suggested. "Even though the nun told us to take the place apart if we needed to, I waited for a warrant. I ran things by the book. And, when the warrant came we did find several knives in the kitchen matching the ones used in both cases."

"That's a start," the investigator suggested. "What about the fruitcake tins?"

"Not a single one," the cop explained, "and there were no signs of the drug used in the drinks. Of course, Joe had plenty of time to get rid of the drug and the cans."

"And," Tiffany added, "If he'd ditched those things he likely would have dumped the knives as well."

"Well," Lane retorted, "perhaps we got there before he thought of that."

"So, Skipper," the reporter noted.

"What's this Skipper thing all about?" a suddenly interested Garner asked.

"I'll tell you later," the woman assured him

231

before turning her attention back to the cop. "Anyway, the only thing you can hold Joe on is the suspicion of sticking a knife in a dead man. Is that even a crime?"

"A minor one," Lane assured her, "but about the only place it would send the guy would be to a mental institution."

Garner took a long draw of coffee before asking, "Maybe Elrod and Saunders had a connection in the past to Joe." He paused and smiled before asking, "Can I call you Skipper, too?"

"No, you cannot," the cop barked. "On the connection, I thought of that link, too. So I visited with both Elrod's widow and Saunders ex-wife. Neither of them knew of any link between the two men. When I showed them a photograph of Joe, they both swore they'd never seen him. I also checked with those at the DA's office. I don't mind telling you that none of them were too pleased to be bothered on the Saturday night before Christmas. I struck out there, too. So, I had six guys from the night crew go through old police case files clear back to the twenties looking for a way to connect Elrod and Saunders. After seven hours of work, we came up blank."

"You're being waved at," Tiffany announced as she pointed to the end of the counter. "I believe one of your men wants you."

The cop pushed off of his stool and ambled across the room to where a uniformed police officer stood by the door. After Lane was out of earshot, Garner spilled a bit of new information. "I can't come up with anything on the fake Santas that doesn't make them appear like candidates for Citizen of the Year. They all seem to be involved in this routine due to the goodness of their hearts."

"Well," the woman wryly cracked, "then why did that quartet of goons go after me Friday night?"

He shook his head, "I'm thinking again they thought you were the real blonde."

"I thought you said Delono's men would have killed me," she noted.

"Maybe they were just trying to scare you," he explained.

She turned until their eyes met. "Has anyone come after you?"

"No," he admitted. "And that kind of surprises me, too."

"Maybe they'll soon figure out their mistake, and when they do, it will take some of the pressure off me."

"That's a nice thought," he mused.

"Shut it down," she suggested, "Lane's coming back and he doesn't look happy."

"You got some news, big boy?" Garner asked.

"Yeah," the cop grimly replied, "the nun can alibi Joe for the night Elrod was murdered and, I can alibi him for the murder that was committed either last night or early this morning in a home in

Oak Park. You two want to join me to look at another man who died exactly the same way as Elrod and Saunders?"

"I've got nothing better to do," Garner noted, "and if we're with you we are likely safer than we are alone."

"What do you mean by that?" Lane demanded.

Before the investigator could explain, Tiffany cut in, "I think he's worried about Delono having a hit out on him."

The cop grinned, "Maybe the safest place for you, Bret, is in jail. I could arrange that."

"I'll just depend upon you to protect me," he quickly answered. "If I am by your side, I feel safe."

"By the way," the cop sternly demanded, "do you have an alibi for the times the second and third murder were committed?"

"Do I need one?"

The cop grumbled, "Now that Joe's off the hook, you've once more emerged as the best guy I could hang this on. I'll be looking for your fingerprints at the scene. If they are there, you'll get a free ride downtown."

"What's the address?" Garner asked.

"1323 Ridgeland Avenue, you ever been there?"

The private investigator smiled. "Sounds familiar. I once dated a redhead in Oak Park, wonder if that could be her place?"

"Are you serious?" the reporter demanded.

Garner grinned. "I guess we'll see. Besides, if it gets any colder outside, sitting under a bright light being grilled for a few hours might be good thing."

"I can make it happen," Lane bragged.

"I'm sure you can," the other man shot back.

Tiffany shook her head. Did Lane actually want his old friend in a safer place or did he have something to tie the former Marine to the crimes? Was that the reason the cop was keeping the investigator close? No matter how this thing played out, this was going to be a very interesting day.

— 28 —

Sunday, December 22, 1946
10:17 a.m.

Though Tiffany trailed both of her companions into the small, brick home where the latest victim had lived and died, she immediately spotted the obvious anomaly in this murder. While the dead man was sitting in a chair, his head leaning forward and resting on a desk, and though he did have a red-handled knife sticking in his back, his wardrobe framed things in a much different light. This victim was wearing a Santa costume. To her recollection this was the first time she'd ever seen a dead St. Nick and even though she was no longer a child, it was a bit unsettling.

"Well, how about that?" Lane noted, irony dripping from his lips.

Garner nodded and frowned, "I wouldn't be the least bit surprised if his name is Kelly."

"You mean like the famous clown?" the cop asked.

"Yeah," the investigator replied, "just like the clown. But my reasons for thinking that have nothing to do with P. T. Barnum."

A short, wide uniformed policeman, his three chins held up by his tightly buttoned shirt collar, stood beside the body. Lane sized him up for a moment before posing an obvious question. "You got an I.D. on this guy?"

"Yes sir," came the quick response, "his name is Royal Ogden. At least I think it is."

The homicide cop frowned, "What do you mean you think it is?"

"Well," the beat policeman answered, "Royal Ogden lives here, and the man's billfold contained information stating that he was Royal Ogden, but the paper in his pocket, the permit for him playing Santa, gives his name as George Kelly."

Lane snapped his head back toward Garner. "How could you have known that?" He paused and then added, "Unless . . ."

"Unless I killed him?" the investigator finished the thought.

236

"Yeah," the lieutenant shot back. "Let's see you dance around this one."

"Why, Lane," Garner chuckled, "in all our years in the Pacific you never once asked me to dance. Shall I lead or you?"

"Quit wisecracking and give me the answer, or I really will be slapping the cuffs on you."

Tiffany smiled as Lane set his jaw in place and stuck his chest forward. He was playing the tough cop to the hilt and it was having no effect on Garner. That had to be frustrating. As Lane continued his bulldog impersonation, the bemused investigator relaxed his shoulders, stuffed his hands into his coat pocket, and grinned.

"Lane, someday you're going to have an ulcer. You've got to learn to relax. Now, on three, let's take a few deep breaths and think pleasant thoughts."

"You're dodging the question," the cop barked.

Garner pulled his hands from his pockets and crossed his arms over his chest. "Well, in truth, the explanation is rather easy. Here's the story. It took me just a couple of hours of sniffing around to discover a good portion of the Santas working in this town are carrying papers with the name George Kelly. I met four of them yesterday."

"What?" Lane demanded. "That's the dumbest story I've ever heard. You can't expect me to believe that."

Tiffany stepped forward. "Lane, it might sound

a bit lame, but it's true. You remember the Santa scam I've been looking into? Well, Bret has been helping me. A lot of the guys in the red suits are carrying legal permits with the same names. It seems the cops just check the permit and not the name written on it."

"Oh," Lane noted, as he turned back to look at the dead man. He seemed to contemplate what he'd just been told before asking, "So, do you now think that Mr. Ogden's death, as well as the other two, are tied to your Santa scam?"

The reporter stepped by the lead cop and walked over to the body still sitting in a ladder-back chair. There was very little blood around the place the knife entered the man, so that likely meant, that like the other two victims, he'd been stabbed after his death. An empty cup of coffee was just to the right of where the Ogden's head lay on the table. She was betting there was a knockout drug in the drink. Beside the cup were the man's Santa hat, beard, and wig. A dented fruitcake tin was resting on the floor about a foot from the man's right foot.

"Well, Sherlock?" Lane quipped.

Tiffany looked back toward the cop. "I don't think this murder has anything to do with the Santa scam, but I will bet you dollars to donuts that there is a connection between this man, Saunders, and Elrod."

Lane snapped his fingers, looked back toward

the uniformed officer and barked, "Who was this guy? What did he do?"

The cop, as if he'd been waiting for that question, eagerly stepped forward, yanked a pad from his pocket and began to read from his notes. "Mr. Ogden was sixty-six and according to neighbors he used to own a gun shop on Marshall Street. He retired about three years ago. He never married and had no children. He lived alone."

"Tell me," the homicide lieutenant quizzed, "how this man could be connected to Elrod and Saunders? After all, we have not yet found any link between those two."

"Are you asking me?" the beat cop asked.

"What's your name?" Lane demanded.

"Bowen."

"No, Bowen, I was not asking you. I was directing my question to the member of the media and the shamus who has attached himself to that woman."

Tiffany shook her head. "So now I'm 'that woman.' I don't even rate a name."

"Where's the link?" Lane barked.

"I don't know," the reporter snapped, "but if you give me the time, then I'll likely find it before the men in blue do."

"And," Lane cracked, "If you do I'll buy you a meal at the best restaurant in town."

"How about second best?" Garner chimed in, "You see, I've already taken her to the best."

Tiffany ignored the investigator's dig and the way the cop rolled his eyes as she shot back, "Listen, Skipper. I'm going to catch a cab and go back to the paper to do some digging. Call me there if you turn up anything new."

"And, Skipper," Garner added with a smile, "unless you want to arrest me, I think I'll be leaving, too. There is an angle I'd like to explore on this case as well."

"You're not leaving unless you tell me what it is." Lane warned.

The investigator nodded, "I'm looking at the obvious one. This guy ran a gun shop, Saunders was a cop who carried a gun, Delono was man whose business needed guns, and Elrod was a district attorney whose was trying to take the crime boss down. To me that seems to be the best connection we have uncovered yet."

"That's not bad," Lane admitted as he turned his gaze to the body. "In fact, that's the first thing that has made sense in this whole mess. Wait until the crime scene guys arrive. As soon as I turn things over to them, I'll work with you on that one."

"Fine with me," Garner agreed. "That should give me access to information that will save us some time."

For a second, Tiffany almost begged off her research to join the men. She figured it would be fun to watch them bicker as they hunted through police files and chased down potential informants, but her gut told her that her angle would bear better fruit. Crossing over to the phone, she dialed the City Taxi Service, set up a cab ride, and then wandered out to the street to wait for the yellow car.

— 29 —

Sunday, December 22, 1946
3:00 p.m.

Three hours of digging through files brought Tiffany Clayton no closer to her quest in connecting the three dead men to one another. Records and news stories indicated they had never even shared a moment in the same room, much less met. She was about to give up when she came up with another angle. What was the story behind the fruitcake?

Sitting in the musty room, the reporter pulled old issues of *The Chicago Star* going back to the 1920s. She found only two references to Jan's Old World Fruitcakes. The fruitcake was first mentioned in connection with the closing of a candy factory. The other time the holiday dessert found its way into print was when the equipment and products of that factory were sold at auction. It seems that among hard candy, candy canes, and chocolate-covered peanuts were one hundred and seventeen tins of Jan's Old World Fruitcake. While reading that story, she was broadsided in discovering that Jan was not a woman, but rather a Polish immigrant whose last name was Lewandowski.

As there was no record of who had purchased the fruitcakes at the auction or even if they had been sold, Tiffany shifted her research to the man who had owned and then lost the shop. For the first time, her digging hit a bit of buried treasure. The maker of Jan's Old World Fruitcake had been convicted of the murder of a local grocer.

In some places, news like that would have been shocking. Murder of any kind had that effect in small towns, but not in a large city. Several times a year business owners developed rivalries that led to assaults and in some cases, murder. Thus, the fact that Jan Lewandowski had been found guilty of murdering Geno Lombardi barely registered on the reporter's subconscious. Rather than see it as sad or scandalous, she latched onto the news as if it were a lifesaver tossed to a drowning woman.

No matter how dated or bizarre, this was the very first concrete lead she had. Perhaps the trio of current murders were tied to events of two decades before. Her excitement grew even greater when she discovered that Jan's Old World Fruitcakes being removed from the showroom window had caused the men's dispute and that the instrument of murder was a red-handled kitchen knife. Grabbing a cup of coffee, she pulled down several months of newspapers and dug deeper.

The scribes of that time described Lewandowski as a quiet, humble man who deeply loved his family. Never once, until that night on December 23, 1926, had he stepped outside the law. Though he claimed his innocence from the moment he was arrested until he was led into the execution chamber, the evidence against him was much too strong for a jury to dismiss. He'd been found with the murder weapon in his hands and he couldn't produce the witness he claimed could confirm he'd only come into the store after a large man with a scar exited. Thus, from the get-go, the candy maker had the whole legal deck stacked against him. He was a lone man fighting the entire Chicago legal machine.

The trial began on February 1, 1927, and the jury reached a decision just three days later. Lewandowski's court-appointed attorney, Raymond Johnson, called three witnesses in an attempt to use the man's outstanding character as a defense. Yet, the words of a priest, a neighbor, and an employee of the candy factory did little to blunt the testimony of the cop who discovered Lewandowski with the murder weapon in his hand. That one witness was Henry Saunders. She didn't know if the guys were finding anything, but Tiffany sensed she was on a roll. Uncovering this small sliver of news suddenly made the world a much brighter place.

As she leaned back in the wooden library chair to consider what she'd just learned, the reporter grimly nodded. Now she knew the man who died in the Stockyards Hotel was the policeman who fingered Jan Lewandowski as a killer. If the candy maker had been innocent, the symbolism of the current murder weapon and even the knife in the back made sense. But why kill Ogden and Elrod? There was no mention of them in the main news stories. Where and how did the other two men tie in?

Spurred on by the finding of one nugget, the reporter spent another forty-five minutes mining every detail on the case written in everything from the trial coverage to police reports to sidebar features, but again she found no mention of Elrod or Ogden. Discouraged, she was about to close the final folder and put it back into the files when she noted a short story on Lewandowski's family. The accompanying photo showed an elderly woman—the candy maker's mother—with her arms wrapped around a teenage boy and a small girl. This one image caught on film put a very human stamp on what had been, up until now, just another research project into an era she'd never known. Suddenly Jan Lewandowski was more than just a convicted murderer: he was a son and a father and the thoughts of those the man left behind hit the reporter harder than a Joe Louis right. Now not only could she not leave this tale alone, it wasn't going to leave her alone either. This was a tragic story of pain, loss, and suffering.

Scanning the human-interest feature that accompanied the photo of the family, Tiffany picked up on something that caused her blood to run as cold as a lakefront winter wind. The sixteen-year-old son was described as crazy and irrational. He'd even been kicked out of school for threatening his classmates and attacking a teacher. According to neighbors, Szymon often screamed at them and gave anyone who came near the family's home menacing looks.

Tiffany pulled her eyes from the copy and back to the photo. Could the boy have been the real killer? Did anyone consider that back then? As she thought about a father who might just have died for his son, she was struck by another even darker chord. What if Szymon was the man behind the current murders? She had no choice; this was something she couldn't let slide. She had to find out what had happened to the son and where he was now.

Tiffany rushed back the newspaper's file index in an attempt to uncover the fate of the old woman and Jan Lewandowski's children. Though she dug through a half a dozen files and hundreds of pages of newsprint, all she found was a short obituary on Petra Lewandowski. The candy maker's mother had died of a heart attack in 1929. There was no mention in the short story of what happened to Szymon or Alicija. With no place left to search at *The Star*, it was time to pick up the phone and dial her contacts at the other newspapers.

A half a dozen calls produced an equal number of dead ends and it was in frustration the reporter went back to rereading stories on the final days of the trial. That led to something she'd missed earlier. Buried on page three was a feature piece on Lewandowski's execution that actually documented the man's last day moment by moment. This final chapter in the candy maker's life was penned on March 29, 1927, and each of the times he was quoted, the convicted murderer still proclaimed his innocence. In his last statement before the state turned on the electric charge that would end his life, Lewandowski shared his love for his family and his faith in the Lord. It seemed those would be his final words, but right before the executioner slipped the hood over his head he yelled out, "The truth will set us free and a little child will lead them to the truth."

Tiffany drummed her fingers on the table as she contemplated the last line in the story. The reference to truth was out of the book of John. She had memorized it as a child during Vacation Bible School. Perhaps because of fear or fatigue,

Lewandowski had misquoted it slightly. He should have said, "Then you will know the truth and the truth will set you free." In using this final statement was the innocent man trying to leave a clue as to who the real killer might be or at least a way of identifying him?

"You need anything, Miss Clayton?"

Pulled from her thoughts of a story almost as old as she was, Tiffany looked toward the custodian of *The Chicago Star*'s records room or, as it was most often called, the morgue. In his seventies, dressed in gray slacks, a white shirt and striped tie, white-haired Oscar Taylor was a cheery man about five-foot seven. A generation before, he had been a top-flight reporter. When he got too old for that job, he was shifted over to the newspaper's morgue. Either unwilling or unable to retire, he kept plugging away. Though he hadn't written a line in five years, the woman still thought Taylor was the heart and soul of *The Star*.

"Oscar," Tiffany asked, "what can you tell me about the line, 'A little child will lead them to the truth?' "

The old man smiled, "We don't get much call for Bible knowledge around here, so you likely came to the only one who could answer your query. It is from the Old Testament, Isaiah as I recall. It reads something like this. 'The wolf also shall dwell with the lamb, and the leopard shall lie down with the kid, and the calf and the young lion and the fatling together; and a little child shall lead them.' You need anything else?"

"What do you remember about the Lewandowski trial?"

"Now you're going way back," he laughed. "And you're lucky, too. I covered a bit of that case."

"I've read all about it," Tiffany assured him. "I read a couple of your stories. What I want to know is not what you wrote, but what you thought. I'm not looking for facts as much as I am getting a feel for your instincts."

The man's eyes grew small and his expression stoic. He balled his hands together as he spilled out his memories. "The evidence clearly showed me Jan Lewandowski was guilty and so my mind agreed, but my gut screamed out that the candy maker was innocent."

"Really? Why?"

"Tiffany, logic can't define gut feelings." Taylor paused, licked his lips and shook his head. "I was one of those that watched the state kill him. That's the way reporters are, we all want to be in the death house. We trade in all our favors just to see that moment when a heart stops beating. It is the ultimate story. And yet to this day, I have nightmares about the moment when Jan Lewandowski's heart beat for the final time. Tiffany, I've watched a couple of dozen men die in the chair and that was the only time I had doubts. And, boy, I had real doubts, the kind that get in your stomach and turn it into a raging sea. I couldn't really eat or sleep for weeks. In fact, I still have nightmares about that night." He paused and looked toward a wall as if suddenly seeing clearly an old memory. " 'The truth will set us free and a little child will lead them to the truth.' Those were his last words and to this day they haunt me." He sadly shook his head, "I'm going to take a break. I'll be back in fifteen minutes if you need anything."

"Thanks," the woman said as she watched Oscar walked off. Turning back to the newspaper resting on the table, she wondered. Was the child in those final words one of Lewandowski's children? That was the only thing that made sense.

"The son," she whispered to herself. That had to be it. Though innocent Lewandowski must have been protecting his own son. She had to find those children. She had to dig up what they knew in order to tie this case together. But where could she start looking?

The reporter's blue eyes fell back to the story. Beside the text was a photograph of Lewandowski being led to death row by a cop and a priest. The condemned man was drawn, thin, his hair almost white, and his face heavily lined. He already looked dead. The policeman walking beside the condemned was stoic . . . his face showing no emotion. Then there was the third man. The tall, thin priest likely best reflected the emotion of Jan Lewandowski's final moments. His eyes filled with tears, the young clergyman was holding a Bible, and staring straight into the camera. The haunting and hollow look captured by the photographer clearly spelled out this man, who was there to represent faith, had none at that moment. He appeared lost and hopeless. She could well imagine how he must have felt. He likely knew Lewandowski well. He'd heard his hopes and dreams and shared his prayers. And now he was going to watch him die, and there was nothing he could do about it.

Tiffany glanced from the priest to the guard and then once again to the priest. Suddenly he looked familiar. Did she know him or did he just remind her of someone? Glancing down to the cutline she read what the copy editor had written almost twenty years before.

Officer Myron Mays leads Jan Lewandowski to the chair as Father J. McBride softly offers a final prayer for the condemned.

That was it! The cloud had been lifted and suddenly everything was clear! She had the angle she needed and knew where she had to go to begin unraveling this bizarre case. The only question was if her link to a twenty-year-old story would know where she could find Szymon today.

— 30 —

Sunday, December 22, 1946
7:30 p.m.

The night was cold, but not bitter, and the cab
Tiffany secured had been blessed with a good
heater. Thus, the twenty-minute ride from her
office to Sister Ann's soup kitchen offered the
reporter a few minutes to forget about the frigid
weather and carefully go over what she knew. So
she paid the cabbie and entered the charity
enterprise, she was more than ready to let the cat
she'd spotted in the newspaper photograph out of
the bag.

A small woman, perhaps fifty, stood just inside
the door, her body wrapped in a wool coat at least
four sizes too large for her tiny frame. One look
assured the reporter that the lady with the dark
brown eyes was not a staff member, but was in the
establishment for a meal and a chance spend a
few hours out of the winter air. Thus, for this
person, the kitchen was a welcome refuge and
maybe even a lifesaver. A quick inventory of the
rest of the room revealed a few dozen other
wayfarers who likely felt the same way. It was
sobering to realize that with so many spending so
much on things that were not really needed that

this place was the final outpost for the lost, misguided, and hopeless who had nothing to spend and no hopes of getting any gifts. Christmas had a unique way of clearly displaying the ironies of life.

"Excuse me," Tiffany asked, after returning her gaze back to the tiny woman, "is Sister Ann in?"

The fragile creature shook her head, but said nothing.

"Is Sister Ann in?" the reporter asked again, this time raising the volume a few decibels.

"She won't answer," a familiar voice called out from across the room. Glancing beyond the woman, Tiffany noted Joe coming her way. As he approached he explained, "Mary's not rude, but she is deaf and mute. So while she can't hear a kind word, she does know the meaning of a sincere touch."

"I see," Tiffany replied as she watched Joe gently pat Mary on the shoulder. After noting the woman's smile, the reporter continued, "In truth, I actually came to see you. Is there a place we can talk?"

The man in black smiled and pointed across the room. "How about the table where you visited with Sister Ann?"

Tiffany nodded and when the man turned and started back to the far wall, she followed. They were both seated before she opened the conversation.

"Joe, why isn't Sister Ann here? I mean, I figured two days before Christmas would make this a pretty big night for the kitchen."

"This is her one evening a week off," he explained. "Even as strong and dedicated as she is, she needs time to regroup. If you want to talk to her, she will be back tomorrow."

Tiffany shook her head. "It really is you that I need. If she was here, I thought you might want her in on this." She paused and looked into the man's kind eyes. She was now sure she was right. "You see, I've got something figured out."

"You are well ahead of me," the man pronounced with a slight smile. "It has been a very long time since I have figured out much of anything. I just kind of wander around in the darkness looking for the light."

"And you found some light here," she suggested.

"More light," he admitted, "than I've found anywhere else in a long time. Sister Ann does the kind of work the church is meant to do but often ignores. What would Mary do without this place?" He waved his hand toward the others who'd sought refuge in the kitchen and then added, "What would any of them do? Sister Ann finds the least of these and lets them know that someone actually cares."

"And," Tiffany added, "I think you do, too."

"I care," he agreed, "but I'm a man without

direction or faith. I'm not anywhere near like she is. I can dish out a bowl of soup that fills their stomach; she gives them something that they carry in their souls."

On the ride over, Tiffany thought this would be easy. She'd simply lay out the truth and listen to the story that followed. Now it seemed much more complicated. She was dealing with a man who was fragile and perhaps even lost. If it hadn't been for a need to solve three murders and perhaps stop more, she would have kept mute and let the man deal with the past in his way.

"Joe," the reporter softly announced, her need to know pushing her to go where she now didn't want to go. "I know why you dress in black and why your pants are patched. I know why the material is so worn that your knees are shiny." She paused until their eyes locked. If he had a clue as to what she discovered, his expression didn't reveal it. That made this even harder. Tiffany was struggling to find a smooth path to gently lead the damaged man where she knew he didn't want to go. "Joe, you spend a lot of time praying, don't you?"

"It goes along with the job," he answered. "There are a lot of people who come in here who need to be prayed for and, if they ask, I pray with them. Ironic, I'm the one without much faith. I need it worse than anyone. So I pray a lot. The problem is that I'm not sure my prayers are heard." His face was suddenly awash in sadness . . . a sadness,

Tiffany guessed, that was born in both a memory and a defeat. She sensed it was also a sadness he probably couldn't shake.

"How do we know if our prayers are heard?" Tiffany asked. "I mean, how do we really know?"

He shrugged, "I'm not sure. I only know about when they're not heard. I know a lot about that. I also know a lot about when prayers are not answered."

She nodded. It was now time to jump in with both feet. It was time to pull back the curtain on the past. "Joe, do you still pray for Jan Lewandowski?"

"I'm not sure I follow you," the man quickly replied, his words not fully masking the recognition she saw in his eyes.

Tiffany didn't let the denial throw her off track. She looked his way and smiled sadly. "I don't know when you quit what you no doubt felt was your calling, but I do know that about twenty years ago you were a priest named Joseph McBride. I have no doubt that the clothes you wear today were once a part of your official garb."

"What makes you think that?" he quietly asked. He was still running from what she knew was the truth.

She shrugged, "I've noticed a lot of priests whose pants have shiny knees."

"So do men who scrub floors," he suggested.

Tiffany reached into her purse and pulled out a

file. After opening it, she produced a photo and slid it his way. She waited for Joe to study what had been captured so long ago in black and white before asking, "Why did you leave the priesthood?"

He glanced toward the street, licked his lips, and frowned. She could tell, even when she'd sprung the trap he still didn't want to share his story. But she was just as sure that if she waited long enough he would cave to her wishes. So the clock ticked. Three minutes later, he broke his silence and proved her instincts correct.

"Jan was innocent," Joe solemnly announced without looking Tiffany's way. "I was sure of it. And for the last six weeks of his life, I tried every avenue I could find to get the evidence to prove it. Still, I couldn't uncover the one thing he needed. When I had exhausted everything I could humanly do, I turned to God. I just knew the Lord wouldn't let an innocent man die. Sadly, even *my* prayers went unanswered. It was if the court system and even God turned his back on poor Jan Lewandowski. It killed him and destroyed me."

"It has happened before," Tiffany suggested. "I mean the execution of Jesus followed that same path. An innocent man paid and a guilty man walked."

The man turned back to the reporter and sighed. "I was with Jan until the end. I watched him die.

I smelled his body burn. You don't forget that smell. As I drove back to my room at St. John's Church that night, I felt like a failure."

"So you quit and walked away?" the reporter asked.

"No," he admitted, "not then. I figured that my feelings would pass in time. So I kept at it for another decade. I said my prayers, blessed babies, heard confessions, led mass, and even assured the lost I had the map to where they needed to go. Then one day, after saying the funeral mass for a three-year-old killed by a hit-and-run driver, I just couldn't do it anymore. So I gathered the tools of my trade, my collar, and even my Bible and left them on the steps of St. John's and just walked away. I lived on the streets; even rode the rails for a while. In my travels, I got to see the dirty parts of America only the lost and forgotten see. I ate out of trash cans and visited with men and women who were alone. I kept looking for answers as I mingled with what the Bible calls the least of these, and I didn't find them. What I discovered was a world where the poor were pushed aside and those weak of mind were despised and abused. Then, two years ago, still just as lost as I was when I left Chicago, I came back here. Not long after I arrived in the town where I'd grown up, I discovered this place."

Tiffany reached across the table and tapped the photo, "Your knowledge of what happened and the fact you were so crushed by what you saw as a miscarriage of justice provides you with a pretty solid motive in this case. You need to understand that when I show this to Lieutenant Walker, he will come after you again."

He nodded, "No doubt, but you likely realize that I also have an airtight alibi for the times the two murders happened."

"There are three now," she coldly chimed in.

"Three?"

"Yes," she continued, "a man named Royal Ogden was killed in the very same way."

"Ogden?" he asked.

"Does the name mean anything to you?" she queried.

"Yeah," he replied grimly, "he was the one juror in the Jan Lewandowski case who held out for acquittal. That was the reason Jan's fate wasn't decided in just a few minutes. In fact, the jury actually went home after ten hours of fighting it out and resumed deliberating the next morning. Overnight, Ogden changed his mind and went with the others. So, just when I thought my prayers had been heard and answered, I was hit in the gut. To this day, the bruise is still there. You can't see it, but it's there."

Though she hadn't enjoyed digging into a man's fragile mind to mine the needed information, it had proven worth it. The reporter now had a second link. Ogden was on the jury, and Saunders was the man who testified against Lewandowski. Therefore, if these murders were tied to that old trial, she had finally gained some traction.

"Joe," she asked, "where did Elrod fit in?"

The former priest shook his head, "I've thought a lot about that in the last day and have come up with nothing. I mean, the fruitcake and knife pointed to evidence that was still fresh in my memory, but I still can't come up a connection Elrod had with the case. I was in the court on all three days of the trial and he was never there. Jan never mentioned him either."

"What about Lewandowski's kids?" Tiffany demanded. "What happened to them?"

He shook his head as he explained. "I only met them once during the trial and lost track of them afterwards. Why do you ask?"

"I read where Szymon had mental issues," the reporter explained.

"The result of an accident as a child," Joe cut in. "Jan always blamed himself for that. It was something about the kid running out in front of a carriage and being kicked by a horse."

"I have a theory that his mental health might still be a problem," she paused before offering an additional thought. "Perhaps his mixed-up mind is causing him to now even the score."

"He'd have to be a magician," Joe suggested.

"What do you mean?"

The man smiled, "The fruitcakes are the problem. I was at the auction of Jan's Candy Factory. No one bought the fruitcakes, so they were immediately taken to a vacant lot and burned. I watched it happen."

"So," Tiffany asked, "where did the three fruitcakes that were used as weapons come from?"

Joe looked back toward the street and suggested, "Jan left five or six for display at Lombardi's store and no one knows what happened to them. I'm guessing that perhaps the real killer took them."

The reporter reached across the table and grabbed the priest's arm. She squeezed it and demanded, "What else do you know that wasn't in the papers?"

The man finally turned his face and locked his eyes onto her. "Jan said that a fat man with a deep scar on his face walked out of the grocery store that night and got into a large Cadillac driven by a younger man. That fat man carried two large sacks. Jan watched them leave before continuing his walk to his shop. The only reason he went into the grocery was because the fruitcakes he'd given the store owner to display in his window were not there. Jan wanted to know why they'd been removed. So he walked in to confront Lombardi. He thought he was alone, but then saw a small boy hiding behind a display. The child ran out before Jan could find out who he was. Jan then saw Lombardi. He studied the dead man's body and even pulled the knife from Lombardi's back. That's when Saunders walked in and Jan's life essentially ended."

"Why was he out that night?" Tiffany asked. "The newspaper account I read said it was bitter cold and snowing."

"Jan told me he was going to get a sled he'd made for his daughter as a Christmas present. In fact, that's the reason I know the fruitcakes were burned. You see I went to the auction to fulfill a promise. I bought the sled and the next Christmas Eve I secretly left it on the steps where Jan's mother and the children lived. That way Alicija finally received the last thing her father made for her with his own hands."

"I need to find the boy who witnessed that murder," Tiffany announced.

"Good luck," Joe grimly replied. "I've been looking for him for twenty years and have come up with nothing. Just like smoke from a fireplace; he disappeared into thin air."

The ringing of the phone brought the man in black to his feet. He quickly covered the twenty steps to the kitchen. A minute later, he reappeared. "Miss Clayton, a Mr. Garner is on the line for you." Joe pointed toward the counter, "The phone is right through the door."

After grabbing the photo and slipping it back into her purse, Tiffany crossed the room and pushed the door open. The candlestick phone was on a small desk to her right. She dropped onto the corner of the desk and picked up the phone. "This is Tiffany and how did you know I was here?"

"Some guy named Oscar at the paper told me where you'd gone. Anyway, Tiff, I was at a store looking for a present for you when I figured something out."

"There are places open on Sunday?" she asked.

"A few," he explained, "why, is that illegal?"

"Maybe," she chuckled, "but the cops often turn and look the other way at Christmas. Anyway, I hope you found something nice for me."

"I didn't get that far," he cracked, "but I do need to pick you up and take you to Elrod's home."

"Why?"

"I think I know where we can find some information."

"You and the cops tore that place apart."

"Tiffany, I now know what we overlooked. I'm 99 percent sure of that. Can you call Mrs. Elrod and arrange for us to get into the study?"

"I've met her several times in the past," the reporter quickly replied, "she's a straight shooter. If it means catching her husband's killer, I think she'll give us access."

"Okay," Garner suggested, "you do what you need to do get us into that man's study, and I'll pick you up in ten minutes in front of the soup kitchen."

— 31 —

Sunday, December 22, 1946
8:30 p.m.

Tiffany spent the half-hour trip across town catching Garner up on what she'd learned in the newspaper morgue and at the kitchen. After they drove through the estate's large gates and up the paved circular drive, the investigator parked in front of the mansion's front doors and posed a question about what he'd just heard. "So this Simon kid . . ."

"Szymon," she corrected him. "His name is a traditional Polish one, not like the game you likely play as a child."

"Fine, Szymon," Garner grudgingly corrected himself. "Do you buy Joe's rationale on why he couldn't be the killer?"

"Not for a second," the reporter assured him. "I think it provides the perfect frame for real murder. After all, if all the fruitcakes at the factory were destroyed, the most logical place for any others to be would be at Lewandowski's home. Thus, Szymon, who is unbalanced, would be not just the best suspect, but likely the only one who might have kept the fruitcakes. I mean, think about this, the guy is crazy, and according to what I read in old newspapers, he is also violent. Who knows where he has been? Maybe he has been confined for years in an institution and has finally been released. All that time locked behind walls he's been waiting for the chance to get back at the men he blames for his father's death. He, therefore, gets the cop who caught his old man. He also murders the one man on the jury who might have saved Jan Lewandowski's life."

"And," Garner cut in, "he started with Ethan Elrod, who had nothing do with the case."

"Nothing that I've found," Tiffany corrected him. "I'm sure there is a connection and we just haven't come up with it yet. But, if you really know where there is some hidden information, maybe that part of the case will fall into place as well." She smugly added. "Still, let's make this exercise in snooping a quick one, because I need to get Lane using all his police resources to find the now middle-aged son of a man who likely was wrongfully put to death."

"You even talk like you write," Garner cracked.

"And what do mean by that?" the reporter demanded.

He smiled, "You use too many words to say what's on your mind. Just keep it simple. Say something like 'I need Lane's police connections to locate old what's-his-name.' "

"Now you're sounding like Skipper."

"Hey, don't insult me."

"Fine," she grumbled, "but let's make this quick. I have a case to crack and I want to beat the cops in unveiling who is behind this series of murders. I'd just love to see Lane as he picks up the paper and finds I wrote about the murderer even before he guesses who he is. In fact, I will probably just hand deliver the first newspaper off the press run directly to his office."

"Let me assure you," Garner replied, as he reached for the car's door handle, "that you won't have to cool your jets for long. It will only take a minute to figure out if we have hit the mother lode or if this has been a dry run. If it is the latter, you can make fun of me all you want. Now, let's get into the house and let me show what I discovered at a high-end gift shop."

A few moments later, Mary Elrod graciously welcomed the pair into the mansion and then ushered her guests to the study where she left them alone. Once their host closed the door, the investigator immediately walked over and tapped on the large wooden globe.

"If you cut it in half," Tiffany noted, "you could have two really large washtubs."

Garner spun the globe and observed it slowly turn until it stopped. Smiling he explained, "These babies were made for two things. The first is looking impressive." As he spun it again he added, "The other has nothing to do with geography."

"So," the reporter quizzed, her bland tone and bored expression giving away that she was unimpressed, "what's the other use?"

"No reason to waste words," he teased. "Just relax and watch."

Garner twisted the top of the brass rod that served to hold the axis that secured the large wooden ball in place. He then put both hands on the top of the three-foot wide representation of the world and spun it to the left. He stopped the globe when he heard a slight clicking noise.

"Did you hear that?" he asked.

"Yes," Tiffany assured him, "sounded almost like a gear snapping into place."

"You're close," he replied as he moved to the bottom of the axis and twisted a brass knob he found there to the left. He then slowly moved the large ball back in that same direction until there was another click.

"And," he noted, as he stepped back and admired the globe, "That should be all there is to it."

"To what?" she asked, her tone indicating she still was not mesmerized by his little show.

"Lane and I figured," he explained, "that Elrod must have stashed the information he'd gathered in a safe or perhaps even placed it in a small hidden room that would be found behind a bookshelf. We were wrong. There was no concealed safe or secret room. Then, tonight, when I was looking for a present to give you, I saw a globe just like the one here. After noting the item's sky-high price tag, I asked the clerk how they ever sold any of them. That's when he showed me the trick."

"The trick?" she asked.

Garner leaned forward, pushed England with his index finger, waited for another click, and then placed his right hand back on the top of the axis and pulled. That action caused the top of the globe to open like a car's alligator hood.

"It's hollow," Tiffany pointed out.

"It is made to hide important documents or even cash," Garner added. "And if I am correct, what Elrod had on Delono might well be somewhere around Brazil." As the pair peered into the hollow square carved into the bottom half of the globe, they spotted a file. "Why don't you do the honors?" the investigator suggested.

Moving to the large desk, a now smug Garner leaned into the top edge, folded his arms over his overcoat, and observed the woman stroll to a chair. After sitting down, she began to leaf through the pages. As he waited for Tiffany to unveil what was in the file, he used the time to study the case he really wanted to win. The woman might not have been the daughter of a diamond dealer, but she was a real jewel. Tiffany's combination of grit and glamour put even the pinup girls to shame. He'd seen Carole Landis,

Marilyn Maxwell, and Dorothy Lamour in U.S.O. shows and none of those movie stars could hold a candle to the reporter. She was not only beautiful, but bright and incredibly intuitive. She was also as tough as nails, as gritty as a Marine gunner, but, somehow still all woman. Though he hadn't known her before this week, he was now sure she was who he dreamed of during those lonely nights in the Pacific.

As she continued to study what they'd found, his eyes fell from her face to her form. Even a heavy, wool winter coat couldn't hide her charms. She wasn't lithe like a model; she was more the athletic type. Her body was toned and strong, but it was still so very feminine, too. He was admiring the way her pump hung from the heel, when the woman's voice pulled his eyes back to her perfectly formed face.

"What we've found . . ."

"What I found," Garner corrected her.

"Okay, fine. What you found ties Jacobs to a former citizen of this city now retired and living in Florida."

He shrugged, "So, what you've got there doesn't tie the judge to Delano?"

"Not directly," Tiffany noted, pulling her eyes from the material to the investigator, "but I would think this might help a bit."

"So this benefactor," he asked, "now lives in Florida? What good does that do us?"

"It might just mean that Jacobs made a deal with the devil," the woman explained.

"I don't see what you're driving at," Garner announced, pushing off the desk and slowly crossing the room to where Tiffany sat. As he arrived at her side, she handed the investigator the file.

"Take a look," the woman suggested, "all that is here are a series of photos of Jacobs with Al Capone. They were obviously taken before Ness and his Untouchables, along with the IRS, got the mobster for income tax evasion and shipped him off to Leavenworth and later to Alcatraz."

His curiosity piqued, Garner glanced through the set of photos. The pictures, taken at various locations and over a series of years, proved the current federal judge was once a part of the crime boss's inner circle. But what did that mean? Closing the file and handing it back to the reporter, the investigator cracked, "Even without the story behind these pictures, *The Star* would love to run them on the front page. Can you imagine the fallout? Imagine a federal judge who spent his younger days chumming around with old Scarface. That is big-time news, even if you didn't have Jacobs considered a shoo-in for governor."

"Yeah," Tiffany agreed as she rose from the chair, "and I'm betting Delono knew about these pictures, too. Maybe he even found them and gave them to Elrod as a part of the deal for the cash and the blonde."

"Okay," Garner admitted, "I'll admit these photos seem to be the nail in the coffin that could have spelled the end of Jacobs's career and killed his chance for higher office, but if Elrod already had them, why make a deal with Delono? Why give him the blonde? What did she have to do with anything? The DA had what he wanted, so why sacrifice a human life?" Garner thought back to the way poor Sunshine had died, before sadly adding, "There has to be a lot more to this. If there isn't, then Elrod is not much better than Capone and his cronies."

"Bret, we have to figure out who that blonde is."

He nodded, "And we need to do that before we confront Jacobs with these photos or before the press runs them. Can you sit on these and not give them to your paper?"

She shrugged, "If they run now or next month, they will have the same effect. So, I'll just hang onto them for a while." Tiffany slipped them into her oversized purse before asking, "Now what do you have in mind?"

"We need to go see a man who lives in a house in Cicero. It's not too far from the Hawthorne Race Track."

"A friend of yours?" she asked.

"No," Garner admitted. "Delono mentioned him

during one of our conversations, and I've done a bit of digging to find out more over the past two days. The guy's name is William Hammer. He used to work for Capone."

"What makes you think he'll talk to us?" she asked as she reached down and pushed her shoe back over her heel.

Garner carefully watched the woman as he explained. "A year ago he likely wouldn't have, but I've found out he's dying of cancer now. So, he's not going to be afraid to tell the truth. In fact, he might just be looking for a pretty reporter to share his story with. Especially one who can dangle a high heel like you can."

"You're horrible," she smirked. "Now, it's a little late for a visit tonight, so let's get some sleep and go over in the morning."

"When a man's dying of cancer," Garner shot back, "you don't wait until tomorrow." He walked back to the desk, yanked a drawer open, and pulled out a phone book. It took him less than a minute to find Hammer's name and get an address. Then, after closing and relocking the globe, he barked, "Let's go."

— 32 —

Sunday, December 22, 1946
11:30 p.m.

One dim light was on in the small, red brick home and that was all Bret Garner needed as an invitation to knock on the front door. Tiffany Clayton, who still felt it would have been better to put off this visit until the morning, stood a step behind on the small front porch, uncomfortably watching the investigator wait for a reply.

"Emily Post would not approve," Tiffany warned.

"Then I'm glad she's not with us," Garner shot back as he knocked again. "Besides, she'd have made a lousy private eye. You can't do what I do and get all hung up on manners."

"Yeah," the reporter grumbled, "I've noticed the folks in your profession and cops seem to lack grace and tact, too." After thirty seconds, when no one had come to the door, Tiffany leaned toward the investigator and whispered, "He's probably asleep. Let's come back in the morning." The words had no more than escaped her lips when the front door swung slowly open.

William Hammer had likely once been a big man, but the disease that was now ravaging his body had robbed him of both muscle and fat, leaving him with little more than skin and bones. Even the stooped, balding man's face was rail thin, so it was not surprising his faded red sweater and blue dress slacks, which surely once fit, now all but swallowed him. Yet, as he flipped on the porch light to intently study his unexpected guests, there was life still evident in his eyes. They literally danced from the woman to the man and back to the woman and when they landed on Tiffany the second time, they lingered so long it made her uncomfortable. As Hammer continued to stare, much like a wolf sizing up a lamb, the woman sifted her gaze to something that didn't have to beg for attention. In his right hand, the retired mobster held a forty-five Colt automatic.

"I guessing you're not here to sell insurance," Hammer finally announced. While his voice was raspy and thin, his gun hand was rock steady. Sick or not, this man was not going to be a push-over.

"No," Garner admitted, seemingly ignoring the weapon and what it had the power to do. "In truth, we need some information."

The old man grinned, "Call the operator. I still don't give information to cops. And I'm guessing that's what you are. Cops have a smell all their own."

"I'm a private investigator," Garner corrected Hammer.

"Well, not quite as bad," the man cracked, "but I still don't really have anything you'd want to know. My glory days were a long time back. So . . ."

"Mr. Hammer," Tiffany piped up. When she was sure his eyes were again locked on her, she continued. "My name is Tiffany Clayton and I'm a newspaper reporter."

"I recognize your name," he answered with a smile. "I've read your stuff in *The Star*, but I always pictured you as more of a fat broad."

"Sorry to disappoint you," she returned.

"I didn't say I was disappointed," he quipped, "just surprised. They'd sell a lot more newspapers if they put your picture on the front page. You are one ripe tomato."

Tiffany forced a smile before pleading her case. "Mr. Garner and I are trying to solve a mystery of two recently murdered people who were a part of a 1926 murder case in Little Italy, as well as the death of one more man who might have been tied to that case. We believe the person executed in that 1926 case was not guilty, and the murders that are happening now are tied to the fact the state killed an innocent man."

"You are one wordy broad," the old man noted. "Besides, if the guy's been executed, what difference does it make? You can't bring him back."

"But," Tiffany cut in, "maybe what you tell us can stop some innocent people from being killed.

You don't hit me as the type who likes to see folks murdered that don't deserve to die."

His mode suddenly changed. Hammer scratched his head with his free hand, shrugged, moved to one side of the door, and pointed with the Colt to a burgundy couch on the far side of the room. As the two stepped out of the cold, the old man shuffled over to a well-worn, green overstuffed chair, sat down, and then covered his lap with a green, red, and tan Indian blanket. Once settled, his eyes followed his uninvited guests until they took their positions. Only when Tiffany pulled out a small notepad and pen did he speak.

"I'm dying," he began. "Have been for a long time. I'm seventy-six and have been shot five different times and yet, the bullets didn't get me. So I spent most of my life feeling like . . ." he snapped his fingers before adding, "What's that comic book kids are always reading? There's a daily radio show that spills out the guy's adventures, too."

"Superman?" the reporter chimed in.

"Yeah, that's it. I felt like Superman. I thought nothing or no one could hurt me. And then a few months ago, I found out that something I can't see is going to take me down for the count. Now ain't that a kick?"

"We're sorry," Tiffany said.

"Don't be," Hammer snapped, "I didn't deserve to live this long anyway. I've done some bad things in my life. If I were a Catholic, my confessions would cause priests to have strokes. I am well aware that my life, the mud I rolled in, is why I'm alone today. I've got no wife, no kids, and the friends I have require me to answer the door with a loaded weapon. Let's not even talk about my enemies; there are enough of them to make an army unit."

"Sounds like a heck of a story," the reporter noted.

"Yeah," Hammer snapped, "but I don't have enough days left to even share the highlights. I mean, I know who was behind the St. Valentine's Day Massacre and that is just the beginning. I could finger a dozen respectable men who had their competition rubbed out." He pointed his hand toward his guests. "And I'm not bragging. I mean, why would I brag about something that I'm now ashamed of? When you know you're dying, when you realize the next breath might be the last, you spend a lot of time thinking about the way things should have been . . ." His voice trailed off and his eyes grew misty. After taking a deep breath, he whispered, "I'm not a nice man."

"No one's perfect," Tiffany offered, all the while knowing her observation was lame at best.

Hammer looked up, pointed a finger at his chest, and sadly shook his head. "I have a ton of excuses I could use for ending up this way. My dad died when I was five, my mom became a prostitute and was never home. I quit school when I was twelve. I fell in with a bad crowd. Yet, they're still all excuses. I had a lot of friends who had it just as bad as I did and they didn't go down the streets I traveled." He paused, looked to his right at some change on the lamp table before reaching over and running his fingers over it. Picking up a dime, he held it up between his thumb and index finger and posed a question. "Did you ever have a hundred bill?"

"I've had a few," Garner admitted.

"Did you hang onto them for a while?" the old man asked. "Or did you spend them as soon as you got them?"

"I always hung into them just as long as I could," the investigator admitted. "In fact, I have one in my billfold right now that I've been carrying for about a year."

"What happens when you break it?" Hammer asked. "Do you hold onto the twenties, tens, fives, and ones like you did the C-note?"

"No," Garner admitted, "they're easy to spend. They don't last any time at all."

Hammer nodded. "I've found that's the way it is with virtue. You hang onto it, you cherish it, and then some little thing, something you really want, tempts you enough to break it. Once you have crossed that line it is easier to step over it again and do the second wrong thing. That leads to others and soon you have traveled so deeply into the darkness you cannot even begin to see the light, much less find your way back to it. You do know that most folks who get lost in the darkness stay there."

"That sounds like a sermon," Tiffany suggested.

The dying man chuckled, "Sinners always give the best sermons. Believe me, I know that for a fact. You see, I've spent most of my life in their company." He took a deep breath before dragging his thoughts back to why he'd allowed the two to enter his home. "Now, why after all this time do you want to talk to me about the candy maker? I mean, we can't bring Lewandowski back from the grave, so what difference does it make now?"

"How did you know it was that case?" Tiffany asked.

"I'm pretty good at both math and reading between the lines," he replied. "It just added up. There is the year, the location, and the fact an innocent man paid for the crime. I mean, that's really why I let you in."

"After glancing over to the reporter, Garner chimed in. "We need to know some of the history, because it might make a lot of difference right now. There have been three murders in the past few days, and we think they are all tied to what happened all those years ago."

"Who's been killed, and what makes you think they are tied to ancient history?"

Tiffany cut in, "A retired gunsmith, Royal

Ogden, a retired cop named Saunders, and the district attorney, Ethan Elrod. Do those names mean anything to you?"

"Interesting combination," Hammer said, "but I don't really know how they tie together with what happened in the grocery back in '26." Perhaps sensing he was safe, the old man pulled the Colt from beneath the blanket covering his lap and set the black gun on the table. He then rubbed his smooth chin before saying, "Saunders I get, he discovered Lewandowski in the store, but Ogden and Elrod don't fit. Back then Ogden was nothing more than a guy who fixed guns, he didn't even own a shop yet, and Elrod was just a young man on his way up when all that happened."

The reporter reached into her purse and pulled out the file they'd found in the globe. Pushing off the soft couch, she took four steps across the room and handed the folder to the old man. She waited in front of the chair as he glanced through the photos.

"Al was never a man who took good pictures," he cracked. "The fact he was fat and had a scar didn't help. Ah, but the ladies loved him. That's what money and power do for a man," Hammer looked up at Tiffany and smiled, "they always make a man so much better looking. Heck, if I was rich, I'd have dozens of people catering to my every need right now." He frowned, "But breaking hundreds got to be a habit with me. I threw away money as easily as I tossed away my life."

"What about the other man in the photos?" the reporter asked.

"Is Ben Jacobs on the hit list as well?" Hammer asked as he closed the file and handed it back to the woman. "And young lady, if you want to ask questions about Jacobs, you better go back and sit down because it will take a while for me to spill that tale."

"What's the story?" Garner asked as Tiffany followed Hammer's suggestion and returned to her seat.

The old man smiled, "What makes you think there is a story?"

"The photos," Tiffany argued. "Jacobs is seen with Capone over a period of several years. What's that all about? I mean, you hinted it was a lulu, so spring the information on us."

Hammer waved, "Jacobs made a deal with the devil. It happens all the time. You have to understand, it's not like in the movies; you don't sell out all at once. Instead, you auction your soul one piece at a time. It takes years."

"You're speaking in proverbs," the reporter shot back, "I don't need a sermon to find this killer, I need the story."

"Why?" Hammer demanded. "Big Al is a shell of the man he used to be. His time on The Rock destroyed his mind. He sits down there in Florida and just babbles about things that don't make any sense. So what if Jacobs was once tied to Capone? What does it matter now?"

"When Elrod was killed," Garner cut in, "he was working on bringing down Delono."

"He's a punk," the old man snarled, "he couldn't shine Capone's shoes. None of the boys today have what it takes to really run a town. They're all afraid to get their hands dirty. They always hire out-of-town talent. They never do anything themselves. To get respect you have to face your enemy and make him feel small. Capone had that kind of style, but it doesn't exist in this world."

"You're probably right," the investigator agreed, "but I get the feeling Delono had something on both Elrod and Jacobs. The Capone connection might just be it."

Hammer leaned back in his chair and frowned. "So you want the story of how they are connected?"

"Yeah," Garner assured him.

"What about you lady?" the old man barked, as he pointed a thin finger in her direction, "are you looking for a story? Are you looking to ruin Jacobs in print?"

Tiffany shook her head, "What I really want to know is why Ethan Elrod was killed. I've done some digging and I think there is a connection to the candy maker being executed. Ruining the judge is not on my list of things I want to do unless I find out, as you put it, Jacobs has broken a few too many hundred dollar bills."

Hammer dropped his hand back to the arm of the chair. His eyes went from the reporter to his gun. He picked up the Colt, fingered it for a few seconds before dropping it into his lap and making an observation. "You do know that Jacobs and Elrod were tighter than ticks on a hound. Even though Elrod was a bit older, they've been friends for years. Jacobs even worked for Elrod for a while."

"That's all public record," Garner pointed out.

"Yeah," Hammer snapped, "so it is. But the connection with Capone isn't. Listen, I'm at death's door. As I have told you, there are a lot of things I've done in my life I'm not proud of, but I've never ratted someone out. Most of what I know I'm taking to the grave. I've ruined enough lives and don't feel like ruining any more."

"So you don't rat Jacobs out," Tiffany said, "but when these photos are printed in my newspaper, the judge is going to be in hot water. He's going to have to explain this to everyone from his staff, to the voters, to the president. So why not tell us now? Give us a head start. I might even be able to frame the news in a way that helps Jacobs."

"Dig it up on your own," Hammer barked.

"What if I told you," the reporter jabbed back, "this is also tied to a blonde that Delono put a hit out on?"

"And," Garner added, "the hit went wrong and a

working girl named Sunshine died because of it."

"Sunshine?" Hammer whispered as his shoulders suddenly sank. "That simple-minded gal never hurt anyone."

"Well," the investigator continued, "Elrod hired her to impersonate the blonde who Delono wanted out of the way. I'm guessing that Delono knocked her off because he believed she was the mystery blonde."

"And why would he think that?" Hammer demanded.

"Because she was wearing a blue jade ring," Tiffany interjected.

"How did she get the ring?" the old con whispered, his eyes reflecting the sadness the reporter noted in his body language.

"Elrod had it," Garner explained, "and I let Sunshine have it."

"You were stupid!" Hammer screamed. "No one should wear that ring except . . ." Rather than complete his thoughts his eyes went back to the gun. Then he went mute.

"Who was she?" the reporter demanded after a minute of complete silence.

"That poor woman," Hammer moaned, "do you know she was beaten as child? Sunshine was abused in ways you can't imagine. And then Delono had her wiped out. Worse yet, it was for no reason." The man raised his hand and formed it into a fist. "Rico didn't care about the blonde.

Yeah, Rico was Delono's name before he became Richard, but changing his name didn't change the fact he was and is a punk. I know for a fact that Sunshine didn't mean a thing to him. He was too high and mighty to care about a working girl."

"He thought she was the blonde with the blue jade ring," Garner cut in. "Delono wanted that woman dead, not Sunshine. Sunshine was just in the wrong place at the wrong time."

"And," Tiffany added, "Why did Delono hire a man to take that blonde out? Who was she? What did she have on him?"

As if the facts were now evidently coming too fast for him to fully grasp, the old man slowly shook his head and squeezed his chest with his arms. After a few moments of silence, he glanced back to his guests. "Jacobs was from the South Side. He grew up with nothing but a good mind. He made great grades in high school and kept his nose clean, but his widowed mother couldn't afford to send him to college. So she made a deal with the devil."

"What do you mean?" the reporter asked.

"In the late teens," Hammer wearily explained, "Jacobs's mother told one of James Colosimo's boys about how smart her son was. Big Jim was then the head of the Chicago underworld and, when he discovered what the woman said was true, Jim paid for the kid's education in exchange for a promise that Jacobs would handle Colosimo's legal problems down the line. There was even a contract drawn up spelling all that out. I witnessed both men signing it. Jacobs's mom was there smiling the whole time. She was sure that she'd found a way for her kid to escape the slums. Now you talk about a pact with the devil."

"Capone wasn't even in Chicago then," Garner pointed out. "He was still a street punk in New York when that deal was made. So what does this have to do with the photos and the blonde?"

Hammer feebly waved his hand, "I'll get to that. You just need to be patient. Johnny Torrio took over the Chicago underworld in 1920. Torrio was behind the murder of Colosimo and he was also the man who was later pushed aside by Capone. Anyway, Torrio also saw Jacobs as an asset and kept paying for the kid to attend the University of Illinois in Urbana. By the time Big Al rose to power, Jacobs was in law school here in Chicago. Capone loved the kid and kept him with him a lot of the time. He even used Jacobs for various errands, but Capone was careful to never get Jacobs involved in stuff that might lead to his arrest. In other words, he protected him. He needed his future lawyer to be as clean as the driven snow."

"So," Garner pointed out, "you're telling me Ben Jacobs owes his career to three of the most powerful men in the history of organized crime in Chicago?"

"Hence," Hammer noted, "my reference to deal

with the devil. Capone saw Jacobs as being his future mouthpiece. So he spoiled him rotten. A lot of good it did him. The kid wasn't old enough or experienced enough to protect Big Al when he faced the Feds and got his ticket to the pen."

"What about the blonde?" Tiffany asked. "Do you know anything about that?"

"I know everything about that," Hammer quickly assured the woman. "She was a local girl and a singer at speakeasies. Al liked her voice and figure, she was long on both of those gifts and had a great face, too, but Al didn't want her hanging around Jacobs. That didn't stop Velma and the kid from getting together. He even took some of the money Al gave him and bought the blonde a big, blue jade ring as an engagement present. To keep Al from ending their relationship, the two eloped in July, 1926. When Al found out he almost blew a gasket. I saw him take a baseball bat and destroy a Lincoln sedan just to vent his rage. If he hadn't thought of Jacobs like a son, I think he'd have killed him."

"What happened to her?" the reporter asked.

"Well," the old man explained, "when Capone didn't like what his boys did, then things changed. So, a few months after Jacobs and Velma got back from their honeymoon, the heat was applied. In time, Jacobs had to choose if he loved a woman more than he loved breathing. When he made that rather easy decision,

Capone's boys moved in and took care of Velma."

"Was she killed?" Garner chimed in.

"No," Hammer quickly replied, "she was just moved to another location a long way from Chicago. Velma and the photos you showed me tonight are likely the only direct links to Jacobs's past. He never appeared on Big Al's payroll. The money that paid for his schooling came through third parties that were not connected to the mob, and he was never arrested. So, he has no police record. I can also guarantee that those in the gang who know the connection between Capone and Jacobs would never talk. What makes no sense to me is why Delono would want to take out Velma. In my mind, he'd want her alive so he could control Jacobs if he became governor. Velma could be his trump card."

"What was Velma's maiden name?" Tiffany asked. "That might help me track her down."

Hammer grimaced, "Your story is about to get really interesting. Her name was Lombardi. Her father was the grocer the Polish candy maker supposedly knocked off. And not long after the murder, the girl was escorted out of town."

"And now we have motive for the current killings," Garner noted.

"But," the old man cracked, "it's not a motive that means anything in court." Hammer waved his hand and smiled. "There's one more bit of information that ties this all up in a real neat package, but you'll have to find that out on your own. I'm done talking. Now, before you leave me alone and let me die, I need for you do a favor for me."

"What's that?" Tiffany asked.

Hammer reached under the blanket and pulled out a worn wallet. He opened it and yanked out several bills. "Here's ten C-notes I've been holding for a long time." He smiled and added, "And you know how hard they are to break."

"I do for sure," Garner quipped.

Hammer's face suddenly grew very serious, "Do you know of a charity kitchen not far from the stockyards run by a nun?"

"Sister Ann?" Tiffany asked.

"Yeah," the old man said, "that's her name. Will you see that she gets this?"

"Why?" the investigator asked.

Hammer shrugged, "I'm not trying to buy my way into Heaven, if that's what you're thinking. I just like what she's doing. If I die with this cash in my pocket then I've got to believe whoever finds my body will spend the grand in a very dark place. I'd rather have it spread around in the light. Now, take this cash and get out of here."

— 33 —

Monday, December 23, 1946
1:01 a.m.

Repeating what Bret hoped would become a habit, he and Tiffany again employed her small kitchen to whip up some bacon and eggs. It had been such an eventful day they used the time preparing and eating to review what they'd learned from Hammer.

"Elrod was no better than Jacobs or even Delono," the woman noted.

"Why do you think that?" Garner asked between bites. "I mean, just because Jacobs's mother made a deal with the devil doesn't mean the judge stuck with it."

"If Hammer is right on Delono," Tiffany cut, "who would want Sunshine dead? I mean, the mob boss told you her death was a present for someone else."

The investigator nodded, "From what we've learned it could be Jacobs."

"And the photos in the globe prove what?" the woman asked.

"On the surface," he admitted, "it would seem like Elrod was keeping them to use on Jacobs."

"And," Tiffany added, "the fact that the DA was

willing to use Sunshine proved a couple of other things. One was that he had little regard for innocent life. Don't forget he also paid you a lot of money for something. Perhaps that was to take out Sunshine. And two, because he had secured the jade ring, he knew where the blonde was. So, was he keeping her alive to control Jacobs? This makes it sound more and more like Delono was working for Elrod, not the other way around."

"That's a lot to chew on," Garner noted, "and at this moment I'd rather put all that on the back burner and finish my late supper."

The remainder of the meal was spent in silence, Tiffany looking as though she was mentally constructing a jigsaw puzzle, while Garner did little more than study the woman. After their meal, they took what had become their usual places in the reporter's small living room and the investigator used the change in locale to deftly shift the conversation's direction.

"So, I know you two have a history, we've talked about that, but how do you really feel about Lane?"

"That came from out of left field," she chuckled.

"I'm serious," he quickly replied. "I really want to know where that relationship stands."

"I'm guessing," she jibed, "that you'd like that information before you buy me a present."

"Now who's being direct?" Garner grinned. "Listen, I've gotten to like you a lot in the past few days. In fact," he paused to measure his words. As he did, Tiffany raised her eyebrows. After licking his lips, he finally looked back to the woman and completed his thought, "I respect you, too."

"So," she laughed, her eyes twinkling, "you both you like and respect me. You have something in common with someone else then."

"Lane Walker?" Garner asked.

"No," she assured her guest, her smiled reshaping into a frown, "my boss. He told me the same thing just before he turned me down for a raise."

With one well-timed sentence, Tiffany had pushed Garner into a box and he didn't really know how to get out. He'd told her as much as he wanted to say until he found out where she stood with Lane, and it seemed obvious she didn't want to reveal that. So, now he was stuck and so was the dialogue. If she hadn't chimed in, he might have sat there mute for the next hour.

"Listen, Bret, you're a nice guy, even if you did threaten to kill me last week, but you're not my boyfriend or my brother. I'm not going to feel obligated to share stuff with you that I've shared with no one else. Besides, I couldn't answer how I really feel about Lane. One moment, I kind of like the guy, but the next I want to strangle him. In the more than five years I've known him, there have been some good times and some that were not so good. What does the future hold for us? If the past is a barometer, then I'd guess more of the same. What you need to know is that Lane's and my relationship is both special and complicated and that's as much as I'm going to tell you."

In a sense, though she probably didn't intend them that way, her words gave Garner hope. He'd feared that she was actually in love with his old friend. If she had shared that, then the investigator was going to walk away. Now, there was opening, a chance for him to press a bit deeper and see if she could see in him what he saw in her. But what was the best way to pursue what he was sure he wanted to do?

As his mind whirled like the propeller on a B-19 bomber, Tiffany reached down to the coffee table and picked up a catalog. She studied its cover for a few moments before pitching it his way. After he caught the Wish Book, she picked up the conversation.

"I like you and I have no doubt you are fascinated by me. I'm cute, at times I'm funny, I'm bluntly honest, unlike most women, I don't play games, I've got a brain, and we've worked pretty well together, but here is the bottom line. Once when I was a kid, I went swimming in Lake Michigan. I got in trouble and would have drowned, except for a man named Paul Warren. I didn't know him until he saved my life. In retrospect, he wasn't that good-looking, just an average guy from small-town America, yet for weeks after he dragged me to shore, I was sure I was in love with him. I didn't care if he was twelve years older than me, or that he was married and had two kids. He'd saved my life and I thought that bonded us together forever. As I look back, I realize I made a fool of myself flirting with him. I said things that I now hope he didn't hear or has at least forgotten."

"I'm not sure," Garner cut in, "what this has to do with anything."

"You saved my life," she reminded him. "You were my knight in shining armor. You arrived just when I needed you. Who's to say what I feel for you now is not just gratitude? Who's to say it goes any deeper than that? It's much too soon to tell."

As he considered the meaning behind her words, the investigator glanced down to the Montgomery Ward Christmas catalog and began to leaf through a few pages. He stopped to admire a large electric train set when Tiffany allowed a few more thoughts to tumble from her head.

"And who's to say I'm not like those toys in that catalog. Kids study those pages for weeks. They imagine what it would be like to play with the toys they pick out. They daydream about all they could do if Santa would just grant their wish. And when he does, when that toy is theirs, it becomes the happiest moment of their lives. Then, after a few days of playing with their toy or toys, they get tired of what they dreamed of for so long and center in on a new wish." When she paused, he looked up until their eyes met. "Bret, you've not known me long enough to decide if I'm the female version of a toy in a Wish Book."

"I don't think that's fair," he quickly argued. Tossing the catalog back on the table, he spat out what was on his mind and heart without measuring his words or worrying about their impact. "I've never met anyone like you."

"That might be a good thing," she joked.

"Be serious," he demanded. "You need to hear me out. I really think I love you."

She smiled. "I'm twenty-seven, my friends are all married, and most of them have kids. I work at a job that pays so little I don't own a car and live in a tiny walk-up apartment. I'm a smart woman trying to make it in a man's field and I don't mind telling you that it's tough. You're not playing with a full deck if you don't think that I dream of marriage and kids."

"And . . ." he began.

She cut him off with a wave of her hand. "Bret, you said you *think* you love me. You're not the first who's told me that. In fact, you're the seventh. And, just in case it matters to you, Lane has not even had the guts to tell me he *thinks* he loves me. But here is what you need to know. I'm not settling for someone or even opening my bedroom door for someone who *thinks* they love me. They have to *know* they love me to get and hold my interest."

He was tempted to blurt it out, to confess that he really did love her, but he couldn't. Though he wouldn't admit it, he wasn't sure enough to say *love* without qualifying it with the word *think*. Why did she have to be so blasted perceptive and smart?

"We've got some work to do," she announced, cutting into the debate taking place between the man's heart and brain. "As tonight has somehow already become tomorrow, you can call me this afternoon and maybe we can meet to discuss the case and perhaps even share a meal. And if you are still in Chicago a few weeks from now, and if you are still making a habit of eating at my table and sitting in that chair, perhaps we can revisit what we talked about tonight."

She pushed off the couch, walked over to the chair, and took his hand. As he rose, she led him to the door. When it was open, they paused there for a moment, his eyes locked onto hers. As he leaned down to kiss her lips, she moved just enough that his mouth landed on her forehead.

"Good night," she whispered as she closed the door and left him alone in the hall.

— 34 —

Monday, December 23, 1946
8:35 a.m.

Tiffany Clayton was shocked. Lane Walker was sitting in one of the back booths at the dining section of Woolworth's looking over a menu. She couldn't believe he was on time. This had to be a first. The cop had called an hour earlier and asked the reporter to breakfast. He even offered to buy. She was tempted to refuse, but then realized now that she had the blonde's name the cop might have the best resources to track the woman down. Thus, even if it meant she'd have to endure a few rounds of verbal boxing, it was likely worth it. Besides, on her salary, who was going to turn down a free meal? Taking a deep breath while secretly promising to try and make this meeting a cordial, civil affair, she strolled across the busy store to where Lane sat.

"You're late," the cop noted as the reporter took a place across the table from him. His words were caustic enough, but the fact that he never looked up from his menu immediately got under her skin.

"Five minutes," she replied after checking her watch. Setting her purse on the seat beside her, she very deliberately removed her gloves, one finger at time as she added, "I'm surprised you even remembered to come at all."

"Must we do this again?" he asked.

"You started it," she snapped.

Thirty seconds later, they were still glaring at each other when a waitress strolled up to the table and popped the question of the moment. "Do you two know what you want?"

"Hot cakes and sausage," Lane replied, his eyes still locked onto Tiffany.

"Short or tall stack?" the tall, thin woman asked between smacks on her gum.

"Tall."

"Ground or link sausage?"

"Link."

"Coffee or juice?"

"Coffee . . . black."

The bleached blonde nodded and smiled while jotting down everything Lane had shared. She then looked back toward the man and asked, "What about your wife, what does she want?"

"I'm not his wife," Tiffany replied, her forceful tone dragging the waitress's eyes to hers. "And even if I was married to that galoot I could and would still order for myself."

"Sorry," the waitress quickly replied, "I just assumed that at your age you'd be married. Besides, I don't get many unmarried people eating together in the morning. Their dates are mainly at night."

The reporter locked onto the waitress like a guided torpedo and cracked, "As a matter of fact, someone asked me last night if I wanted to be his wife and I'm thinking about it." She smiled before placing her order. "Now I want one scrambled egg, bacon, toast, and I've been feeling really adventurous today, so bring me a glass of tomato juice and a Coca-Cola."

"Yes, ma'am."

After writing Tiffany's order down the woman turned on her heels and hurried back to the kitchen. When she was gone the cop smugly said, "Well, I figured Garner would move in on you. He always went after my women. Every time anyone showed any interest in me in Hawaii or anywhere else, he immediately locked his sights on her. As soon as he meets one of my women, he just has to try to take them from me. That guy has always been so jealous of me."

"Excuse me," Tiffany shot back, her finger pointing at the man's nose, "since when have I been *your* woman? I'm the woman you forgot, stood up, made excuses to, didn't buy presents for, and insulted far more than you have complimented, but I'm not *your* woman and I don't want to be *your* woman."

"So," Lane noted, seemingly ignoring the fact he should apologize, "at the very least you had the sense to say no to Bret."

She shook her head, "I didn't say anything to

298

him. I suggested he give it some time before he rushed into a relationship with me."

"Well," the cop grinned, "you gave him the same advice I would have."

"Why," Tiffany grumbled, "did you ask me to meet you?"

"The case," he replied. "I wouldn't have called if it wasn't for this stupid case. The heat's on, everyone from the mayor to the chief is on my back, we need to solve it before Christmas or there's going to be coal in my stocking. Now did you find out anything?"

She was tempted to keep him in the dark. He deserved that for the way that he treated her, but this was about murder and he needed to know what she knew in order to do his job. So, even though the woman in her told her not to, she leaned back in the booth and quickly brought him up to speed. When she finished her story, she could tell he was impressed.

"Tiffany, with the information that you dug up . . ."

"The information Bret and I dug up," she corrected him.

"Whatever," Lane snapped, "this information gives me all I need in order to go visit with Jacobs."

"Just hold your horses," the reporter suggested. "I think we need to find out if Velma is still alive. When we boil this all down, she is the key. So why don't you spend your day tracking down the woman? I think we'll only get one chance at this, so when we hit the judge and put him on the grill, I want to combine what we have about the blonde."

"What about the priest?" Lane asked. "Do you think he knows anything else?"

"No," she assured the cop, "Joe spilled what he knows."

"Okay then, Tiff, let me ask you a harder question. Based on what you've learned, do you think Jacobs knows who the killer is?"

"Have you considered this?" she asked. "What if he is the killer?"

"The judge?" Lane gasped. "That's not even on my radar."

"Well," she suggested, "widen your radar's range. It seems to me that each of these men must have known and trusted the man who killed them. After all, at none of the scenes were there any signs of the victims having fought back. Somehow, the killer was able to make these men feel so comfortable and secure, he could drug their drinks and then coolly go about his business. When you think of it, other than Santa, who better to trust than a federal judge?"

The cop nodded. "And the blonde was not only the woman he loved, but the daughter of the man killed in 1926. Hence, the symbolism fits. But we still have no direct connection to Elrod and that twenty-year-old crime."

"Just because we haven't found it," Tiffany assured him, "doesn't mean there isn't one. For the moment, let's discover what happened to Jacobs's first wife. She might give us the tie to Elrod."

"I'll spend my day on that," Lane replied as the waitress brought their orders. "Now, let's sit back and enjoy a quiet meal."

Fifteen very quiet minutes later, as the cop finished the last of his hotcakes, Tiffany put in a second request. "Tomorrow is Christmas Eve, the last day the Santas are raising money on street corners. Tonight, we need to find out what's happening to the money the bogus Santas are collecting."

"So," he stoically replied, "You're still concerned about that."

"I'm going to do this with or without you," she warned. "Now, Bret learned the cars come by about nine to pick up the day's take. All we have to do is follow the cop car that picks up the kettles and see where it goes. As a cop is working this scam, it also means that you can find out who's dirty in your own department."

"Fine," the cop agreed, "I owe you that much. Where do we meet?"

"I've done a bit of homework," she assured him. "There's a fake Santa, another one whose permit has the name Kelly, working at the corner of Randolph and State Street. Let's just meet at half past eight at that location and follow the ride until it arrives home." She paused, drained the last swig of the Coke from the bottle, and then issued two warnings. "Don't bring a marked car or it will tip them off, and don't be late or stand me up."

Tiffany smiled, grabbed her bag and coat, and slid out of the booth. After all the times she'd paid in the past, there was a certain satisfaction in glancing over his shoulder seeing Lane digging out his billfold. He deserved that and a lot more for calling her *his* woman.

— 35 —

Monday, December 23, 1946
11:00 a.m.

Even as Lane Walker searched through files and made calls, he was kicking himself. Once again, he'd fallen into the trap of having a verbal war with the woman he cared more about than any person in the world. Was his inability to open up and tell her the way he really felt due to a clash of personalities or the fact the war had so changed him that he no longer felt capable of being honest? He decided that it was likely a bit of both with one more wild card added in the mix. Though he didn't know why, he was scared of love. Love required leaps of faith, thus allowing a myriad of illogical thoughts and feelings to push their way into his head. To avoid that jumble of confusion the cop had built a high wall to keep love out. So far it had worked. In his world, life and actions made sense and work provided him with a security he figured love couldn't give. Still, did that justify constantly tossing verbal volleys at a woman who defied his longing for security, order, and logic? He knew what Emily Post would say . . . he was guilty of bad manners and had been for years . . . but, on the positive side, being rude had kept him single. And most of his married friends complained so much about the way their wives badgered them, that perhaps single was the only way to go.

During the time his mental debate over love waned, the cop stumbled down blind streets leading to nothing but dead ends. Velma Lombardi had disappeared off the face of the planet in 1926. There were no records of her in Illinois. She wasn't on either tax or voter rolls in the dozen other states he checked. If she'd ever been legally married to Jacobs there was no record of it, just like there was no record of a divorce.

Giving up on his local and state contacts, Lane turned to the FBI. Though J. Edgar Hoover's men worked with him, they were also no help. No one with the name Velma Lombardi had ever been arrested and fingerprinted. Thus, the cop had to believe she apparently didn't have a record. Why was it the innocent were so much harder to find than the guilty?

Just before one, with the early afternoon sun now pouring through his window, the cop gave up. He had exhausted his sources and was forced to admit he was beaten. The frustration brought on by this blind pursuit so dimmed his senses he barely heard a uniformed officer ask, "Need something, Lane?"

Looking up, the homicide lieutenant noted Rankin O'Toole. O'Toole had been on the force for more than thirty years and even on the darkest days, the rock solid six-footer's smile lit up the room.

"I'm whiffing at curve balls," Lane replied with a forced smile. "I guess you could say I'm digging through haystacks and finding no needles at all."

"It's like that some days," the beat cop laughed as he pulled an apple from his coat pocket, rubbed it against his sleeve, and tossed it to Lane. "Eat this, it might just give you a new perspective."

Lane turned the apple over in his right hand and laughed. "Rankin, if that's the secret to thinking clearly, you should have shared it with me much sooner."

"Lane, it might not be the answer," the beat cop admitted, "but we always think better when we get the clutter out of our brains. For me, that moment comes when I eat an apple. Just biting into it takes me to a different place. Suddenly it's late summer, I'm sitting in the shade of a tree by a stream watching the sunset. I've got a fishing pole in my hand and a line in the water, but I don't care if I catch anything. I'm just enjoying being there. When I'm in a place like that, it is easy to figure out what matters and what doesn't matter. For me, all it takes is biting into an apple."

Leaning back in his chair, propping his feet on the desk, Lane took a bite. As O'Toole watched, the homicide cop grinned. "You're right, the taste does take me back a bit." He took another bite before posing a question that had nothing to do with either man's occupation or the apple. "Rankin, how long have you been married?"

O'Toole grinned, "Thirty-three years and they have been great ones, too. Sally is one heck of a gal."

"Is she a good cook?" Lane asked as he continued to work on the piece of fruit.

"Not really," came the quick reply. "And before you ask, she doesn't look like a movie star either, but that really doesn't matter. I just love her and having her in my life gives me something to look forward to and someone to laugh and cry with. It's nice having a person to share your dreams, no matter how humble, and to be there when you get home." The cop stopped, smiled, and then dropped a question of his own. "You're not married, are you?"

Lane shook his head as he tossed the apple core

305

in a trash can. "No, that's one road I haven't traveled."

"I guess you haven't found the right girl," O'Toole observed.

"Not sure."

"You don't sound too convincing," the beat cop observed. "In fact, you sound like a man trying to talk himself out of being in love rather than a man trying to decide if he is." O'Toole looked down at his chest, rubbed his sleeve against his badge to shine it up a bit, before adding, "What are you not sure of? Are you questioning yourself or the woman?"

"The woman is amazing," Lane explained as he dropped his feet from the desk and stood. Walking over to a window and looking out at the holiday traffic on the street, he added, "It's probably me. I just can't seem to . . ." His voice tailed off.

O'Toole waited a few moments before joining Lane at the window. "What can't you just seem to do?"

The homicide cop turned to face the man in uniform. "How would you describe me?"

"Smart and cool."

Lane shook his head, "I'm cool on the outside, but on the inside I'm all jumbled up."

"Why? Is it the job? If it is, get a new one."

"No, Rankin, it's not the job, it was the war. I just can't leave it behind me. There was a kid always pushing to get out of me before the war

306

started. I joked and laughed all the time. Each day was kind of like a gift. Then the war came and I killed for the first time. I didn't realize it then, but killing another man took a bit of the kid in me away. Each time I killed, another part of that kid died. By the time the war ended, the kid that used to live in me had been buried on some island in the Pacific. He didn't get to come home when I did."

O'Toole rested his right hand on Lane's shoulder. "The kid can still come home."

"How?"

"Kids take leaps of faith," he explained. "They reach for things they can't see and accept things they can't understand. It doesn't matter if they fall down; they just get up and keep trying to reach up. When you bit into that apple, where did it take you?"

Lane grinned. "I used to climb an apple tree when I was a kid. I used to sit up in the branches, lean up against the trunk, pull an apple from a branch, and look out over my yard. Things looked different from up there. They were always bigger and more exciting. It was like I was on top of the world and nothing could knock me down. That's where I went a few minutes ago. For just a little while, I was sitting on top of the world."

O'Toole gently smiled. "Ah, it seems the kid did return from war with you. You just forgot to look for him. If you eat more apples, then you might just discover a few more things to like about yourself, and I'll bet that kid who likes to laugh and have fun will demand a bigger piece of your life. Now, I've got to get back to my beat."

"Stay warm," Lane suggested.

"Even if I don't," O'Toole laughed, "I have Sally to go home to. I find the warmth that lasts the longest comes from the heart and pushes out."

Lane watched the uniformed cop stroll from his office before returning to his desk. Sitting down in his chair, he picked up a pencil and jotted down a reminder to pick up some apples on his way home from work.

— 36 —

Monday, December 23, 1946
1:15 p.m.

Two hours of hard digging led to one two-line story on page thirty-four of a 1926 issue of *The Star*. When she finally stumbled onto it, Tiffany Clayton read the short notice a half dozen times.

Benjamin Franklin Jacobs married Velma Louise Lombardi. After a short honeymoon, the couple will live in Chicago while Jacobs goes to law school.

In all the stacks of newspapers there was nothing else about the marriage and not a single record of a divorce. Perhaps Capone spirited the woman to Mexico to end the union, because it certainly didn't take place in Chicago. If it had, *The Star* would have run it somewhere.

Using old phone books, the reporter found a listing for Benjamin Jacobs in 1930. She followed that lead to discover the recent law grad had landed a position as an assistant with the District Attorney's office. Having his protégé in the courthouse must have been a dream come true for Al Capone. Still, with Capone being shipped off to a federal pen the next year, Tiffany doubted that Jacobs had an opportunity to pass along much information to the crime boss. As she pushed on through the years, Tiffany found a story published in a 1931 issue of *The Star* noting Jacobs had been married to Elizabeth Deborah Starnes. The best man at the wedding was the groom's supervisor, Ethan Elrod. Further research indicated the union between Jacobs and Starnes lasted until 1944, when the woman was killed in a car wreck. The couple had no children.

As she leaned back in the hard wooden chair and stretched, the newspaper's records clerk strolled into the room with a Coke. "You look thirsty," Oscar Taylor noted.

"Thanks," Tiffany answered with a smile. After taking the hobble-skirt bottle from the small man's hand, she took a quick sip and noted, "That's a really red bow tie you're sporting today."

"My wife hates it," Taylor laughed. "So this is the only time of the year I get to wear it or my green sweater. You should see the sweater, it's so bright you need sunglasses when you greet me." Smiling more with his eyes than his mouth, he observed, "You've been here a long time and pulled out a lot of back issues. Your fingers are black with newsprint. So, what are you looking for?"

After taking another swig of the soft drink, Tiffany pushed her hair off her forehead and asked, "What can you tell me that I don't know about Ben Jacobs?"

After releasing the button on his herringbone sport jacket, leaning up against a bookcase, and folding his arms, Taylor shrugged. A second later, the man who knew more about Chicago than anyone else painted a brief verbal sketch of the judge. "His life is pretty much public record. Worked in the DA's office, met the right people, the party gave him the job he has now, and they are grooming him to be our next governor."

"You used to cover the Windy City on a daily basis," Tiffany noted, "you know anything about his younger days?"

"Not much," Taylor admitted. "I do remember he was from a poor family, father died early in some kind of accident, some unnamed benefactor saw Jacobs's potential and paid for at least some of his education. Still, it took him a while. He was over thirty when he finally got his law degree. My guess is that during those years he was working odd jobs and going to school part time."

"No hint of any scandal?" the woman probed.

"Nothing," came the quick reply.

"Oscar, ever hear of a woman named Velma Lombardi?"

"Hear of her?" he laughed. "I had a crush on her. Back in the flapper era, she sang in a few local clubs . . . a couple of them were speakeasies. She was a blue-eyed blonde with the finest set of pipes in town. She could sing ballads and blues equally well. She worked a lot for a few years, and from what I heard back then, Capone got a piece of the action wherever she performed. As a side note, her father was murdered around Christmas of 1926 in that case you and I were talking about the other day. The one where Jan Lewandowski was executed for the crime."

"Where was Velma at that time?" Tiffany asked.

"Not at the store or the upstairs apartment," Taylor explained, "and she never came to the trial. In fact, she'd dropped out of sight about that time."

"So Velma wasn't performing when her father was murdered?" the reporter asked.

"I'm not even sure she was still breathing," the old man answered. "Her last performance that I remember was early in the summer before her father's death."

"I need to find that woman," Tiffany explained.

"I doubt that will happen," Taylor announced as he pushed off the wall and rebuttoned his jacket. "If she really did work for Capone and she somehow crossed him, she will never be found."

"That's not the news I need to hear."

He chuckled, "Reporters rarely get the news we need. We therefore have to find a new way to frame a story. In other words, we think beyond the subject. That's what separates the good scribes from those who are hacks."

She considered the man's words. Hammer swore that Velma wasn't murdered, but just relocated. So, in the past twenty years what had happened to her? What would she being doing with her life at this moment?

"Oscar, what kind of contacts did Capone have in the music business?"

"He might have had some ins at record companies, but I never heard of it. I know he was connected with nightclubs."

"Where did he hang out when he wasn't in Chicago?" she asked. "Was it New York or Los Angeles?"

Taylor laughed, "Big Al loved Hot Springs, Arkansas. He had a suite at the Arlington Hotel. Back then, that city was wide open. It was no problem getting booze, there was gambling and all kinds of nightclubs. I went down there with a couple of friends who were getting divorced and saw Clark Gable, Wallace Beery, and a bunch of other stars just walking down the streets. It was an amazing place in the twenties and thirties."

Tiffany smiled, "You said your buddies went down there to get a divorce?"

"Until Reno changed its laws," Taylor pointed out, "Hot Springs was the easiest place in the nation to end a marriage." He checked his watch. "My break's over, so unless you need something else, I should get back to my desk."

"Do we have a Hot Springs, Arkansas, phone-book?" she asked.

"There should be one on the back wall," he assured her.

"Thanks."

As Taylor shuffled off, Tiffany refocused her energy. If her hunch was right, Velma might still be in Hot Springs. She might have changed her name, but the reporter was betting that the woman was still singing. Thus, Tiffany was going to spend the afternoon trying to find a forty-something blonde blessed with, as Oscar had described them, a fine set of pipes.

— 37 —

Monday, December 23, 1946
4:42 p.m.

Undeterred by what he'd been told the night
before, Bret Garner spent his day carefully
looking for that perfect gift to present to Tiffany.
As he shopped, he realized he was walking a
fine line. While the gift couldn't shout his
feelings—that might scare her off—it still had
to paint him as being serious. That way it might
help remove the damage his use of the word
think had caused while not shutting the door for a
time when he could say *love* without adding the
think.

The sun had set by the time he walked into
Marshall Field's and found a gold chain necklace.
Was it a bit over the top to give to someone he'd
only known for a week? There was no doubt
about it, yes it was! But he'd already talked
himself out of perfume, a bracelet, a sweater, and
a dozen other things as being too much or too
little. It was time to act. After having his choice
wrapped, he slipped out of the store via a side
door and began the walk back to his hotel.

The night was crisp, the wind strong, and
shoppers crowded the streets. He could hear

carolers in the distance, mixed with piped holiday music over store loudspeakers, blasting car horns, and the ringing of Santa bells. This mishmash of disharmonious sounds should have caused him to grit his teeth and cover his ears, but instead he found it heartwarming. It was Christmas and for the first time in years, there was peace on earth. On top of that he'd found an angel in high heels that charmed him in ways he'd never been charmed. Maybe he had been a good boy after all. How could life get any better? Noting a phone booth, he stepped in, closed the door, dropped a nickel into the machine, and made a call to *The Chicago Star*. It took a minute for the switchboard operator to track down his party. Just hearing her voice proved that it had been time well spent.

"Tiffany Clayton," she announced, her tone so coldly professional it almost made her seem aloof. Still, it was music to Garner's ears.

"It's Bret."

"How are you *thinking* today?" she jabbed.

"I've decided to never actually use that word again," he explained.

"What word?"

"Think."

"Well," she chided, "it's not even New Year's Day and you've already messed up that resolution. While you *think* about *that* I will tell you I might be close to finding Velma. I'll know something concrete one way or the other tomorrow."

"Good detective work," Garner announced. "Now, how about dinner?"

"Can't tonight," she quickly explained, "I'm waiting on calls. But why don't you meet me at Randolph and State Street at eighty-thirty? Lane and I are going to follow the trail to the missing Santa money. I think you need to be with us as we wind this case up. After all, we don't know what we're running into, and Lane might need some backup."

"I'll be there with bells on," he replied, trying to hide his disappointment in having to share Tiffany with his old friend. "Should I wear a Santa suit and go undercover?"

"No," the reporter chuckled, "the thought of a Santa hit man is kind of upsetting."

"I was undercover then, too," he argued.

"I'm still not convinced."

"Tiff!"

"Don't be late," she advised. "Bye."

"Bye."

As he placed the receiver back into the pay phone's cradle he frowned . . . so much for a romantic night alone with the city's most attractive single woman. Now it looked like he'd be eating by himself in some cheap diner and then listening to the radio in his hotel room for a couple of hours. Opening the phone booth's folding door, he stepped back into the cold wind. Remembering he'd skipped lunch and suddenly longing for a warm meal and a hot shower, he took a shortcut across the lot, waving at a man running a Christmas tree stand, and then made a left down an alley. Taking the short detour quickly proved to be a big mistake.

Chicago alleys were never pretty sights. Even on the best days, they were filled with trash cans, litter, and grime. At Christmas, it was even worse. The cans were spilling over onto the streets, the smell was anything but fragrant, the brick-covered surface was icy and slick, and there was so little light the investigator could only see a few feet in front of him. He was fifty feet in and was about to turn around when, with no warning, a shot rang out, the bullet coming so close to his head Garner heard it race by his left ear before the lead projectile buried itself in a trash can. A normal man would have seen this as a time to duck and run, but thanks to his years of fighting close battles in the Pacific, Garner was no longer a normal man. In less than a blink of an eye, he'd fully evaluated the situation. There was no place to hide and it was another two hundred feet to the corner. If he ran, within two steps whoever had fired the first round would squeeze off five more. Even if the guy were a horrible shot, at least one of those would surely find its mark. So, rather than race for his life, the investigator grabbed his head, screamed, and fell into the thick blanket of snow topping the pavement. As he played possum, his body unmoving, he snuck his right hand into his belt and grabbed his gun. Now it was just a matter of waiting the guy out.

The shooter didn't immediately approach, but thankfully, he also didn't fire off another round. Thus, for both men the waiting game continued. That wait was likely much better for the shooter than for Garner.

The investigator had not had the time to pick the spot where he staged his death tumble. If he had, he would have avoided landing on an empty wine bottle. While it thankfully hadn't broken, it didn't feel good pushing into his side. The fact his face was half-buried in dirty, wet snow was creating a bit more discomfort. Still, all things considered, this beat playing dead on Wake Island while a hungry Japanese soldier was searching through his pockets for something he might eat. Now, lying still, Garner ignored his discomfort and tuned out all the sounds of a noisy city as he listened for footsteps. Finally, after two long minutes, he heard crunching in the snow. The sound continued until the shooter stood just to the left side of the investigator's body. What would he do now?

Garner grinned when he felt a gloved hand on his shoulder. The prey was falling into the trap. As the shooter tried to turn his target over, the investigator sprang into action. Grabbing the surprised man's weapon with his left hand, he pushed it to the side while he shoved his own gun into the man's gut.

"Drop it," the investigator ordered. Initially, the shooter struggled to pull his weapon away from Garner, but he lacked the war vet's strength. Growing tired of the game of tug-of-war, the investigator cracked, "If you want to live to see Christmas, drop that gun, step back, and hold your place until I get off the ground. Then we're going to have a little talk."

"A talk?" the man whispered.

"Yeah," Garner assured him, "unless you want to make it more than that. That's your choice."

A second later, the weapon landed in the snow. When it did, the investigator kicked his size eleven right wing tip into the other man's gut, driving him into the overflowing trash cans. By the time the failed assassin pulled himself up, the investigator was towering over him. Even in the dim light, it was clear the prey was nothing more than a short, thin teenager.

"You shave yet, boy?" Garner asked.

"I'm older than I look," he spat as he tried to brush some coffee grounds off his brown jacket.

"Well," the investigator noted, "if you keep up this line of work you're not going to get much older." Though he knew better, Garner was now feeling his oats and opted to make his point by spewing out a bit of overused radio crime show dialogue. "Listen punk, the only reason you aren't dead now is that it's the holidays and I hate killing people at Christmas."

The young man shrugged, "You might as well, I ain't got nothing to live for."

"Listen, kid," Garner asked. "What's this all about? Are you short on holiday cash? You looking for a loan?"

"Just doing a job," came the shaky reply.

"You new at this?" Garner asked.

"I've done a few," the man assured him.

"Where?"

"Cleveland, Newark."

"Let me explain something to you," Garner snarled, "a hit man who fails in a hit dies. So, you are nowhere near a veteran or you would have dropped a kill shot into me the first time you squeezed the trigger. Let me tell you something else someone in *your* profession should know. You were too far away when you pulled the trigger to have any experience at this and you're using a twenty-two. That, my friend, is not a hit man's choice of weapons. Now how old are you?"

"Twenty."

The investigator shook his head, "You're not a day over seventeen, and you've never killed anyone in Cleveland or Newark or anywhere else. Admit it!"

"Maybe," he answered. "But if that news got out, I wouldn't have been hired for this job. I had to look like a pro. So I had a friend play me up big."

"You got a record?"

"No, sir."

"Where are you from?"

"Memphis."

"Okay, here's my Christmas present to you. I'm letting you continue to breathe, but you have to do me a favor."

"What's that?" the kid asked, his voice unsteady.

"Who hired you? And don't make up a name or I might change my mind about giving you a pass."

There was no hesitation. "A guy named Dominick. He wanted to give his boss a special present and was looking for outside talent to deliver. He told me if I pulled this off, he could get me a sweet job. I was supposed to stop your heart. I didn't know you, I was hungry, and I'm tired of being a loser, so I talked my way into it."

Garner grinned. Dominick Gigabbo was a one of Delono's boys. The investigator met him a couple of times when he'd first rolled into town and was setting up the job with the crime boss.

Sticking his gun in the kid's face, Garner barked, "Before you get out of town, you make sure Dominick gets this message and gives it to his boss." The investigator paused, reached forward, grabbed the kid by the collar, and yanked him closer to the weapon. "You listening?"

"Yeah."

"This move cost Delono dearly. If he doesn't take his sights off me, I'll make sure this Christmas is his last. Either he backs off or the final present he gives anyone will be that car he bought for his wife. You got that?"

"Yeah."

Garner relaxed his grip and stepped back. The kid took a deep breath and started to make a move to pick up his gun.

"Don't try it," the investigator warned. "You just turn around and walk down this alley. And kid, forget you ever bought that weapon and don't buy another one."

The shooter nodded, spun, and took five slow steps before breaking out into a full gallop. Once he had turned the corner and was out of sight, Garner reached down, picked up the twenty-two, dropped it into his pocket, slipped his own gun back into his waistband, and casually continued his trek to his hotel assured that his warning would be shared. But sharing was only a part of the equation. Would Delono listen? Likely not, so Garner probably wouldn't be safe until the crime boss was either dead or behind bars. Now that was a very sobering thought to consider two days before Christmas.

— 38 —

Monday, December 23, 1946
8:25 p.m.

Tiffany was the first to arrive at Randolph and State Street. The scene stretching before the woman looked like something staged for a Hollywood Christmas movie. Music was blaring from loudspeakers, traffic was bumper to bumper, and the sidewalk was bustling with thousands urgently trying to find a few more items to stick under the tree and into stockings. Yet, on this night, the reporter had eyes for only one element of this festive holiday parade. Dressed in a long, gray coat and red slacks, her head covered by a dark green hat, Tiffany stood in front of a dime store window watching a lone Santa ring his bell on the corner across the street.

"Did you have a good day?" Bret Garner asked as he waltzed up Randolph and took a place beside her. After pulling his coat collar up to cover a bit more of his neck, he added, "And by the way, you look kind of like an elf in that get up." When she shot him a cold stare, he amended his observation. "A cute elf. In fact, you are the best-looking elf I've ever seen."

She leaned close and noted, "I *think,*" she drew

the word out a bit, "you're off to another rocky start. You might want to . . ." she smiled before saying, "*think* before opening your mouth."

Feeling like a little kid caught with his hand in a cookie jar, Garner grumbled, "I'll make a note of that."

"Now," the woman continued. "Since we last spoke I've managed to find out a bit more about Velma. By tomorrow, I should know if she is still alive, and, if she is, I will have a way to contact her. How about you? Did your day offer any excitement?"

He shrugged, "Not really. I spent most of my time shopping," he paused, "actually mainly window shopping. Then I cleaned up and came over to meet you. I see our favorite cop is late."

"He's always late," she cracked. "Just in case he doesn't get here in time, where is your car?"

"Across the street," he answered, "about a quarter of the block back. It's parked in front of a drug store. If we need it, I have a full tank of gas and it's ready to go."

"Never mind," Tiffany said. "I see Lane's old Ford. He's parking it about forty feet behind the Santa. Let's head on over there. It's bound to be warmer in the sedan than standing out here in the wind. Besides, I wouldn't want to have some random kid come up and ask me about working at the North Pole. Elf, indeed . . ."

The pair waited for the light to change and the

bell to ring before hurrying over to the gray sedan. Garner quickly rounded the car and piled into the front seat, forcing Tiffany to open the rear door and slid in the back.

"How long do you figure we'll have to wait?" the cop asked.

"Hello to you, too, Lane," the woman said. "I hope you had a good day. And, thanks, I'm fine."

"Sorry," the cop quickly replied, "I guess I'm a bit focused."

The woman checked her watch. "Based on what I've been told, the car comes by here at fifteen until nine to pick up the money. So not long at all. And about you being focused . . ."

"Let's not go there," Lane suggested. "I struck out on the woman. What about you?"

"Got a couple of leads," Tiffany admitted. "It will be tomorrow before I find out if they take me anywhere. I'll let you know."

"Yeah," the cop shot back. "I'm sure you will."

"Nice weather we're having," Garner noted.

Lane looked toward the other man and frowned. "It suddenly got a bit frosty in here."

"Maybe we need to turn the heat up," the woman suggested.

"It's fine," Lane grimly assured her.

For the next few minutes, the trio opted to remain mute. The silence might have continued for hours if the investigator hadn't picked up on something.

"He's early tonight," Garner pointed out as a black marked police car rolled up to the corner where Santa was working. The three watched the uniformed officer get out and then the jolly, red-suited elf hand his black kettle—likely filled with a lot of monetary gifts—to the cop. The Santa and the man in blue shook hands before the pot was placed in the back seat of the sedan. After a hearty "Merry Christmas," St. Nick waddled off down the street while the cop got back into the car and pulled out into traffic. Lane dropped the Ford into first and followed a few seconds later.

"He's not in any hurry," the reporter noted.

"No reason to call suspicion on himself," Garner added. "Lane, do you recognize the car?"

"It looks like one of ours," the cop explained, "but it's not. We have numbers on the back designating each car's unique I.D. That's how a cop knows which one to take out of the garage."

"There's a number on this one," Tiffany pointed out. "It's eleven."

"Yeah," Lane replied, "and car number eleven was totaled in an accident last week. So that's how I know it's not ours."

"Let me guess," the reporter cracked, "you know because you were likely driving it."

"That's none of your business," the cop replied with a frown. "Let's just keep our eyes on the prize. Talking will just break our concentration."

"Sounds good to me," Tiffany shot back.

The trio rode in silence for the next several miles as the car they were following stopped at a dozen more corners and picked up a like number of black pots. Finally, after taking the contributions gathered by a short, rather thin Santa whose corner was just at the edge of the business district, the driver picked up his pace. When he drove beyond the shopping area, it was apparent his rounds were completed.

"Okay," Lane suggested, "let's see where he leads us. My guess is he's heading for the bank."

Car number eleven drove west on Twenty-Sixth until it passed the jail. Coming to Pulaski, the patrol car's driver made a left, going by Sportsman's Park Race Track and over the river. After crossing the canal, it continued south until Fifty-Fifth Street, then it turned back west until the driver drove through an open gate leading to a warehouse. As the car pulled up beside two other police vehicles and parked in front of a loading dock, Lane continued down the street, only rolling to a stop after he pulled around the corner.

"Doesn't look like he ever knew he had a tail," Garner pointed out.

"He's likely been driving this route every night for weeks," Lane surmised. "So, as he has not been followed before now, he was probably not even looking for someone." He glanced toward the other man and asked, "You got your gun with you?"

"I do," the investigator assured him. "In fact, I've got an extra one that I plan on giving you later. There's a story that goes with it, but I'll save it for now."

Lane looked over his shoulder into the backseat, "I suppose it wouldn't do me any good to ask you to stay in the car."

Tiffany grimly smiled, "No, this is my baby, I uncovered it, and I want to be there when we discover who's behind it."

"Then let's go," the cop announced, "though I still feel it would be a lot better if you stayed here. This might get ugly, and if you get killed I don't want you complaining to me about it."

"That observation has so many flaws it doesn't even deserve a reply," the reporter cracked.

Following the men's lead, Tiffany pushed open the door and stepped out into the cold night air. It was so dark she could barely see her feet on the cracked and uneven sidewalk. Turning up her collar to shield her neck from the cold wind, the reporter ducked her head and walked beside the two men down the lonely, deserted block. When they arrived at the gate, they stopped.

"No one is guarding the door," Garner whispered.

"Have your gun ready anyway," Lane suggested. "And let's not waste time. Unless you have a better suggestion, we'll sprint up to the back of the sedan, work our around to that lighted window, and take a look at what's going on inside through the glass. I don't want to charge into the building until we gauge their numbers and firepower. If there are too many of them and they are armed, we'll find a phone and call for backup."

"Reasonable thinking," Tiffany noted.

"Thank you," the cop sarcastically shot back, "now let's get moving."

It took the trio about forty seconds to jog across the gravel parking lot to the side of the car marked with the eleven. They then crept up four badly weathered wooden steps leading to a concrete loading dock. Lane was the first to get to the window. Garner and Tiffany joined him a few seconds later.

Stealing a glance inside proved the building was still being used. There were hundreds if not thousands of boxes and containers stacked in neat rows from the front to the back of the large interior space. Judging from the writing on the sides of some of the wooden crates, it seemed Chicago's own Montgomery Ward Company leased the storage facility.

"So this is where they stash all the stuff they advertise in their catalogs," Tiffany noted.

"Likely the stuff they don't sell," Garner suggested. "There's a lot of dust on those crates. It's pretty obvious this place doesn't get visited much."

"Which," Lane pointed out, "makes it a perfect place for those behind the fake Santa scam to hang out and count the loot. There are four of them inventorying the night's haul right now."

A portable table was set up in the middle of the open area beside the building's large rear receiving door and the men were pouring the contents of black kettles onto the eight-by-four-foot wooden table top. Three of them were dressed like cops. The other appeared to be a member of the clergy.

"Do you see anyone besides the quartet?" Tiffany asked.

"No," came Garner's whispered reply. "But this looks way too easy. You'd think there would be someone watching the door. I mean, those cops aren't even armed."

"It's close to Christmas," Lane noted, "I'll accept any gifts that are tossed my way. Get your gun ready, Bret, and let's see if that side door is open. When we get inside, I'll do the talking."

Lane eased over to the designated entry and twisted the knob; it moved freely. He looked back at his team and nodded. With Garner and then Tiffany close on his heels, he crept into the room. The men were so caught up in their bookkeeping they didn't even notice they had company.

"Everyone keep your hands on the table," Lane called out while pointing his service gun toward the quartet. As the shocked four looked up, he identified himself. "I'm Lieutenant Lane Walker of the Chicago Police Department."

"What's this all about?" the man dressed as a priest asked.

"I'll ask the questions," Lane replied. "Now, as it is well past Halloween, why are you boys dressed up like policemen?"

"I can explain that," the priest cut in, "and the guns aren't needed."

"Bret," Lane suggested, "why don't you search them? You boys stand and raise your hands."

Tiffany watched as the investigator pushed his weapon back into his coat pocket and strolled over to the now-standing quartet. After patting each of them down, Garner nodded his head.

"I told you we weren't a threat," the priest chimed in. "Now, can we lower our hands?"

"I'll let you do that," the cop sternly agreed, "but only if you'll pipe up on who you are and what this racket is all about."

The priest appeared to be about forty. He was tall, his dark hair cut short, his blue eyes set deep, and his jaw square. As he lowered his arms, he glanced at each of the three uninvited guests, as if sizing them up, before telling his story.

"These guys are friends of mine," he explained. "They are also members of the clergy representing three different denominations. Until you hear me out, I would like to leave their names out of this."

"So," Lane cut in, "there are pastors behind

this racket? This will shake things up back at headquarters."

"I'd rather not call it a racket," the man replied. "Now, for the moment, you can call me John."

"Okay, John," the cop cracked, "how much have you taken in?"

"About a hundred thousand. I think when we finish counting tonight's donation it will equal or slightly exceed that amount."

"Not bad," Lane noted, "of course you know that you have stolen funds that were supposed to be used by the city to provide Christmas for those who lost fathers and husbands during the war."

"Actually," John explained, "we have donated more than twenty-thousand to that fund. This hundred thousand is on top of that. It's thanks to our help that the city actually exceeded its 1946 goal by more than fifteen thousand dollars. So, because of our Santas, the kids and widows will actually get more than was planned."

Tiffany had held her voice as long as she could. After listening to the priest's bizarre rationalization, she decided it was time to prove she could speak, think, and judge. "And the fact you gave some to a good cause makes stealing the remainder of the money all right? That leads me to believe that you can't be a real priest."

"I'm not sure you would call it stealing," John replied, his eyes locking onto hers. "And, I am a real priest."

"This beats all I've ever heard," Lane noted. "Now we've got clergymen entering the crime game."

"Listen," John suggested, "this is not really the way it looks. In my coat pocket I have a letter signed by Judge Ben Jacobs granting me immunity if something happened during our little ruse."

"Ruse?" the reporter shot back, "you call skimming a hundred grand a ruse?"

"Miss . . ." the priest stopped as if waiting for a response.

"Tiffany Clayton, I'm a reporter with *The Chicago Star.*"

"Miss Clayton, I know your work. In fact, earlier this year, you wrote a story on the large number of children in Europe who were being warehoused in overcrowded orphanages."

"Yes," she quickly replied. "Many of the kids affected lost their parents in either the mass extermination of Jews in concentration camps or due to Allied bombing. Who knows how many more are living on the streets, even now?"

"Have you done a follow-up story?" he asked.

"No," she admitted. "I did that one piece and moved on."

"You should write another," he grimly replied. "You need to expose the red tape we have to go through to get those children into the United States. These kids are lost, hungry, and because there is no longer room in the orphanages and they have no families, many are living on the streets, sleeping in doorways, and digging through trash for food."

Tiffany nodded, "So the money you collected is to feed them?"

"Not exactly," he explained, "we have families right here in Chicago willing to adopt some of these children, but we can't legally bring them in. The money we are raising is to create false papers and pay a few bribes. What we have in our fund will pave the way for almost eighty children to become a part of a family here."

"That's illegal," Lane noted.

John looked toward his three companions in crime. "We have found these children very good homes. They will be loved and well taken care of. But if they stay where they are most will likely die long before their reach their teens. None of them will probably ever have a chance at an education. No child deserves to grow up like this. We have the means and those willing to save them right here in the United States."

"That's noble," Lane noted, "but it is still against the law."

"Are you suggesting we wait on Congress to change the law?" John asked.

"That's the way things work," the cop argued. "When the law is changed then you can bring the kids in."

The priest looked to Tiffany. "Do you think that's right?"

It was an interesting question, and she really didn't know how to begin to answer it. Lane was correct, these clergymen were breaking the law, but if put into the same position wouldn't she have done the same thing as the priest? Wouldn't she have done whatever it took to save as many as she could? She didn't know.

"Father John," she began, "there are times when the law keeps us from doing what in our hearts we know is right. At that time, we have the right to push our government to change the law. That's the way that the system works."

The priest nodded as his eyes moved from to Lane and then to Garner. "Were you two men in the service?"

"We were Marines," Garner answered.

"Did you kill people?" John asked.

"Yes," the investigator replied, "we both killed many people. But that was in war."

The priest looked back to Lane, "Did you ever kill someone who didn't have a gun in his hand? Did you ever shoot a man who was resting and not fighting?"

The cop shook his head, and, in a weak voice asked, "If you made it to one hundred grand, exactly how many could you save?"

"Seventy-seven," came the quick reply.

Tiffany studied Lane as he lowered his gun,

slipped it into his coat pocket, slowly walked over to a crate, and sat down. As she watched the man's eyes fill with tears, she didn't know what to do. Glancing over to Garner, she lifted her eyebrows. All she got back was a weak shrug.

"Lieutenant," the priest broke the now painful silence, "I need to ask this again. Did you ever shoot someone who was not prepared to fight?"

Lane took a deep breath, rubbed his brow, and nodded.

John solemnly asked, "Then, was that, by the laws of the United States, not legally murder?"

"War is different," Garner quickly chimed in. "You are assigned to kill people. If you don't, they might well come back to kill you or one of your buddies."

"I know that," the priest said, "I'm not judging you. I'm just pointing out that in a court of law there might be times, even in a war, when a man could be considered legally guilty of murder."

"We could argue the merits of law," the investigator suggested. "We could debate them all day long. If you want to consider me a murderer, I guess you can. I have killed men during lulls in battle when they were resting and didn't know they were about to be shot, but my country would not look at what I did as legally wrong, and even though I did end more lives than I could possibly know, I don't believe I ever committed a crime." Garner glanced toward the cop, and added, "and neither did Lane. He's a moral man and, because of that, he carries the weight of what we were ordered to do with him every day. Thousands of us do, but what happened in war can't serve as a justification for what you're doing now."

The priest sadly nodded, "I've listened to the confessions of many men who brought the horrors of war home with them. I have assured them of the same thing you have just told me. But I would argue there is justification for our actions. You fought to protect the children whose lives we four are trying to save. You said that if you did not kill certain men when you did, they might have later killed you. If we wait until the government changes the law, then the children we have picked out to come to Chicago might die as well. Now, I will agree that what we are doing is not technically legal, but it is moral."

As a strange silence fell over the room, Tiffany looked from the money still on the table to Garner. The investigator's eyes were locked on Lane. Moving her gaze to the cop, she noted the tears now rolling down his cheeks. She almost moved forward to comfort him, but she knew that was not what he would have wanted. He had to face the past alone and he had to find a way to reconcile that past with what was going on in the present. So she held her ground and waited for the cop to regain a sense of control. It took several minutes. During that time, no one moved or spoke.

Lane, his voice thin and unsure, finally broke the silence. "Father John, you mentioned that Judge Jacobs knew about this."

"He does," the priest replied. "In fact, after a trip to Europe a few months ago, he fought to get laws changed. When the powers didn't move quickly enough, he hatched up this plan with us. He arranged for us to get papers and uniforms so we could appear to be just a part of the group raising money for the local charity. We all agreed that we would first make sure the local needs were met before we diverted funds to our cause."

Tiffany looked to Garner and noted, "By participating in this Jacobs was risking his spot on the bench and his shot at being governor. If this had gotten out it would have killed his political career."

"Yeah," the investigator agreed. "It would have done even more damage than the photos we found."

"For the time being," Lane asked the priest, "where do you keep the money?"

"It's hidden at my church," John quickly replied.

The cop pushed off the crate and walked over to the quartet of clergymen. After sizing each of them up, he asked, "When do you have to have this money in order to fulfill your mission?"

"The day after Christmas," the priest explained.

"For the moment, I won't write this up," Lane promised. "Tomorrow I'll talk to Jacobs. If he confirms your story and is willing to risk his future for these kids, then I will look the other way. Where can I find you?"

"St. John the Baptist," came the priest's reply.

"Okay," the cop shot back, "why don't you finish the count and get this cash put away."

Wordlessly the quartet retook their seats and continued their work. Meanwhile, as Tiffany watched, Garner walked over to Lane and put his hand on the other man's shoulder.

"You sure about this?" the investigator asked.

"Did I ever tell you how many?" the cop sadly noted.

"How many what?" Garner asked.

Lane shook his head, "It was seventy-seven. That's how many I killed as a sniper."

Tiffany marched quickly forward to join the men and made a suggestion, "Maybe this is God's way of evening the score. Maybe he's giving you a chance to save seventy-seven as a way of you forgiving yourself and moving on."

"You believe that?" Lane asked.

"Yeah," she assured him. "I mean, look at it this way. I stumbled onto this little scam when no one else did. Your friend from the war helped me investigate it, but rather than write a story, which is what I do, I turned to you for help. Why? Because I wanted to see the money get to the place it was meant to be. That was a lot more important to me than a byline or a bonus. So I think there are far too many ifs there to just have happened by chance."

"She's right," Garner agreed. "Lane, Christmas is a time of light and it's way past time some light shined into your life. If this puts the war behind you, and lets you get back to being who you were before this all happened, then I can't think of a better gift for you or for those who love you."

"And," Tiffany added, "there are two people here who do love you." She waited until Lane's eyes caught hers before adding, "Even if you have stood me up and stuck me with the check more times that I can count."

— 39 —

Tuesday, December 24, 1946
10:05 a.m.

It was a few minutes after ten when Bret Garner walked into the main door of *The Chicago Star.* After climbing a flight of stairs, he strolled into the second-floor newsroom to find a whirl of activity. More than twenty people were busily pounding away on typewriters likely attempting to finish stories so they could leave early and spend Christmas Eve with their families. Thus, it was almost as noisy and as much a madhouse as the scene he witnessed in Marshall Field's the day before. What was it about this time of the year that made people crazy and happy at the same time? After a quick survey of the chaos masquerading as a major newspaper, he spotted Tiffany Clayton, a phone to her ear, sitting on the corner of a desk near the back of the large room. She appeared more together than anyone in the entire building. That in itself was kind of scary. He was about to head in that direction when he felt a firm hand on his shoulder.

"I'd wait until she ends the call," Lane Walker suggested. "I've found that she doesn't like people listening as she talks."

Garner nodded while glancing to his former war comrade. The cop looked like he'd gotten a good night's sleep. Maybe the events in the warehouse had proven sound therapy.

"Bret," Lane asked, his tone relaxed and easy, "do you know how Tiffany got her name?"

"I've heard the story," the investigator replied with a sly grin.

The cop folded his arms, rocked on his heels, and nodded while shooting his friend and rival an admiring smile. "It's still hard to believe that her father once worked selling diamonds to folks in New York City and gave it all up so his daughter could have a normal life. I mean, that's so noble and unselfish. I wonder if I would have done that if I had been in his place."

One look convinced Garner that Lane had

actually bought Tiffany's story. The investigator was tempted to set the record straight, but as he considered how to best break the news, it dawned on him that it would be just like telling a kid Santa wasn't real. So, rather than burst the bubble, he let the moment pass. A few seconds later, the reporter dropped her phone back into the cradle. It now appeared to be time for the meeting they'd scheduled the night before.

Rather than give them a chance to walk over to her desk, Tiffany strolled across the newsroom and waved for the men to follow her out the door. The pair continued to walk just behind the reporter up a flight of steps, down a hall, and into *The Star*'s records room. She ushered them over to a table and pointed to chairs. Only after all three were seated did she open what appeared to be a staff meeting, and there was no doubt who was the chairman.

"When are we going to confront Jacobs?" she demanded. "Now I've even got a few more things I want him to explain."

"I've done some checking," Lane explained. "He has a meeting this afternoon and is scheduled to be home around four. He gave his maid and cook time off for the holidays, so he should be there alone. I think around five would be the best time for us to spring what we've learned and see if we can get him to confess what he knows about the killings."

Garner nodded, "That sounds good to me, but I need to have some questions answered before we get there."

"As do I," Tiffany added. "Let me go first. Based on what we found out last night, why would a guy who is dirty take a chance on the Santa scam? Why back the four clergymen? And if he is not dirty, then why take the risk of killing his reputation and costing himself the opportunity to be governor by becoming a part of this scheme?"

Lane smiled, "I've actually done a bit of homework on that. According to his friends, his wife, Margaret, who died a couple of years back, had a huge impact on him. She got him going to church and pretty much changed his outlook on life. Though he has not used it for publicity, thanks to her he became more focused on charity work. After she died, he doubled up his efforts. It seems she was very big into children's programs so, when you look at it in this light, what he is doing for the orphans makes perfect sense."

"I can buy that," Tiffany assured him. She smiled and added, "Woman do have the power to actually push men in the right directions." She raised her eyebrows and chuckled, "Though I have not had much success in that area with you. So I will give Margaret credit for last night, but that doesn't begin to answer all I need to know."

"I can accept the charity part as well," Garner agreed, "but what bothers me is why did Jacobs order the hit through Delono on Velma? I was there, I got the orders, this was about as cold-blooded a job as I have ever seen. It had to come from Jacobs. Nothing else makes sense."

"That's bothering me too," Lane admitted. "That's one of the areas I'm going to corner him on this afternoon, along with why Elrod would be a party to it."

Tiffany rapped her hand on the table to get the men's attention. "Along that line, I tracked Velma down."

"Really?" the cop asked.

"Why would I lie about that?" she shot back.

As Lane drew back and licked his wounds, Garner broke in, "So, what did you find out?"

"Velma Lombardi Jacobs is now known as Betty Hopkins. She's lived in Hot Springs ever since Capone spirited her out of town and got her a divorce. Big Al changed her name, set her up with some money, and thanks to her talent, she worked her way into singing at some of the clubs and casinos in the city. She was absolutely sure she'd left the past behind until a few months ago when Ethan Elrod caught her act and came to her dressing room after the show."

"How did Elrod find her?" Lane asked. "Had he been looking? Did he put investigators on the trail?"

"Who knows," Tiffany explained, "but Elrod told Velma it was nothing but blind luck. He was in Hot Springs on a vacation, picked The Vapors to catch a show, and she was on the bill. But here is where it gets interesting; according to Velma, they'd never met. Yet, he knew all about her marriage to Ben Jacobs right down to the blue jade engagement ring."

"How?" Garner chimed in. "I thought Elrod and Jacobs met after all that went down."

"I don't know," the reporter admitted, "and he wouldn't tell Velma either."

"So," Lane asked, "what was this meeting between Elrod and the woman all about?"

"From what I could gather," Tiffany explained, "when the DA spotted the woman, two things entered his head. The first was the ring. When he found out she still had it, he demanded she sell it to him. As she never wore it, his generous offer was easy to accept. The other thing he told Velma was to stay away from Chicago."

"So," Garner noted, "he was protecting her."

"Or," Lane cut in, "he was protecting his friend."

"But," the woman asked, "why sacrifice Sunshine? Why be noble and save one woman just to set up another to be killed?"

Lane nodded. "This is going to sound cold and harsh, but if you work in law enforcement long enough there are times you cease looking at the criminal element as people. You see them as cogs in a machine, and it's your job to stop that machine from working. It doesn't matter if it is a petty crook, a prostitute, or a mob boss, they all seem to lose their humanity after a while. You just want them gone and there are times when you even celebrate their deaths. After all, when they die that's one less problem you have to deal with."

"That's horrible," Tiffany chimed in. "People are still human. Anyone with a soul has to believe that."

"No," Garner corrected her, "it is understandable. No doubt most of the Japanese men I fought in the war were pretty good guys. They had families they loved and dreams they wanted to live. Yet, it became so engrained in my psyche that I ceased looking at them as real people and instead saw them as a cancer that had to be removed in order for the right side to live and prosper. I feel horrible for thinking that way now. I mean, each life has value, but when I was in the war it was all about conditioning. I was conditioned to think of the enemy not as people, but as a disease that had to be cut out. After all the years Elrod served in the office of the District Attorney, after all he saw, then it is not inconceivable he might have fallen into that trap as well. Thus, even though it breaks my heart to think of this, he might have gotten to the point where he no longer saw Sunshine as a person. To him she might have become a problem to be eliminated in order to make the world a better place."

"Wow," the reporter sighed. "This makes me want to go home and take a bath. I feel dirty."

"The human mind," Lane noted, "is a fragile thing. Believe me, I know that for a fact." He paused, looked toward Garner, and then suggested, "If no one has anything else to add, let's break this meeting up. I have some things I need to do."

"As do I," Garner chimed in.

The cop stood. "Why don't I pick you two up in front of this building around four? We'll go over to the judge's house and spring all we know on him. Then we will see how he reacts. If we get lucky we might put this case to bed before Santa leaves the North Pole."

"Sounds good," Tiffany replied. "I didn't like the direction this conversation was going anyway."

With not even a good-bye, a suddenly focused Lane walked out of the room. As the door swung shut, the woman looked toward the investigator.

"I don't think I realized the effects of war until the last twenty-four hours."

Garner shook his head, "You're a bright girl, you are perceptive, too, but you will never begin to know the real cost of war. Unless you have been there you can never fully realize how much it changes you." He paused, "I'm going to spend a bit of time observing people shop. Maybe by watching the faces of children excited by a visit from Santa, I can once again absorb a bit of the Christmas spirit. I'll be back here this afternoon."

Before leaving, he leaned over and kissed Tiffany on the cheek, then, while humming "Jingle Bells," he followed in Lane's footsteps. As he stepped outside, he was greeted by the cold north wind and a chilling thought. What if Richard Delono was still on his tail?

— 40 —

Tuesday, December 24, 1946
4:46 p.m.

As the police car pulled up the long, paved drive of the large, stately, red brick home on the city's north side, Tiffany smiled grimly. Perhaps now she would find the answers to the reason three men and one woman had died and if Ethan Elrod, a man she had once so admired, had pulled the wool over her eyes.

Turning her gaze to the front door and noting the porch light was not on, she sighed. Had Lane messed this up? Was Jacobs home or would this be a dry run?

"Are you sure he's here?" she asked. "The place looks deserted."

"I know he is," the cop assured her. "I had a

man stationed about a block away and he called the station when he spotted Jacobs. So the judge is home." As Lane switched off the engine, he sounded like a father laying down the rules for his kids before they entered a strange home to meet an important person. "Okay, Jacobs and I know each other pretty well, so let me take the lead. I'll start with the Santa deal. That provides me with a reason for bringing the two of you along on this ride. Still, it might be best if both of you didn't actually speak unless you're spoken to."

Tiffany frowned, "Yes, you have done such a good job of that in the past. Might I remind you, it was your surefire plan that placed me in the car with a hit man."

"I wasn't a real hit man," Garner argued.

"Yeah," the woman agreed, "but Lane didn't know that."

The driver turned toward the woman in the back seat, "I should have left you at home."

"You've forgotten me before," she snapped.

The cop shook his head. "Just follow my lead. Please?"

"In truth, I think it is a good plan," Garner cut in. "I believe you need to start with the Santa thing, and, as you are the only real cop here and Jacobs is a judge, you need to take the lead. But I'm wondering how you're going to open the door to the real reason we came? This is about more than a hundred grand in charity skimming; it's about four murders and how they tie together."

"I'll play it by ear," Lane suggested, "and just hope for the right opening."

"I hope you're a smoother operator here," Tiffany cracked, "than you are on dates." She let her verbal blow sink in before adding, "And if you don't find the opening, I will. We aren't leaving here without my knowing why he wanted Velma dead, and if he's still in bed with the mob. After all, those are his roots."

The cop ignored the opportunity to jab back, pulled up on the handle, pushed the driver's door open, and stepped out. It was already dark and there was a light snow falling.

"The weather forecast called for it to be clear by midnight," Tiffany noted as she got out of the car. "Doesn't look like it right now."

"Still got some time," Garner observed, "and at least it's not falling very hard. This is more of the kind of snowfall they use to illustrate Christmas cards." He leaned over and lightly elbowed Tiffany, before adding, "Wonder if the judge has any mistletoe hanging over his door?"

"If he does," Lane chimed in, "Jacobs can kiss you first. Now, let's get going."

As the cop moved forward, his two companions followed close behind. After strolling up the front walk and onto the porch, Lane pushed on the doorbell. It took almost a full minute for the judge to finally open the door.

"Lieutenant Walker," Jacobs announced, his voice registering a bit of shock, "is there something I can do for you?"

"Yes, there is," the cop assured him. Maintaining a friendly but serious tone he added, "The three of us are here on official business. I think you know Tiffany Clayton. The other man is a friend of mine from the service and a licensed private investigator. His name is Bret Garner."

"Good to see you again, Miss Clayton," the judge said with a forced smile, "and nice to meet you, too, Mr. Garner." He turned back to Lane. "You said this was official, does that mean you need a warrant issued so that you can do a search? This is Christmas Eve, can't that kind of thing wait?"

"We don't need a warrant," the cop answered. He looked back to the reporter as he continued the explanation for the visit. "Miss Clayton uncovered something a couple of weeks ago. Bret helped her dig into it, and when it became obvious things were amiss they brought the matter to me. So far, I have kept it off the books, so I can assure you that no one at the department knows about it, and Tiffany has not sought to publish the story either. I felt we needed to talk to you first. As this might take a while, can we step inside?"

"Excuse me," Jacobs said quickly, as he stepped to one side. "Where are my manners? Please come in. We can visit in my study, but I must say you have me completely baffled. I can't begin to imagine what you are talking about."

"Let's get inside," Lane suggested, "and after we are comfortable, we will get into it."

Much like Ethan Elrod's, the home was impressive. Two stories tall, the foyer looked like the lobby of a grand hotel. Walking across marble floors, the trio's host led them by a large, impressively furnished living room, down a twenty-foot-wide hall and into a study that was at least seven-hundred-square-feet. Even a casual examination of only the study proved the man knew how to live and live well. The room's huge, high-backed, twelve-foot-wide couch and four matching chairs were covered in red leather. The side tables and bookshelves were walnut, and the judge's desk was made of tiger oak and large enough to set a pool table on. The walls were covered with framed, antique maps, and the room's brass and glass lights likely cost more than a new model Ford.

"Please be seated," Jacobs suggested. "I'll take this chair at the end. Lane, why don't you land in that one at the far side of the coffee table, and Miss Clayton and Mr. Garner you can take the couch. If you want to take off your coats, just place them on that far table." After their coats were removed, and the trio positioned themselves in their assigned spots, the judge asked, "Now, what is this all about?"

Crossing his legs and brushing a bit of snow from his cuff, Lane smiled and opened for the group. "A few weeks ago, Tiffany noticed there were too many Santas on Chicago street corners."

The judge chuckled, "Too many Santas at Christmas? Is that even possible?"

Ignoring Jacobs's attempt at seasonal humor, the cop explained. "I got involved in finding out why there was a St. Nick population explosion, and last night we tracked the cash the extra Santas were raising to a warehouse in the canal district. I think you know where this is going."

"Do I?" the judge asked, as he leaned forward.

Tiffany had been quiet as long as she could. So before the cop could follow up, she chimed in. "We learned the whole setup from the priest. Father John told us you were involved in the plan to raise extra money to help bring some children illegally into the country."

Jacobs shrugged. "The way you just put it, Miss Clayton, makes it sound so unseemly."

"It's against the law," she pointed out. "There can be no doubt about that. So it does seem strange that a federal judge would be the person pulling the strings. Now, was the priest lying to us or is it time for you to make a confession?"

"Miss Clayton, that was a brilliant play on words," the judge noted with a wry smile. "You speak almost as well as you write. Now you deserve the truth, and I will be happy to share it with you. I recently made a trip to Europe and I was overcome by what I saw there. When I discovered that laws of European nations and those here in the United States were preventing couples in America who would adopt these children from doing just that, I worked to get them changed. I was told it would take time. Some of the kids I saw didn't have that much time. The more than seventy we are trying to sneak in are the kids who likely would not live long enough for the govern-ment to change the laws and allow them access to our country."

"But no matter how you frame it, it is still breaking the law," Lane pointed out. "The way the money was raised was illegal and deceptive. You took advantage of a city charity drive. Then there is the smuggling of kids who are illegal aliens into Chicago."

"We are not cheating the city," Jacobs answered. "There has been much more money raised for the local cause than is needed."

"But why this way?" Tiffany demanded. "Why not be open and straight-forward?"

"Because," the judge explained, "Americans gave and gave and gave during the war. They are tired of giving, even to good causes. For months, churches have been trying through special offerings to raise money to feed these children and it has not worked. Yet, put a Santa out there with a bell and a pot and, for whatever reason, it causes people to give. We didn't have much time. So when Father John made his suggestion, I did what it took to make it work."

"But," Garner chimed in, "if it got out that you were running an illegal operation like this, it might ruin your career."

"If it does," Jacobs snapped, "then hang my career. As long as those kids get to come into this country and live, I don't care. You see, my late wife drove into me that helping people in need is our most important job on this earth. All I am doing with this is living out what she would have surely urged me to do." His locked his eyes onto Lane, "Are you going to arrest me? Are you going to confiscate the money that's been raised? Are you going to sign a death warrant for those special kids I've picked out? The ones who need it the very worst? The ones Christ called the *least of these?*"

"No," the cop admitted.

"And I'm not going to run the story," Tiffany added.

"Well," the judge sighed, "thank God for that."

Lane looked at Tiffany and Garner and then back to the judge. He spoke slowly as he pushed forward.

"Judge Jacobs, were you aware that Ethan Elrod had discovered a connection between you and Richard Delono?"

"Now that's an unexpected change in direction,"

the man acknowledged. "You should warn a man before hitting him with a low blow. But, nevertheless, I will answer you. Yes, in fact, I told him I'd been in contact with Delono. I had a job that needed to be done and I couldn't use normal sources. But, just in case things blew up, I wanted Ethan to know what was going on."

Tiffany reached in her purse and pulled out the file. She handed it to the judge and waited for him to open it and look through the photos. She was hardly surprised his jaw dropped as he studied the images.

"We found out how you got your education," Tiffany noted. "These photos were hidden in Elrod's office."

"Delono had them," the judge explained. "He was holding onto them to threaten me if I made the run for governor. Ethan managed to cut a deal to get them from him. Ethan was just trying to protect me. Friends do that for each other."

"So Elrod was willing to break the law for you?" Garner asked.

Jacobs shook his head. "The law might be black and white in my courtroom, but in real life there are a lot gray areas. Technically, maybe Ethan made a deal with the devil, but he didn't break the law. He just bought photos for a very high price."

"That price being Velma Lombardi," Garner coldly suggested.

"What do you mean?" the judge demanded. "I have no idea what you're talking about."

"Delono took out a hit on Velma," the investigator explained forcefully, "he told me that killing the woman was a favor he was doing for someone else. It was a special Christmas present."

"No," Jacobs said, his head shaking, "he was supposed to find her for me not kill her. That wasn't a part of the deal."

"Why?" Tiffany demanded. "We know you were married to her back in 1926 and then Capone ended it. So why were you looking for her? The only logical reason would have been to have her eliminated, so that she couldn't be used against you in your race for governor. Get rid of the pictures of you with Capone and knock off the woman you married twenty years ago and you're home safe."

"No," he sternly answered. "That's not it at all. I was looking for Velma because I wanted to reconnect. After all, I'd lost my wife, I was lonely, and if Velma hadn't remarried . . . well . . . I was hoping to see if the feelings were still there. You know she had a voice that lingers in your heart and mind long after she's finished her final note. It is still there. I still love her. Delano was supposed to find her through his contacts. When he located her, Ethan was to pay him off."

"So," Lane demanded, "Elrod went along with this?"

"It took me weeks of arguing with him about it," Jacobs admitted, "for him to buy into the deal."

"Why was he against it?" Tiffany asked.

The judge shrugged, "He thought it would ruin my chances to become governor. Finally, even though it likely meant ending his crusade against organized crime, he told me he'd help me out. But every time I checked, Ethan claimed Delono hadn't found her. So, I'd pretty much given up."

"Delono didn't find her," Tiffany explained, "but Elrod did. He bought the blue jade ring from her and told her to never come to Chicago." She stopped, glanced back to Lane, and then posed a question. "Did Delono know what Velma looked like? Had he ever met her?"

"Not really," Jacobs answered, "he was working off a picture taken more than twenty years ago."

"Well," Garner angrily snapped, "Elrod not only told the woman you were looking for to stay away, he set up a prostitute who looked a bit like her to be delivered to Delono. That woman is dead. She was knocked off by one of Delono's hit men."

"Why?" the judge demanded. "I had nothing to do with it. I wanted Velma alive."

"It might have been Elrod's way," Lane suggested, "to have you and Delono believe Velma was dead. As Elrod is now dead, that's a question we can't answer. But here is one question that you might be able to help us with. We know you drove for Al Capone when you weren't at school. Did Al kill Lombardi?"

"I hate to remember those days," Jacobs sighed. "And I swear that when I drove over to the grocery store on that night I didn't know what was planned. Even after we left, I didn't know what had happened. But to answer your question, no, Capone didn't kill the grocer. When he wanted to make a point, Al worked people over with baseball bats. In this case, he hired another thug for that job . . . an ex-boxer named Rocko Falconi. They called him the Fatal Falcon. He liked the moniker so much he used a red knife as his talon when he did his work. But I swear, I just thought we stopped by the store because Falconi wanted something. I didn't know he was going to kill Velma's dad. I only found out about that the next day when I read the story in the papers. When I confronted Capone, he laughed and explained that it was his way of teaching me a lesson for going behind his back and getting married. He added that he took Velma from me to teach me who was boss and killed her father to scare her into never opening her mouth. That's the way the mob worked. To this day, I have to live with the memories of the kind of world my mother sold me into."

As the magnitude of the vicious nature of the underworld took root, the room grew deathly silent. It was Tiffany who first worked her way beyond the brutality of the underworld to pose the next question.

"The man convicted of the crime, Jan Lewandowski, told his attorney and a priest that the big guy, the person you just identified as Falconi, carried out two big sacks when he left the store. What was in the sacks?"

"Fruitcakes," Jacobs explained. "He loved them, but he never got to eat any of those. He died in a car wreck the next day. As a part of my duties, I cleaned out his place and gave four of the cakes to some little kid who said he was a friend of the store clerk who got killed. I felt sorry for him. He told me Lombardi gave him a candy bar and a bottle of pop each day and even helped him with his homework. He swore he loved the old man like a dad. What the kid didn't know was that I loved a member of that family, too, and she was dead to me as well. I guess we were both heartbroken."

Garner shook his head as he reentered the verbal fray. "Did Elrod have any association with Lewandowski's trial?"

"Yeah," Jacobs wearily admitted, "a few years ago, when we were discussing the case and I told him I'd been the unwitting driver of the car that took the hit man to the crime scene, and the guilt for not coming forward was still eating me alive. Ethan shared that during that trial he was working as a clerk at the DA's office and some kid had cornered him as he went to his job one morning. That young boy swore that someone other than the candy maker had committed the murder. The kid was raggedly dressed and looked hungry, so Ethan figured he was just trying to get attention and looking for a handout. Anyway, Ethan gave the kid a buck and sent him on his way. He never passed along the information to the DA. That omission ate at him, too. An innocent man died because he didn't act on what a little boy told him."

Jacobs shook his head. "Miss Clayton, back in my office you asked me about the fruitcake. Everyone has long thought it was just a gag gift. It was a lot more than that. That cake came from the place Velma's dad was killed and had been made in Lewandowski's candy shop. Ethan and I both could have kept the wrong man from dying for that murder and yet we didn't. That cake reminded us of our past sins and pushed us to never be cowards again. So, I swear on all that is holy, Ethan did not finger that prostitute for murder. He had some plan that would have kept her alive after he'd used her as bait for Delono. He had to have."

"We might never know that," Tiffany soberly added, "but we do know that Elrod, a retired cop named Saunders, and a gun shop owner named Odgen were all killed in the same way. Now that we know the full story on Elrod, we can tie each of those men to the Lewandowski case. So if it wasn't you who killed them, then who was it?"

"I don't know," Jacobs admitted. "Maybe the candy maker's kids. One of them was crazy."

With everything else off the table, that was about the only thing that made sense. As Tiffany studied Jacobs, now looking like a completely beaten man, she heard a deep, unfamiliar voice bark, "Lewandowski's kids had nothing to do with this!"

Jerking her eyes in the direction of the study door, she saw a man she didn't know. He was about five-foot ten, perhaps one hundred and sixty pounds, clean-shaven, close cut, dark hair, intense and deep-set dark eyes. The stranger was holding a chrome-plated pistol in his left hand and a large sack in the other.

— 41 —

Tuesday, December 24, 1946
5:26 p.m.

His unvoiced theory proven correct, Garner calmly studied the completely unexpected guest. As their eyes met and the visitor flashed a sign of recognition, the investigator smiled and announced, "Stuart Grogan."

With the mere mention of the name, the others in the room must have been completely taken aback. For the past week, anyone who read the newspapers or listened to the radio knew that Grogan was dead, but Garner had never bought the story.

The visitor smiled. "It's been a while, Bret. The weather was a lot different in Honolulu than it is here." He waved his gun a bit before adding, "I wasn't expecting to see you here, and I'm a bit surprised you're not surprised."

"You mean," the investigator replied, "surprised to see the Ghost of Christmas Past or are you the Ghost of Christmas Present?" Garner shot the guest a dry grin before adding, "Stuart, the Japs thought you were dead and you came back to haunt them, so why should you treat us any differently?"

The gunman shrugged. "Why shouldn't I, indeed? Now in answering your first question, I think I am more the Ghost of Christmas Past. In fact, I think Dickens might have enjoyed this rewriting of his old tale. It has all the classic plot elements; revenge, retribution, and righting a wrong." The visitor chuckled, "I think I just invented a new version of the three 'R's'."

"You were always clever," Garner admitted. "You broke codes and figured out potential enemy moves much more quickly than the rest of us."

"I must have been a step ahead of you on this

one, too," Grogan observed, "and that's not easy to do. Okay, I know the judge, but who are your friends?"

"The blonde is a reporter for *The Chicago Star*, her name is Tiffany Clayton. The goofy-looking guy in the chair is a homicide detective named Lane Walker."

Taking advantage of being introduced, the cop jumped into what had been a two-way conversation. "This can't be Stuart Grogan. Grogan's dead. We've been fishing him out of the river one piece at a time for the past week, and Morelli tells me that the pieces we've found likely went into the water in late November."

The uninvited guest kept his gun aimed toward the judge and grinned, "Your timeline is right but, as you can see, it looks like someone put Humpty-Dumpty back together again."

Garner nodded. "I always figured Delono hadn't gotten you. After all, even when the Japanese Army took out your whole unit they couldn't kill you."

"Yeah," Grogan grimly replied, "I do seem to have a number of lives. Maybe you should call me The Cat."

"You seem more the rat type to me," Lane chimed in. "Whose body did you use to fake your death?"

"About a month ago, Delono got wise to what I was doing," Grogan explained. "He actually figured out that I was planning on taking him out. So, rather than hire it done, he pulled the trigger this time and watched me fall into the river. I was nicked but not badly injured. I pretended to sink as he fired a few more slugs at me. I then held my breath and swam. I still almost froze to death before I could get far enough down the river to come up for air. Then I headed for shore. As luck would have it, I found a dead bum that night under a bridge."

Tiffany chimed in, "Sounds like the bridge down by Division Street. A lot of hobos stay there. I've done a story on them."

"That's the place," the visitor assured her, "and the dead guy I found didn't seem to mind changing clothes with me. Though I didn't want to do it, I then went to work dropping him into the river piece by piece to assure Delono I was no longer his concern. But, you have my word, I didn't kill him, he was already dead."

"Hard to take the word of someone who's holding a gun on me," Lane mockingly noted.

"And," Grogan noted, "speaking of guns, you all are likely packing. So, while I keep my weapon pointed at the woman's head . . ."

"The woman's name is Tiffany," the reporter reminded him.

"Fine, while I keep my gun pointed at Tiffany, you men reach in and retrieve your guns with your left hands, drop them on the floor and kick them over my way. I wouldn't want to have to shoot such a pretty lady, and Bret can tell you I'm a crack shot."

Garner looked over to Lane and nodded. Opening up his jacket, the investigator showed Grogan his gun before reaching out and pulling it from his waistband with his left hand. He then dropped it to the floor and used his foot to slide it toward the guest. Following his war buddy's lead, the cop did the same thing.

"Thank you, gentleman, I have no quarrel with either of you or Tiffany. I'm here to visit with the judge."

"What's this about?" Jacobs demanded from his chair.

"I've got a job to finish," Grogan explained. "I've been waiting a long time for this." The grin left his face. "Too long, I guess. When I couldn't make things right back then, I pledged I would correct a wrong when I had some power in my hands."

Garner glanced to the judge and then back to the man with the gun. He knew the war had played horrible games with Grogan's mind. When they'd served together, he'd seen the man lose it on several occasions. Back then there had always been a trigger, a song, a word, or seeing someone who looked like a member of his unit. What had pushed him over the edge this time and why was he directing his actions toward Jacobs?

"Stuart," the investigator said, "whatever this is about, you know as well as I do there is a right way to do things."

"They didn't do it the right way," the visitor explained.

"Who didn't?" Lane demanded.

"Those who had the power to make a wrong a right," Grogan answered. "When they found me alive on that island, when they got me up and I looked around and saw all my buddies dead, the medic told me that I'd lived to even the score. That it was my job—to kill each one of the Japs who had killed my brothers. A few months later, I was in a group that overran the same Japs that had destroyed my unit. We had them cornered but I wouldn't let them give up. Like that medic told me, I had a score to settle. I grabbed a machine gun and mowed them down. You know what the Marines did? They gave me a medal for that. They told me how proud they were of me."

Grogan's eyes were misty and a tear ran down his face as he solemnly added, "Then I remembered I had another score to even up and another death to avenge."

"Why Chicago?" Garner asked.

"This is where the battlefield is," the man explained. "It's where the enemy lives." He smiled, "Bret did I ever tell you I was raised in Little Italy? My mom was actually born in the old country and came here as a child."

"You never mentioned that," the investigator answered.

"My childhood wasn't all that great," Grogan added sadly. "Anyway, when I got back here, I needed a job. I wanted to do something that would give me a way to accomplish two things. The first was to get near my targets. The second was to do something good. A few days later, I ran into Ethan Elrod. I'd met him a long time ago when I was a kid, but he didn't remember me. Yet, when I told him I served with Naval Intelligence, he got real interested. When I shared that I was an expert marksman, he offered me a chance to do some work for him. He said I had the skills he needed. He wanted me to get close to Richard Delono, and thanks to Elrod putting out the word that the DA was looking for a former Marine who'd become a hired gun, through one of his underlings Delono sought me out. Once inside, it was my job to feed Elrod information that would help him bring Delono down."

"There had to be a guy on the inside," Jacobs noted. "Ethan never told me about him, but he did share that he had an ace in the hole."

The gunman grinned. "I did a lot of little things to prove myself and then Delono gave me a big job. I was the guy who was supposed to knock off the judge's ex-wife. I shared that information with Elrod and he figured a way to make it appear that I'd killed her, but I really hadn't. That was

368

all set up and then someone ratted me out and Delono took me to the river and pulled out his gun. I ran and got lucky."

Garner turned to Lane. "Did Elrod know that Grogan was supposedly dead?"

"Maybe not," the cop admitted, "we'd just discovered the first body part, complete with an I.D., the day the DA died. If he hadn't read the afternoon paper or listened to the radio news, he could have missed it."

"Then," the investigator said, "Sunshine was never supposed to die. Elrod wasn't planning on sacrificing her. He was clean."

"Not totally clean," Grogan cut in as he turned his eyes back to the judge. "You see, I was in the store that night Mr. Lombardi was killed."

"You were the little child in Lewandowski's last words," Tiffany cut in.

"Yeah," Grogan assured her, "And I was the kid Jacobs later gave the fruitcakes to, as well as the one who went to Elrod telling him what I had seen that night. Jacobs, you could have come forward, and Elrod could have accepted my information, but you didn't. Both of you allowed Jan Lewandowski to burn for killing Geno Lombardi." He shook his head before grimly adding, "You see, I watched Geno die. I was bent over him when the last bit of breath left his body. That's not an easy thing for a little kid to absorb. I'd forced myself to forget what I'd seen

369

until the war. Then it all came back to me. Then I knew what I had to do. I had to get even, just like when I mowed down those Japs. But this time I had to be clever."

The judge's face turned ashen white as a foreboding silence fell over the room. Grogan, his gun now trained on Jacobs, dropped the sack he'd been holding in his right hand to the floor.

"The last fruitcake is in there," he explained. "There's a knife as well. Once this job is finished the score is even again."

"Wait," Garner suggested. "Stuart, you're trying to do the right thing, I know that, but you're going about the wrong way."

"It is all black and white," Grogan answered. "They taught us that in the service. We take out those who are fighting against good."

"But you were working for Elrod," the investigator pointed out, "he was on the right side."

"That doesn't matter," the visitor explained. "I only worked for him to get him to trust me. They taught us in the war the enemy had to pay for Pearl Harbor and they had to pay for Wake Island. You see, once you step over that line between right and wrong someone has to make you pay. No one else was going to make them face their crimes. So it was my job."

Grogan was even further gone than Garner had imagined. He couldn't escape the training or the propaganda. He somehow saw himself as being an instrument of justice. Looking back to the man who'd once been his colleague, the investigator asked, "May I stand?"

"Yeah," came the response, "if you keep your distance. I don't want to be forced to hurt you. But, take this as a warning, those who stand between me and my objective often have to pay the price, too."

Garner stood, slowly walked over to the edge of the desk, and leaned against it. After folding his arms, he noted, "I'm guessing you know a few things about Delono. At the very least you said the guy shot you."

"He did," Grogan acknowledged, "but there is a lot of other stuff, too. When he drank, he liked to brag. He told me a lot because he wanted me to think he was bigger and smarter than Capone."

"How does Delono rank on the list of bad people you've known?" Garner asked.

"At the top," the gunman admitted.

"Then" the investigator suggested, "stop trying to right a wrong from twenty years ago and turn your attention to bringing down a guy who is behind crimes today. Delono's ducked the law long enough. Make him pay for those he's killed and all the pain he's inflicted in this world."

"After I finish this job," Grogan assured his old friend, "I'll be happy to share that information with you. I'll sing like a canary."

Not bothering to ask, Tiffany stood and turned toward the guest. "Can I call you Stuart?"

"Sure."

"Stuart, I understand you wanting to get Elrod. He didn't act on your information, but why the cop?"

The gunman looked toward the judge. "You want to tell her, Jacobs?"

The oldest person in the room sighed. "I found out through one of Capone's men that Saunders was on the take. He was watching the store that night. After the hit was done and the Falcon was gone, he was supposed to wait for someone to walk into that store. His job was to frame them for the murder." He looked at the gunman and asked, "How did you know?"

"About ten years later," Grogan explained, "I was in a bar and everyone was talking about the good ole days when Capone ruled the town. Saunders bragged about doing jobs for Big Al, and even how he once got paid five grand to frame a guy for a murder that happened in Little Italy. I put two and two together."

Tiffany nodded, "Okay, that explains that, but why kill the man on the jury? There were ten others who voted guilty was well."

"Ogden initially felt Lewandowski was innocent," Grogan sadly noted, "and he wanted to do the right thing. He held out until he was offered enough cash to open his own shop. He was also promised the mob would come to him for their special purchases. He sold his soul just so he could own a gun shop. To him the value of a good man's life was measured in a few thousand dollars."

"So," Tiffany suggested, "everything was symbolic."

"First," the gunman explained, "I got them to confess. Then I had them drink the drug so they wouldn't feel the pain. I used one of Lewandowski's fruitcakes because it was as close as I could get to an innocent man coming back from the grave to gain his retribution. The knife was the instrument that tied it back to Mr. Lombardi's murder and symbolized betrayal."

"You can't make that happen tonight," Garner noted. "We won't let you. You're not alone like you were the other times."

With no warning Grogan moved forward. Lane was still on the couch, Jacobs in the chair, Garner ten steps to his left, and Tiffany three feet to his right.

"I don't need symbolism now," the gunman explained as he stopped. "This is the final one. When I do my job tonight, the score is settled. Now, where do you want it, judge? And don't worry, Bret, as soon as I know Jacobs is dead I'll turn my weapon over to the cop. You see, my personal war ends here when the last guilty person pays for the crime. When this is finished, I will finally have peace on earth."

"Don't stop this," Jacobs announced as his eyes flashed to Lane and Garner. "In a strange sort of way, Grogan is right. I got caught up in a web and let an innocent man die. I was a coward." The judge then looked to the gunman. "Give it to me in the heart."

Grogan shrugged, lowered his gun a bit, and tensed. As he prepared to fire, Garner, ignoring Jacobs's orders began to move forward, but he was a bit late. Just as Grogan squeezed the trigger, a huge purse flew out of nowhere and Tiffany's bag knocked the gun from Grogan's hand. The bullet intended to settle the old score found the floor. As the gunman scrambled to pick up his weapon, the cop and the investigator jumped forward and subdued him. The holiday nightmare had finally ended.

— 42 —

Tuesday, December 24, 1946
9:00 p.m.

After Lane filed his report, Tiffany phoned in her story, and Grogan was sent to a psych ward, the trio piled into Garner's Oldsmobile. Falling all over themselves in an attempt to appear noble, the men gave the reporter the chance to choose where to eat. She surprised them by asking to go to Sister Ann's.

"I'll spring for a steak," Garner suggested. "The city is safe, let's make this night special."

"I'll take the soup at Sister Ann's," Tiffany said again.

"I'll buy you the best Italian dinner in the world," Lane chimed in. "I want to celebrate."

From her spot in the back seat, with both men looking at her with hopeful expressions, Tiffany stuck out her bottom lip, crossed her arms, and announced, "I want to go to Sister Ann's." Fifteen minutes later, after a ride spent in complete silence, her wish was granted.

With Tiffany leading the way, the trio marched into the soup kitchen. Even though it was late there were at least three dozen souls sitting in mismatched chairs near an old wood stove intently listening to the nun reading the story of the first Christmas from the second chapter of Luke. Tiffany stood quietly and absorbed the words as if hearing them for the first time. It was if the old familiar story was brand-new. Smiling, she realized the holiday once again had meaning.

As the disappointed men pouted, the woman studied a ragged evergreen tree with a dozen secondhand ornaments hanging from its drooping limbs. The tree that no one likely wanted and the decorations that had probably been thrown out, then Sister Ann reclaimed, kind of represented the folks who came into this place. The world might have forgotten them, but in this building they once again had value.

As the nun finished her reading, Joe got up and began singing "O Come All Ye Faithful." Within seconds, the ragtag band of visitors joined in. Their harmonies might have been strained, but the song took the reporter back to her youth and Christmas Eves spent with her family in church. Suddenly, she felt warm and blessed. It was almost like being home.

"I guess being here," Lane whispered just loud enough for Garner and Tiffany to hear, "is like eating an apple."

"What in the heck does that mean?" the investigator asked.

"Eating an apple takes you back," the cop explained.

"Where?" Garner asked.

"Never mind," the cop answered. "Let's find a place to sit."

"Sounds good to me," Garner agreed. "How about that empty table in the back?"

Tiffany, still intently listening to the words being sung by the unique choir, was only vaguely aware of the men guiding her across the room. After they'd sat down, Garner on one side and Lane on the other, the cop spoke.

"I'm suddenly filled with a sense of irony."

"Why?" Tiffany asked, her eyes still on Joe, as he now began singing, "Away in a Manger."

"That passage of Scripture Sister Ann was reading when we came in," the cop explained, "is where I jotted down the information my men would need if we'd not come back from that trip to the house on Elmwood. And that's where this whole thing started."

"I believe," Garner noted, "that is also where I came in."

The reporter turned her gaze from the singers to the investigator and smiled. "Your name was Rawlings then. I still think I might have liked you better that way. You seem to have a bit more class."

"Yeah," Lane laughed, "class has never been Bret's strong point."

"And," Tiffany pointed out, "Lane, you were the reason I was left with the hit man."

Satisfied she'd put both of her escorts in their place, she turned back to Joe as he led the humble visitors in a chorus of "Silent Night." When they concluded that old carol, the music stopped and the kitchen's patrons began to stand and visit with each other. Some were even laughing and calling out "Merry Christmas" or "Happy Holidays." Turning her attention back to Garner, Tiffany announced, "I believe you have a thousand dollars that was given to us to present to Sister Ann."

The investigator nodded. "I'd almost forgotten about Hammer's gift."

"Well," Tiffany warned, "we're not leaving until you make that delivery."

"So," Garner noted, "that's why we're here. You wanted to make sure I played Santa."

"Great," Lane suggested, "give the gift and let's get out of here. I have a plan . . ."

"Your plans never work out anyway," the woman jabbed, "so just forget it."

"Well," the cop smiled, "I guess you're right." He reached into his pocket and pulled out a small box. He studied it for a few moments and sadly smiled.

"What's that?" the reporter asked.

"I'd almost forgotten it," Lane admitted. "It was given to me by Mary Elrod. She'd bought it for her husband. She asked me to keep it and open it on Christmas."

"Well," Garner suggested, "do it."

The cop fumbled with the paper and when he finally tore it off, he found a box. Once the box was open, the trio spied a watch and a note. Lane set the gold timepiece to one side and picked up the note.

"What's it say?" Tiffany asked.

"Always find time for those who matter," Lane read.

"Wise words," Garner noted.

The cop slipped the note into his coat pocket and then retrieved another wrapped box. He handed this one to the reporter. "I bought you a little something."

Tiffany slowly unwrapped the green paper.

Inside was a bottle of perfume. She opened it, took a whiff, and sighed. After dabbing a bit on she smiled. "Joy. Seems appropriate to get a hint of happiness during the holidays. Thank you."

Lane shrugged, "The clerk told me it was hot this year."

"This stuff is hot any year," she assured him.

"Not to be outdone," Garner chimed in. "I have something, too." He reached into his pocket to retrieve the wrapped box.

"The paper is nice," Tiffany noted. After eagerly tearing into the gift, she smiled and held the necklace up for both men to see and then placed it around her neck. "My two wise guys gave me gold and spice for Christmas. Thank you both."

"Pretty," Sister Ann announced as she walked over to the table. "And Merry Christmas to each of you." After she took a seat opposite Tiffany, she inquired, "To what do I owe this honor? Surely there's a better place for each of you to be on Christmas Eve than a soup kitchen."

"Not that I can think of," Tiffany replied with a bright smile. "I wanted to be here and even if they didn't realize it, Lane and Bret wanted to be here, too." She stood and waved toward Joe. "Can you come over for a moment?"

The man in black shyly stuffed his hands into his pockets and ambled across the room to join them. After he was seated, the reporter put her elbows on the old wooden table and made an observation.

"On this Christmas Eve a lot of things have been settled. The guys and I have solved a mystery and, in the process, we've gotten a bit closer to once more feeling the spirit of the season." She paused and smiled at the nun, "But there is still more truth to be revealed. There is still part of this story that has not been written."

"You sound a bit like one of those radio dramas," Sister Ann noted.

"I guess I do," Tiffany admitted. "Bret told me not long ago that I tend to drag things out when I talk. So maybe I better just cut to the chase." The reporter turned toward the man dressed in black. "Joe, you told me that nineteen years ago tonight you played the part of Santa for a little girl. On December 24, 1927, you took the time to make a very important delivery."

"Yes," he admitted. "I had to fulfill a promise."

The reporter smiled, "And you also told me you never saw that little girl again. You never knew what happened to her. Did you ever wonder where she is and what she's doing?"

"I think about it from time to time," he admitted. "I hope she's happy and maybe has found a bit of the faith I lost."

"I think she is," Tiffany assured him, as she looked to the nun. "Do you still have the sleigh Santa brought you on Christmas Eve 1927?"

"How did you know about that?" a shocked Sister Ann softly asked, as a stunned Joe looked her way.

"It was a hunch," the reporter admitted as she glanced toward the man in black and smiled. "You shared that you were an orphan and raised by nuns. It didn't take me much digging to find out which convent that was. A nun there told me the name your parents gave you . . . Alicija."

"That's a little hard for most Americas to say and remember," the nun explained, "so I kept the first initial and changed it to Ann when I took my vows."

Tiffany turned and looked toward a solitary man sitting by the Christmas tree. "The man you take care of, the one who stays in this building, he must be your brother."

"I lost track of him when I was placed in the convent," she explained. "All I knew was that they put him in some kind of institution. He was on the street when I found him. That was about five years ago."

"And," Tiffany suggested, "that gave you the idea for this mission."

Sister Ann nodded.

"Ann, there's something I need to tell you tonight," the reporter continued. "When you pick up the newspaper tomorrow, you will read that your father was falsely accused and should have been found not guilty in the murder of Geno

Lombardi. My story will explain who committed the crime and why. The words I wrote won't bring your father back, but I hope they will help restore his good name. You also need to know that one of the men your mission helped and another who supported you played a part in sending your father to the chair." Tiffany paused, "I hope you can forgive them."

Sister Ann nodded. "In the end good always triumphs over evil and the light comes to the darkness. Sometimes an innocent man has to die because of the sins of others."

Tiffany sadly smiled. "I think your father would have been very proud of the work you do here." She paused as she looked toward her escorts. "You know, I was going to buy these two lugs something for Christmas today, but decided instead to save the money and give it to you." She reached into her oversized purse, pulled out two twenties, and tossed them in the middle of the table.

"Thank you," the nun replied.

"Here's something from me to match that," Lane added as he tossed two more twenties to the pile.

"Well," Garner grinned, "I guess all eyes are on me now. First, here are ten one hundred dollar bills. These are not from me, but rather from a dying man who chose your work as where he wanted his last dollars to go. He told me that you brought light into the darkness, and that guy knew all about the suffocating nature of darkness." After tossing the C-notes on the table, the investigator shrugged. "In truth, I do have something for you that comes from me as well. And, Tiffany, I want you to know that this was not prompted by any challenge you set forth. I brought this in with me when we entered the kitchen a few minutes ago. So this was planned." Reaching down beside the tabled he picked up a large attaché case, unzipped it, and dumped a huge pile of money on the table. As everyone looked on, Garner explained, "This comes from a honest man and a dishonest man, and neither one will be needing it anymore."

"You always have to top me," Lane grumbled.

"Amazing," Sister Ann whispered. "God is good."

"Merry Christmas," Tiffany announced as she pushed away from the table and stood. Taking it as a cue, the men did as well.

"We need to move on," the reporter explained, "There's another place we have to visit tonight."

"Where's that?" Garner asked.

"I'm kind of curious myself," Lane chimed in. "I hope we can grab a good meal there."

"Last night you said you had gas in that Oldsmobile," the woman said to the investigator. "Is that still true?"

"Almost a full tank," Garner assured her.

"Great," Tiffany announced with a smile, "then we are going to Wisconsin for Christmas."

"What?" the investigator asked.

"We're heading to my folks'," she explained. "I called earlier, they're waiting for us."

Lane frowned and stuck out his hand. "Congratulations, old boy, can't say I'm happy about it, but I will honor Tiffany's decision. Hope you enjoy the holidays."

The woman shrugged, "Lane you're going, too."

"All three of us?" Garner asked as he suspiciously eyed his old friend.

"Yeah," Tiffany replied. "All three of us."

"But," the investigator argued, "Lane likely needs to write up some reports on the case we just solved for him. He probably shouldn't go. You know duty calls and all."

"My crew can fill out any paperwork that's left," the cop said with a grin. He then looked back to Tiffany and asked, "Do you suppose your father will let me look at some of his diamonds?"

"About that . . ." the investigator cut in. "There's something you should know."

"Don't go there, Bret," Tiffany suggested, "or you'll be sleeping in the barn rather than a guest room."

"Fine," he grumbled.

As the two men once more suspiciously eyed each other, Tiffany walked out of the soup kitchen and stepped out into the night air. As promised by the forecasters, the skies were now clear, the wind was calm, there was snow on the ground, and for the first time in years she was going home for Christmas.

— Discussion Questions —

1. The book begins with a reality many don't want to consider: what if the wrong man or woman is executed for a crime? We know that it has happened in many times in the past. Does the fact mistakes have been made in capital crimes have any affect on your feelings of the death penalty?

2. Lane Walker and Tiffany Clayton have a unique relationship. Do you think the way they spar with each other is destructive? Why do they do it?

3. Tiffany is trying to make her mark in a world that, at that time, was normally reserved for men. Would you have encouraged her to pursue this course or pushed her into an area usually reserved for woman? Are there still places in our modern world where qualified women are not considered for certain types of jobs?

4. Morelli is surrounded by death and therefore its impact affects him differently than it does Lane. He often uses dark humor when dealing

with others. Where do you see him most clearly reveal his humanity? Could you do what he does?

5. Wars deeply alter people's perceptions of life. How does Lane's guilt affect his choices?

6. Who do you think is the deepest and wisest of our three leads? Is it Lane, Tiffany, or Bret Garner? Why?

7. Why do you think Tiffany clings to the yarn she has spun about her first name?

8. A mother's desire for her son to succeed caused her to compromise her values to ensure her son a better chance at success. Do you believe Judge Jacobs's decisions were an attempt to make up for his mother's choice? Do you believe he resented her for essentially selling him to the mob?

9. Was what Jacobs and the clergymen were attempting to do for the orphans in Europe wrong or right? Should they have waited for the laws to change? And is it all right to circumvent the legal system when lives are at stake?

10. The homeless man named Joe was lost. He didn't feel his prayers were being answered

and he wondered if God even existed. So, why do you believe he continued to try to help others? What was his motivation?

11. We never did find out why Sister Ann opened the kitchen. Why do you think she did it?

12. Though there is a lot of comedy in this book, it also examines the way war affects the human mind. There are three veterans in this story and each brought the war home in a different way. What drove Grogan to feel he needed to become an agent of revenge? How did the war affect Bret? Why did what Lane saw in combat make it so hard for him to show his emotions?

13. What are the spiritual lessons found in *The Fruitcake Murders*?

14. The book doesn't answer the question about the men in the car who shot at Tiffany as she ran down the street. Who do you think they were?

15. Finally, Tiffany took two men home for Christmas? Which one of them do you think she should choose to love and which should remain just her friend? Why?

Want to learn more about author Ace Collins?

Be sure to visit Ace online!

www.acecollins.com

Follow him on Twitter @acecollins and join him on his author page on Facebook

Center Point Large Print
600 Brooks Road / PO Box 1
Thorndike, ME 04986-0001 USA

(207) 568-3717

US & Canada:
1 800 929-9108
www.centerpointlargeprint.com